TEARS OF THE SUN

OTHER BOOKS BY AL LACY

Angel of Mercy series:
A Promise for Breanna (Book One)
Faithful Heart (Book Two)

Journeys of the Stranger series:
Legacy (Book One)
Silent Abduction (Book Two)
Blizzard (Book Three)
Tears of the Sun (Book Four)

Battles of Destiny (Civil War series):
Beloved Enemy (Battle of First Bull Run)
A Heart Divided (Battle of Mobile Bay)
A Promise Unbroken (Battle of Rich Mountain)
Shadowed Memories (Battle of Shiloh)
Joy From Ashes (Battle of Fredericksburg)

TEARS OF THE SUN

AL LACY

Multnomah®Publishers *Sisters, Oregon*

This book is a work of fiction. With the exception of recognized historical
figures, the characters in this novel are fictional.
Any resemblance to actual persons, living or dead, is purely coincidental.

TEARS OF THE SUN
© 1995 by ALJO PRODUCTIONS, INC.

published by Multnomah Publishers, Inc.

Edited by Rodney L. Morris
Cover design by David Uttley
Cover illustration by Terry Hoff

International Standard Book Number: 0-88070-838-7

Printed in the United States of America.

For information:
Multnomah Publishers, Inc.
Post Office Box 1720
Sisters, Oregon 97759

or my brother,

Jim Lacy,

who will always have a special place
in my heart.
I love you, Jimmy

PROLOGUE

———◆◆◆———

At the beginning of the nineteenth century, the Indian tribes of the Old West were proud, secure, and free as the wind. From the wide Missouri River to the eastern ramparts of the Rocky Mountains, buffalo ran thirty million strong, and other species of wild game roamed the plains and hills in countless numbers. Within the Rockies were bear, moose, elk, and deer, and across the sandy deserts westward, wildlife abounded.

Before the nineteenth century was five years old, explorers Meriwether Lewis and William Clark were making tracks on Indian land in the West. They returned to the East with wordy descriptions of snow-capped peaks, gurgling mountain streams, white-foamed rivers, sky-blue lakes, lush green valleys, grassy rolling plains, vivid desert colors and rock formations, and wild game aplenty. The tide of white settlers began to flow westward, and it increased steadily in volume until late in the century. When gold was discovered in California, Nevada, and Arizona in mid-century, the lure of sudden riches brought even more white men to the red man's territory.

Two hundred thousand Indians roamed the vast land from the Missouri to the Pacific. They were assembled in tribes running from a few hundred members to several thousand. Each tribe had established itself as an independent nation, except the Apaches. They remained in eight fragmented bands—the Aravaipa, the Chiricahua, the Jicarilla, the Mimbres, the Nedni, the Pinal, the Tonto, and the White Mountain.

Most of the tribes resisted the white invasion into their homeland, but none with such uncompromising ferocity as the Apaches. Military historians agree that the toughest, most unrelenting, and fiercest fighters in human history were the Apaches, who themselves, some two hundred years earlier, had been invaders. They were then known as Athapascans, a tribe from the far north. They migrated south into the north of what would become New Mexico and Arizona. They pushed on to the Mogollon Rim, that gigantic upthrust of red and sandstone rock bearing the massive canyon scar of the rambling Colorado River. From that rocky rim they set their gaze across the arid desert toward the majestic peaks of the Sierra Madre in Mexico.

All of this land became the Athapascans' as they drove back Mexicans from the south, moved against the cliff-dwelling Zunis in the center, the Comanches to the east, and the Yumans to the west. The Athapascans carved out a range five hundred miles from east to west and as far north and south. In that rugged desert land, sheltered in wickiups, they lived as nomadic hunters.

The vast wilderness was divided among the loose-knit confederation of warriors and their families, but the various peoples with whom they came in conflict saw them as a single foe. Indeed, the name *Apache* was applied to the Athapascans by the Zunis from their word for "enemy"—*apachu.* It caught on quickly amongst the Mexicans, the Comanches, the Yumans, and the Spaniards who dared cross Athapascan land…and eventually the white men who came as invaders of their territory. Each successive intruder soon learned to fear and respect the name Apache, the antagonist who gave no quarter.

So great were the casualties among the troops of the U.S. army forts in Arizona in the late 1860s, General William Tecumseh Sherman wrote half-jokingly to the secretary of war in Washington, D.C., in 1870, "We had one war with Mexico to take Arizona. Now we should have another war to make her take it back!"

It would appear on the surface that all Apache warriors were fierce, heartless, and without compassion. Of most, this was true. However, Cochise, a chief of the Chiricahuas, and Alchesay, a chief of the White Mountain Apaches, were brave and fierce fighters, but never killed an enemy who was wounded or defenseless.

This is the story of another Apache warrior, a subchief who beneath his fierce exterior had a tender heart. Let us follow John Stranger into dangerous Apache territory.

ONE

In spite of the brilliant noonday sun, death hung over Prescott, Arizona's, main street like a black pall. It was mid-October, but the last heat of summer still clung tenaciously to the desert, pressing down on Prescott like a suffocating shroud. It was quiet as a graveyard as wide-eyed men, women, and children lined the boardwalks.

There was no breeze.

The birds in the trees that towered over the street and its sun-bleached clapboard buildings had suddenly hushed their chatter. The saddle horses at the hitch rails, and those harnessed to wagons and buggies were strangely silent. The only sound that could be heard by anyone along the boardwalks was the beat of their own heart.

And the three rough-looking men who faced the lone sheriff in the middle of the wide, dusty street were cocksure that very shortly, the lawman wouldn't even hear that. Within minutes, Yavapai County Sheriff Brett Holden would be dead...and they were going to do the killing. But first, they would have fun toying with him.

Sheriff Holden was in his late forties, tough as nails and wholly dedicated to his job. In the ten years he had been sheriff, he had cleaned up Yavapai County, especially Prescott, the county seat. When he was elected sheriff, Prescott was a haven for drifters, riffraff, and men on the dodge. Smaller towns in the county were also beginning to attract the same kind of troublemakers.

The county was now a place where decent people could make their homes, raise their children, and live in relative peace.

Jake Maldrum and two of his younger brothers, Harold and Rufus, were about to shatter that peace. And it wouldn't be the first time. They and their youngest brother, Arlo, had come into Prescott drunk a week earlier and started one fight after another. Sheriff Holden and deputies Warren Candler and Jimmy Yarbro had stopped a brawl in one of the town's saloons—a brawl started by the Maldrums—and had run Jake and his brothers out of Prescott.

The next night, Yarbro had been shot dead from ambush while making his rounds on Main Street after the saloons were closed. Sheriff Holden suspected the Maldrums, but had no way of proving it. Neither was there any way of knowing where the killers might have gone.

Four days later, the Maldrums rode back into Prescott, knowing that Holden was out of town. They entered the Yavapai County Bank and demanded all the money. When they came out of the bank with the money sacks in their hands, Deputy Candler and a new deputy, Bud Saxon, were coming on the run.

Candler cocked his gun and commanded them to halt, but they opened fire. Bud Saxon was killed instantly. Candler dropped Arlo Maldrum with a bullet in his shoulder. Candler was then hit twice and went down, but he managed to keep firing rapidly enough to make the other three Maldrum brothers mount up and gallop away, leaving Arlo lying wounded in the street.

Sheriff Holden had arrived back in Prescott within minutes after the robbery and shootout. The town's physician took two bullets out of Candler and assured Holden he would live, then turned his attention to Arlo. After Arlo's bullet had been removed and the doctor had patched him up, Holden locked him up in a private cell in the Yavapai County jail.

Now the Maldrums were back, and Sheriff Brett Holden stood facing them in front of the sheriff's office, alone, his double-barreled, twelve-gauge shotgun in steady hands and his holstered sidearm on his hip. He was not about to back down. It wasn't in his nature to give in to anyone. Nobody broke the law in his county and got away with it. Nobody. Not cowhands on a drunken spree, not a band of troublemaking desperadoes, not a gang of bank robbers. The law was the law. Brett Holden was paid to uphold it, and uphold it he would.

The sheriff was ready to die before he would give in to the outlaws, yet not a single citizen of Prescott had made a move to help him. And Holden was too proud a man to ask for help. There were at least two dozen men in the crowd who wore sidearms, but not a one seemed ready to get into the fight.

There was forty feet of breezeless desert heat between them as Jake Maldrum said in a husky voice, "Now, Sheriff, I think we're bein' plenty fair with you. All we're askin' is that you let our baby brother outta your rat-hole jail, and we'll let you live to pillow your head tonight."

"Yeah, Sheriff!" Rufus Maldrum said. "It's just your stubborn pride that's keepin' you from givin' in here. Is that all your life means to you? I mean, is keepin' Arlo in that jail really worth dyin' in a hail of bullets for?"

"While I'm going down in your hail of bullets, I'll take a couple of you boys with me," Holden said. "Since we're weighing things out here, maybe you boys better take a look at the scales. Not one of you is fast enough to take me out before I unleash both barrels. I'll get one of you good, and another almost as good. One will die. The other might live. Now, just which one of you is going to die? Which one will lose a healthy chunk of flesh? And which one will be left alive to walk in there and let Arlo out?"

"You're forgettin' somethin' Sheriff," Jake growled. "You ain't cocked them hammers yet. In the time it takes you to do that, we'll cut you down."

"That's just talk, Jake. My thumb's a lot closer to these hammers than your fingers are to the butts of your guns. Now, do like I told you at the first. All three of you move your hands *real slow-like* and unbuckle those gunbelts. You're under arrest for murder and bank robbery."

A tight smile spread over Jake Maldrum's face. "Now, Sheriff, ol' boy, seems to me you ain't usin' your head 'cept to give your hat a place to rest. We came here to get Arlo outta jail, and no matter what kind of talk you come up with, that's what we're gonna do. I'm offerin' to let you live if you'll only cooperate. Play the fool, and they'll dig your grave before the sun goes down."

The people on the street stood mesmerized. The Maldrum brothers saw the frightened look on their faces and enjoyed knowing they were feared.

Holden gave Jake a stony gaze and said, "I'm running out of patience, mister. Now all three of you drop those gunbelts like I told you."

But Jake was enjoying the standoff, confident that he and his brothers had the upper hand. He laughed and told Holden they couldn't drop their gunbelts because if they did, it would mean jail for them, too. Harold and Rufus joined in, making light of Holden and telling him it was time for him to put down the shotgun and bring the game to a peaceful end…or die where he stood.

Some of the people on the boardwalks noticed a lone rider on a large black gelding coming into town from the north. The bridle and saddle were as black as the horse.

Holden's eye caught the movement on the sunstruck street behind his challengers, but paid it little mind. He was concentrating on the three outlaws, watching their eyes and their gunhands closely.

Jake continued to taunt the sheriff while his brothers waited for the secret word to go for their guns to pass his lips. Both were wishing their elder brother would speak the word and get the thing over with.

The people who fixed their eyes on the lone rider saw that he was tall and slender, yet broad-shouldered and muscular. Except for his white shirt, he was dressed in black all the way to his boots. There was a black string tie on his neck, and on his head was a black flat-crowned hat.

The tall man in black hauled up to a hitch rail and swung down. He wrapped the reins around the rail and left his horse, patting him on the rump. The sharp words were still going on between the sheriff and the outlaws as the mysterious stranger strode toward the boardwalk. The Colt .45 Peacemaker that hugged his hip in a low-slung fashion had bone-white grips on the handle. He wore a well-trimmed mustache that matched his dark hair, which was slightly flecked with gray. On his right cheekbone was a pair of twin white-ridged scars.

Those who gave him a close look could testify that his gun-metal eyes seemed to look *through* you, rather than *at* you. He gave off an air of alertness, of perpetual watchfulness. The look in his cool gray eyes, the way he moved, everything about him said this was a man who could handle any situation that came along.

Only no one in the middle of the street knew he was there…not the sheriff, and not the outlaws.

The tall stranger sidled up to two men who stood side by side. One was evidently the town barber, and the other his customer. The barber still held his straight-edge razor. The customer's face was lathered for shaving, and he wore the customary apron.

Many eyes were on the man in black as he spoke to the barber and the man with the lather on his face. "Looks like your sheriff's about to shoot it out with those three hombres."

"Yeah," nodded the barber. "They been causing trouble around here for a week. Six nights ago, they ambushed one of the sheriff's deputies and killed him. Then three days ago, they rode

into town, robbed the bank, and killed another deputy. They've
come back to spring their brother Arlo out of jail. Sheriff Holden's
gonna get himself killed sure as anything."

The tall man looked around at the crowd on both sides of the
street. "Well, there are plenty of men here wearing guns. How come
they don't jump in and help?"

The barber was unarmed, but his lathered customer had a
revolver on his hip. The customer's face crimsoned, then paled.
"Well...uh...it ain't our responsibility to face gunmen who ride in
here. That's what we pay the sheriff for."

The stranger's iron-gray eyes seemed to penetrate to the man's
very soul. The lathered man swallowed hard and looked away. The
barber swung his gaze to four armed townsmen who stood close by
and had heard the tall man's words. They gave him a blank stare,
looked sheepishly at each other, then watched the man in black as
he hurried down the boardwalk and disappeared between two
buildings.

TWO

Sheriff Brett Holden knew the talk he was getting from the Maldrum brothers was about over. Holden would have to back up his words with action.

Jake Maldrum's bold, sneering face was cast in a mold of sinister intent. He was about to say the secret word that would trigger the shootout with Holden when his attention was drawn to a tall man in black emerging from between the sheriff's office and jail building, and the hardware store adjacent to it. He was behind Holden, and the sheriff was unaware of his presence.

The people that lined the street saw the man moving up behind their sheriff. Nerves all along the boardwalks tensed even tighter.

Jake Maldrum and his brothers eyed the man in black who wore the low-slung Colt .45 as he moved silently up the sunwashed street.

Brett Holden's own nerves could take it no longer. "Enough talk!" he shouted. "You men are under arrest! If you don't drop those gunbelts this instant, I'll use this shotgun!"

Jake would have laughed and dared Holden to go for it, but the sight of the strange man coming up behind Brett Holden gave him a chill.

The sheriff could see that something had changed the atmosphere of the moment, but he was puzzled, wondering what it could be. Then he saw the man in black move up on his left side. The man's steady gray eyes were fixed on Holden's opponents.

The sheriff wasn't sure what to do. Keeping his eyes on the Maldrum brothers, he was about to ask the stranger what he was doing there when his question was answered for him.

The stranger spoke so only Holden could hear him. "Be ready to cut loose with both barrels if they go for their guns. Work from right to left. I'll go left to right."

Brett Holden had no idea who the man was, but it wouldn't have taken much to convince him he was an angel sent from heaven. He nodded slowly, gripping the warm metal of the shotgun and licking his lips.

Rufus and Harold eyed their older brother as he stood between them, his gaze fixed on the sheriff's new partner.

"Seems I heard the sheriff tell you boys to drop your gunbelts," the tall man said. "You deaf?"

Anger clawed at Jake's insides. His eyes were coldly venomous beneath the shadowing brim of his dirty Stetson. "He's got our brother in jail, mister! We want him out. And we'll have him out one way or another!"

"You've got it all wrong. Your brother's not getting out…you're going in! Now do like Sheriff Holden told you and unbuckle those gunbelts. Move real slow when you do it."

Harold and Rufus were like statues, waiting for their brother to speak the word…and eager to get it over with. Their own faces were beaded with sweat.

"You're buttin' in to somethin' that's none of your business, tall man," Jake said. "Best thing for you to do is back off and go back where you came from."

"What, and put the odds back where they were? Not a chance, pal. You really think the three of you can come away from this unscathed?"

"I'm countin' on it," Jake said.

"There's an old saying that seems appropriate here."

"And that is?"

"Convincing yourself that a bad idea is a good one, is a bad idea."

Jake chuckled hollowly. "Philosophy won't work here, mister. Now, unless you're a complete fool, you'll disappear and let us get on with our business. We're takin' Arlo outta that jail."

"No you're not!" Even as he spoke, Holden snapped back the hammers of the shotgun.

Reflex sent Jake's hand for his gun. It was too late to use the secret word. Harold and Rufus clawed for their weapons, both shouting vile profanities.

The stranger's gun was in his hand and spitting fire before the first barrel of the shotgun roared. The fingers of Harold's gunhand had barely gripped the butt of his revolver when his heart exploded from the .45 slug that ripped into it. Jake had his weapon on the way out of leather, but died with a bullet in his heart before he could bring it clear. The charge from the shotgun tore into Rufus's chest, knocking him flat on his back before he could draw his gun.

In the crowd, women and girls shrieked and looked away while boys drew sudden sharp breaths and men gasped. Some of the horses along the street nickered. Since there was no breeze, the acrid billows of blue-white gun smoke hung motionless over the street like a fog.

The Maldrum brothers lay sprawled in the hot sunlight, never to move again. Men and boys stepped off the boardwalks from both sides of the street and moved to the corpses, forming a circle around them. Low voices spoke of the lightning draw of the stranger and expressed their relief that the incident was over. Women and girls remained on the boardwalks and began to walk away, their faces pale and twisted from what they had just seen. Some entered stores and shops with proprietors and clerks on their heels, ready to resume the day's business.

Sheriff Holden eased the hammer down on the unused barrel, sighed, then turned to the tall man and said, "Mister, I don't know who you are or where you came from, but I'm mighty pleased you showed up. And I'm at a loss for words when it comes to thanking you properly. If…if you hadn't stepped in to help me, it'd be me lying in the dust dead. You're name isn't Michael or Gabriel, is it?"

The tall man broke his Peacemaker open, punched out the empty cartridges, smiled, and said, "No, sir."

"Well, them's the only angels' names I know, but right now I'd swear you just dropped out of the sky."

"Not quite," replied the tall man, pulling two cartridges from the loops on his gunbelt and sliding them into the empty slots in the cylinder. He snapped the cylinder into place, holstered the gun, and set his firm gaze on the circle of men who stood around the dead outlaws. Several were now looking his direction.

When they met his gaze, he moved toward them. Sheriff Holden followed. The tall man drew near the curious group and noted that most of them wore guns on their hips

"I see you gentlemen are wearing sidearms," he said, fixing his level gaze on them.

They stared at him blankly, but no one responded to his words.

"Seems to me that you wear them, but are afraid to use them. You all look able-bodied. Tell me…were you just going to stand there and let those killers gun your sheriff down?"

The group took on a shame-faced look, eyed each other in awkward abashment, then turned and walked away in silence.

Sheriff Holden noticed the town's undertaker, Lester Pettiman, standing near the hardware store, looking on. He caught his attention and motioned for him. Pettiman, a tall, skinny man who resembled Abraham Lincoln, strode to him.

"I s'pose you want 'em buried now, eh, Sheriff?"

"Yes. As soon as possible. The county will pay you as usual."

"Okay," nodded Pettiman, giving the stranger a slow glance.

Being six-three himself, the undertaker figured the man in black had him by a good inch or two. *Before* he put on his boots.

The sheriff turned to the man who towered over him and extended his hand. "You already know my name's Brett Holden. Since you aren't Michael or Gabriel, what *is* your name, stranger?"

"That's good enough, Sheriff."

Holden used his free hand to push his hat up a little and scratch his head. "Pardon me?" he said, brow furrowed.

"I said that's good enough. Just call me Stranger. John Stranger."

"Now, wait a minute. You're tellin' me your name is *John Stranger?*"

"Yep."

The sheriff chuckled. "Sure. Sure it is. I'd come closer to believing your name's Michael or Gabriel. C'mon, now. Nobody's name is John Stranger."

The tall man grinned. "Well, meet *nobody,* because my name *is* John Stranger."

Suddenly Brett Holden's jaw slacked. He blinked several times, snapped his fingers, and said, "Wait a minute! There's a bell ringing in the back of my head. I've heard of you! You're a gunfighter, aren't you?"

"Well, not exactly."

"Don't give me that! You're the fella who took out Tate Landry up in Wyoming! Right?"

"Well, yes, but only because I had to. I'm not a gunfighter. I—"

"Wait a minute!" Holden said, snapping his fingers again. "It's coming to me now. You do favors for that top-dog U.S. marshal in Denver. What's-iz-name? Ah—"

"Chief Solomon Duvall."

"Yeah, Duvall. So what brings you to Prescott?"

"Well, it just so happens that I'm on a mission for Chief Duvall."

"Oh?"

"I was riding west with a wagon train. Started in Wyoming and stayed with the train till it was safely over the Sierras and down on the other side."

"Riding as a guard?"

"Sort of. There was someone in the train who means more than all the world to me. I wanted to make sure she made it through Indian country and over the mountains safely."

"*She*, eh?" grinned the sheriff. "You married, or is this your intended?"

"My intended. Anyway, Chief Duvall knew I was with the wagon train and left a message for me with the town marshal at Placerville. Duvall asked that I get down to Apache Junction as quickly as possible. Seems Marshal Ben Clifton's got a serious problem."

"Apache or otherwise?"

"Otherwise. Duvall's wire said that gold miners in the area are trying to take over the town and put their own man in as marshal…a gunslick known as Hardy Bell."

Holden's eyebrows arched. "Hardy Bell!" he echoed. "I know about him. Fast and deadly. Men cower when he comes around. Bad dude."

"Mm-hmm. I've heard of him, too."

"Well, ol' Ben's getting up there in years. I'm sure he can use your help. Haven't seen him in a spell, but if I recollect right, he's gotta be pushing sixty-five."

"Duvall's wire said he's in his mid-sixties. I'm afraid the miners may have already murdered Clifton and taken over the town. I'd send a telegram down there to Clifton to see if he's all right, but if the gang has taken over the town, they'll control the telegraph office. I sure don't want them to know there's an adversary on his way. So, I've got to keep moving."

"Have you had lunch?"

"No."

"Well, even though you're in a hurry to get to Apache Junction, you've got to eat. Can I buy you lunch?"

"I don't usually take time to eat at midday, Sheriff," grinned Stranger, "but I'll take time to eat a bite with you…and I'll buy."

"Well, we'll argue over who pays after we've eaten. Let's—"

Sheriff Holden's attention was drawn to an Arizona Stagelines stagecoach rolling down the street, coming in from Flagstaff. As it passed them, he saw a familiar face in one of the windows.

"Uh-oh," he said, rubbing his chin. "Guess I won't be able to eat lunch with you after all, Mr. Stranger."

"Problem?"

"Yeah," nodded Holden, watching the coach draw up to the stagelines office a half-block away. "On that stage is the newly made widow of my deputy, Jimmy Yarbro. Bonnie was visiting her parents in northern Wyoming when the Maldrum brothers ambushed and killed Jimmy last Wednesday. I wired Bonnie, and she answered back that she would be on the first available stage south. The stages don't run often in that part of Wyoming, so it's taken her almost a week to get here."

"Poor little gal," Stranger said. "They have any children?"

"No. Only been married a few months." Holden sighed. "I've got to go console her as best as I can…and I'll have to take her to Jimmy's grave. You understand."

"Of course. Anything I can do?"

"Not that I can think of. I want to thank you again for siding with me against the Maldrums. I'd be dead for sure if you hadn't."

"Glad I showed up in time, Sheriff. You go on now and tend to the widow."

Holden started to turn away, but then saw that Bonnie Yarbro was surrounded by several women who were her close friends. He paused, looked back at Stranger, and said, "I'll give it a couple of minutes. Let her friends offer their condolences first."

Stranger nodded, his gaze on the widow and her group of consolers.

"I'm…ah…curious about something, Mr. Stranger," Holden said, turning to face the tall man once again.

"About what?"

"Where are you from?"

Stranger let a wide grin curve his mouth. "Well, Sheriff, I'm from a far country. No time to explain. I'm sure Mrs. Yarbro needs to see your face right about now, in spite of the group that's surrounding her."

Even as he spoke, Stranger reached into a pocket and produced a silver disk the exact size of a silver dollar. He placed it in Holden's hand and said, "Here's a little something to remember me by."

The sheriff closed his fingers around the disk without looking at it, assuming it was a silver dollar. He glanced toward the stagecoach, then smiled at Stranger and said, "My friend, how could I ever forget you? Every time I look in a mirror and see Brett Holden alive, I'll think of you. But I will keep the dollar as a token of friendship. Thank you."

As Holden walked the dusty street toward Bonnie, he took in a deep breath, thankful to be alive. In all his years wearing a badge, he had never come any closer to dying than he had that day. *You may not be Michael or Gabriel, Mr. John Stranger,* he thought, *but you sure were heaven's gift to me today!*

Brett Holden was almost to the stagecoach when the odd feel of the silver dollar caused him to stop and examine it. He was surprised to see that the medallion was emblazoned with a raised five-point star in its center, and words were inscribed around its circular edge: *THE STRANGER THAT SHALL COME FROM A FAR LAND—Deuteronomy 29:22.*

Holden whipped around and looked back where he had left John Stranger. The mysterious man was gone.

THREE

———◆———

John Stranger skirted the barren Bradshaw Mountains along their eastern foothills and headed due south. He figured to reach the southern tip of the Bradshaws an hour or so after dark. He would camp on the bank of the Aqua Fria River, allow a good night's rest for Ebony and himself, and ride out a couple of hours before dawn. He knew there was good grass for Ebony along the river's edge. Stranger would satisfy his own hunger with hardtack, beef jerky, and strong coffee.

When he pulled away from the Aqua Fria in the morning, he would angle southeast across the sandy valley just west of the Mazatzal Mountain Range toward Apache Junction, bypassing Phoenix some twenty-five miles to the west. If all went well, he would make it to Apache Junction sometime in the afternoon day after tomorrow, Thursday, October 17.

A broad sweep of sandy desert lay off to Stranger's left as he held the big black to a steady walk. It was still hot enough that he didn't want to overwork Ebony. Rocks and boulders were scattered across the open land eastward amid patches of catclaw, rabbitbrush, squat cacti, and the towering saguaros. About a mile to the east, he could make out a thin line of mesquite trees growing along a long wall of great jagged rocks, deep red and shaped like tongues of flame.

Westward, to Stranger's right, the bald, sun-scorched Bradshaw peaks cut a jagged bite out of the azure sky, their magnificent shapes sculptured by centuries of desert winds.

John Stranger saw smooth-skinned salamanders sunning themselves on hot rocks, occasionally accompanied by their lizard friends. There were signs of desert night creatures in the pliable sand, and he caught sight of a diamondback rattler slithering among the squat cacti and the rocks.

Stranger was aware that Apaches roamed the desert where he rode, and he kept a wary eye out for them. He had been in Apache country many a time, and knew that they gave no quarter to white men...though he was dark enough that he had often been accused of being part Indian. He had befriended a few Apaches and had learned enough of their language to understand much of what they said. He had given the gospel to some of them, but found it very difficult to get them to listen.

Soon a massive tower of rock jutting up like a church steeple came into view, nestled in the edge of the mountains. He knew at the bottom of the rock formation was a small village. He would stop there, water Ebony, and fill his canteen.

Another few minutes brought him into Alexandra, which according to the weather-beaten sign at the village's outskirts boasted a population of 211. The main street was wide, but had no boardwalks. There was a saloon and a small general store opposite each other in the center of the village, and next to the general store was the Arizona Stagelines office, which was nothing more than a clapboard hut. In front of the stage office was a water trough. On both sides of the street were scattered shacks and rustic cabins.

John veered his mount toward the water trough full of cool, clear water. He left his saddle, patted Ebony, and said, "There you go, boy. Get yourself a belly full." As John lifted the canvas strap of his canteen over the saddlehorn, he saw the agent step out into the sunlight and smile.

"Hello," said the agent.

"Howdy," grinned Stranger.

"Sorta hot for mid-October, wouldn't you say?"

Stranger lifted his hat and wiped his brow with his sleeve. "Yep. A bit warm. I guess it's all right to pump a little water into my canteen?"

"Sure. That's what it's for. Take all you want."

"Much obliged." Stranger began working the well pump at the end of the trough.

A wagon came rattling up and stopped in a cloud of dust. In it was a well-dressed man with silver hair and a younger man, obviously a rancher, who held the reins.

"Good afternoon, Clarence," the rancher said. "You remember my grandfather. He came in on your stage three weeks ago."

The agent smiled. "Sure do. How are you, Mr. Scott?"

"Just fine, sir. I'm finding it necessary to leave a little sooner than planned. If I remember right, the stage coming from Phoenix and heading for Prescott comes through here about three o'clock, doesn't it?"

"Uh…no, sir," Clarence said. "It's due in here at *four* o'clock."

"Oh," said Scott, pulling his watch from a vest pocket and checking it. "Two-forty. Well, that won't be too long a wait. That is, if there is a seat available."

"There is, sir. In fact, *exactly* one seat."

"You're sure?"

"Oh, yes. I always receive a wire from the Phoenix office after the stage has left there so I'll know if there's room for additional passengers."

"Good," Scott said. "Then, I'll take it."

"All right. Come on in the office, and we'll get you a ticket."

Stranger finished filling his canteen as the men headed toward the office. "Thank you for the water, sir!" he called.

Clarence raised a friendly hand and said, "My pleasure. You watch out for Apaches now!"

"I will," Stranger said. He patted Ebony's neck. "You get enough, boy?"

The big black nickered.

"Good," he said, swinging into the saddle. "You can drink out of the Aqua Fria tonight."

Stranger and Ebony headed south and were almost out of Alexandra when the tall man's attention was drawn to the backyard of a tumble-down house some thirty yards to his right. A man, whose back was toward Stranger, was angrily swearing at a young woman hanging up her wash on a thin rope strung between two Palo Verde trees.

Stranger drew rein and watched. Neither the man nor the woman noticed him. While the man grew louder, the woman spoke to him in low tones, punctuated periodically by a "Shh!"

Stranger was about to ride on when he heard the man's voice grow louder yet, then his hand flashed out and slapped the woman, knocking her down. There were other houses close by, but no one else was in sight.

John Stranger put Ebony to a gallop, his own anger rising. The man had the woman down and was straddling her on his knees, cursing and slapping her face. She was weeping and begging him to stop and trying to fend off his blows with her hands.

Stranger slid from the saddle and saw the frightened faces of two small children in a window at the rear of the house.

The man gripped the woman's long black hair and jerked her head back. "You're my wife, Marie, and you'll do *what* I tell you *when* I tell you!"

Marie's face was blotched from fear and bright red where the open-handed blows had struck her. She saw the tall man just as his voice cut the air.

"Let go of her, mister! Now!"

The man's head snapped around, but he made no move to release his hold on Marie's hair.

"I said let go of her."

The man swore and yelled through clenched teeth, "Get off my property and mind your own business! This is between me and my wife!"

"I made myself a promise years ago to *make* it my business whenever I see a man rough up a woman. Now, I'm telling you once more…let go of her hair and get off her."

The man swore at him again. "I told you to get off my property, mister! Now do it!"

Stranger swatted the man's hat off his head, sank strong fingers into his thick hair, and gave it a savage twist. The man yelled and let go of Marie. Stranger yanked him off her and held him low to the ground.

Marie was sobbing as she worked her way to her feet and began straightening her hair. She glanced toward her frightened children, who knew not to come out of the house unless they were invited.

Stranger kept her husband on his knees by the grip he had on his hair. The man was sucking air through gritted teeth.

Stranger looked at the woman and asked, "What's your last name, Marie?"

"Standish."

"And this is your husband?"

"Yes. His name's Curt."

"Let go of me!" Curt screamed.

Stranger twisted the hair a little tighter, and Curt wailed.

"I'll talk to you in a minute, Curt," Stranger said, then looked at Marie. "Why was he beating on you, ma'am?"

Marie glanced toward the window where her two children watched with tear-stained cheeks, then looked back at Stranger and said, "Curt has a gambling problem, sir. He came home from the saloon last night, reeking of whiskey—" She interrupted herself long enough to sniff, then continued. "He was half-drunk and told me he'd lost this week's wages in a poker game."

"Shut up, Marie!" Curt yelled. "You don't have to tell him anything!"

Stranger gave the hair a yank. "Just be quiet. I said I'll talk to you in a minute."

Curt Standish let out another wail, breathing hard and grinding his teeth.

To Marie, Stranger said, "You were saying…"

"He told me he lost this week's wages in a poker game at the saloon. We have three children, sir. One is a tiny baby. We have very little food and now no money to buy any more. Curt works for a rancher about two miles east of town. Instead of going to work this morning, he stayed in bed to sleep off his drunk. He got up a little while ago and ordered me to stop washing the clothes and scrounge him up enough food for breakfast. I told him he would have to wait a few minutes while I hung up this batch of clothes. He lost his temper and started beating on me."

Stranger nodded and yanked Curt's head back like the man had done to Marie. "I want you to know exactly how it felt to your wife when you did this to her, Curt. You like this? Do you?"

Standish stared at Stranger with hate-filled eyes, but did not reply. Stranger twisted harder.

"I asked you a question, woman-beater! You like this?"

Curt wailed, then gasped, "No! No, I don't like it!"

"Well, Marie didn't like it, either. You know what I think of a brute who manhandles a woman, Curt?"

"No."

"I think he's a sniveling coward. Don't you?"

"Yes. Yes, whatever you say."

"When you married Marie, did you vow to love, honor, and cherish her?"

"I suppose."

"What I just saw you doing to her…do you call that loving, honoring, and cherishing her?"

Curt groaned. "You're killin' me, man!"

"You didn't answer my question."

"No!" he gasped, closing his eyes and biting his lips.

"Then you broke your vows, didn't you?"

"Yes."

"And Marie deserves an apology, doesn't she?"

Curt's pain-filled eyes rolled to his wife. "I'm sorry, Marie. I'm sorry I hit you."

"You ever going to do it again?"

"No! Never!"

"Is that a promise?"

"Yes!"

"How about the gambling? You going to stop gambling so you can provide for your family?"

"Yes!" came the pitiable answer.

"Promise?"

"Yes!"

Stranger looked at Marie. "Do you believe him?"

"This has happened so many times...both the gambling and the beatings. I don't know whether to believe him or not."

"I mean it, Marie!" bawled Curt. "I really do! Believe me!"

The children at the window could be heard whimpering. Marie said, "I need to go to my son and daughter."

"Go ahead, ma'am," Stranger said. "Curt and I will wait here."

Marie rushed to the back door of the house and went inside.

"A man who'd beat up on a woman deserves a real horsewhipping, Curt," Stranger said. "You understand me?"

As he spoke, John Stranger released his hold on Curt's hair and took a step back. Curt Standish struggled to his feet, his eyes bulging and fiery, his mouth hardset. Suddenly he roared like a maddened beast and charged the man who stood six inches taller than he. He swung a haymaker at Stranger's jaw, but missed. He swore as he attempted to regain his balance.

"Better get a grip on that temper, Curt," Stranger said. "You try hitting me again, I'll have to put you down."

Enraged, Curt charged again, both fists pumping. Stranger dodged the blows and landed a punch of his own that sounded like an ax hitting the bark of a tree. So great was the impact that Standish's head whipped sideways and his feet left the ground. When he landed, he was out cold.

Stranger headed for the house leaving Curt spread-eagled on the ground. Marie was standing at the back door with a tiny baby in her arms and the older son and daughter pressed close on each side. Her right eye was swelling and bruises were evident on her cheeks.

"Is…is he all right?" she asked in a tremulous voice.

"He'll come out of it in a few minutes. In the meantime, I want to take you to buy some groceries."

Marie's jaw slacked in astonishment, and there was a flash of tears in her eyes. "But…sir, why would you do this? You don't even know us."

Stranger knelt down to the level of the little boy and girl, smiled, and asked their names and ages. He learned that Bobby was six and Emily was four. He took both children in his arms, hugged them, and looked up at their mother. "Ma'am, I may not know you, but I know you need some help. How about we take your wagon and go to the store?"

Curt Standish felt as if the ground beneath him was whirling in a tight circle. He opened his eyes, then closed them against the afternoon sun. He moaned, trying to recall what had happened to him. Then it all came back. The tall man with the scars on his cheek. His punch was like the kick of a mule!

Curt rubbed his eyes, rolled over, and opened them again. This time the sun was behind him. He rubbed his sore jaw and worked his way to a sitting position. He shaded his eyes with his hand and looked around for Marie and the stranger. There was no sign of them. The big black gelding was gone, too.

With effort, Curt worked his way to his feet and stood swaying for a few moments. He stumbled to the back porch and used one of the posts that held up the weather-beaten porch roof to support him until his head grew clearer. Then he staggered into the kitchen.

"Marie!" he called out. "Marie!" No response.

He moved into the small parlor. When he saw that it was unoccupied, he went to the children's bedroom, then his and Marie's bedroom. No sign of his family. Even the little crib was empty.

What had happened to them? Where had they gone?

He made his way onto the front porch and looked both ways on the dusty road. It was empty. He rubbed his jaw, then his temples, and went back into the house, mumbling to himself. His head had been aching from a hangover; the punch had made it much worse.

He returned to the kitchen and stepped out on the back porch. It was then that he noticed the family wagon was missing. It was always parked next to the small barn and corral. His two mules were not in sight, either. They could be inside the barn, but he doubted it. Since the wagon was gone, the mules were probably gone, too.

But where?

Could Marie have run off with the strange man? She hadn't taken any clothes for herself or the children, at least not that he could tell. But then if she was leaving in a hurry, she wouldn't have had time to pack.

A sick feeling washed over Curt Standish and a lump rose in his throat. Suddenly a cry escaped his lips. "No, Marie! No-o! Come back! I'm sorry for the way I've treated you! Marie—"

Curt's cry was interrupted by the sound of a wagon rattling

into the yard. He bolted off the porch and saw Marie and the children on the seat. Bobby was holding the baby so his mother could handle the reins. Tears filled Curt's eyes as he ran to meet them. Marie pulled rein and looked at him coolly.

Curt ran up to Marie's side of the wagon and blurted, "Honey, I'm sorry! I'm so sorry! I thought...I thought—"

"That we'd gone off and left you?"

"Yes," he sobbed, thumbing tears. "I'm sorry, honey. Please forgive me! Bobby! Emily! Please forgive your Daddy for the awful way I've been treating all of you!"

The children stared at him but did not reply.

"Curt, did you mean it when you promised never to gamble again?" Marie said, her eyes stern.

"Yes...yes, I meant it. And I'm never going to drink again or lay a hand on you. I've been a horrible husband and father. It'll be different, now, I promise. Please forgive me!"

Marie looked at Bobby and Emily and said, "I believe Daddy means it this time, children. Can you find it in your hearts to forgive him?"

With his lower lip quivering, Bobby set tearful eyes on his father and said, "I forgive you, Daddy."

"Me, too," chimed in Emily.

"And so do I," said Marie. "And I hope eventually that I'll be able to trust you again."

Curt wept while he reached up and embraced each one.

"Curt, take a look in the back of the wagon," Marie said.

Curt wiped his eyes and looked in the wagon bed. It was loaded with several boxes of groceries. "Wha— How? Who?"

"That stranger," said Marie.

"You mean he—?"

"Yes. I tried to talk him out of it, but he wouldn't listen. Said it was his pleasure to give us the food."

Shaking his head in wonderment, Curt looked toward the road for some sign of the man. "Where is he, Marie?"

"He's gone," she said with a sigh.

"Gone?"

"Yes."

"But…but I want to thank him. For the groceries, yes…and even more for beating some sense into my thick skull! Do you know where he went?"

"No. He was in a hurry to move on, but he gave me something to remember him by." Marie reached into her dress pocket and produced a silver medallion the size of a silver dollar.

"What's this?"

She laid it in his palm and said, "If he didn't have those scars on his face, I'd think maybe we had a visit from one of God's angels."

Curt Standish stared at the silver disk in his hand. It had a five-point star emblazoned in its center and raised lettering around its circular edge that read: *THE STRANGER THAT SHALL COME FROM A FAR LAND—Deuteronomy 29:22.*

"A far land," Curt said in a half-whisper. "Marie, maybe angels can have scars."

"I don't think so. No, I'm sure he's human and mortal. But he sure has been a messenger from heaven to the Standish family!"

"Yeah, you're right, I'm sure. But I wonder what far country he's from?"

"I guess we'll never know," she sighed. "At least while we're wondering, we won't have to do it on empty stomachs!"

CHAPTER

FOUR

———◆———

J ohn Stranger rode south, watching the shadows change along the east side of the Bradshaw Mountains as the sun crept westward. The warm, fragrant desert wind caressed his face as Breanna Baylor touched his mind. He missed her and longed to be with her.

The winding dusty road lay before him like a smooth, tan ribbon as it skirted the edge of the foothills and wended its way toward Phoenix. The Bradshaw Mountains were impressive. The great heave of splintered rock amid massive mounds of sand dwarfed Stranger, making him feel small and insignificant.

Off to his left, as far as the eye could see, there arose blunt, broken ranges of sandy hills in isolated groups, with dark pockets of rock imbedded in their sides. The desert floor stretched away between and beyond them, dotted with giant saguaros standing as sentinels over the arid wilderness.

Ebony carried his master into a deep draw, then trotted up the steep incline toward its crest. When they reached the top, Stranger suddenly drew rein and backtracked quickly at the scene taking place not more than a hundred yards in front of him.

The Arizona Stagelines stage from Phoenix—the one the man

named Scott was planning to ride from Alexandra—was stopped in the middle of the road. Four men wearing bandannas for masks had dismounted and were holding their guns on the driver and shot-gunner, whose hands were lifted over their heads.

There was a rocky ridge rising up out of the desert floor to a height of some ten or twelve feet along the edge of the Bradshaws' foothills. The ridge was broken in places, leaving room enough to ride a horse through. Stranger figured the outlaws had filed through one of the openings and surprised the crew.

If the broken places in the ridge could serve robbers, they could serve John Stranger to *stop* robbers. He spurred Ebony to a gallop, rounded the rise westward, below the crest, and darted behind the rocky ridge. Soon he skidded Ebony to a halt on the opposite side of the ridge where the stage was stopped.

He drew his Colt .45, pulled a second one from a saddlebag, and hurried into the same opening where mingled hoofprints indicated the robbers had been. He kept himself out of sight and appraised the situation.

The coach was about forty feet away. All four robbers were off their horses. One was taking a cash box, which had been under the seat up top, from the hands of the driver. Two had the passengers out of the coach and were relieving them of their valuables. The fourth outlaw was standing with his back to Stranger, holding a revolver in a position to shoot anyone who made a threatening move.

Stranger stepped from the shadowed opening, cocked the hammers to his revolvers, and yelled, "Everybody make like a statue!"

Shock showed on the faces of the three robbers who could see him. The one whose back was toward him started to turn. Stranger's left-hand gun roared, and the bullet plucked the robber's hat off his head. The man froze, dropped his gun in the sand, and threw his hands in the air, crying, "Don't shoot me!"

Stranger moved up quickly beside him and yelled, "The rest of you! Drop your guns!" The other three obeyed without hesitation.

Three of the passengers were men—one in his thirties and the other two in their fifties. The woman was portly and in her early sixties. She smiled at Stranger and said with trembling voice, "God bless you, mister! You sure came along at the right time!"

"You folks climb back in the coach," John said. "We'll retrieve your valuables in a moment."

While he spoke, the driver and shotgunner climbed down. The driver, a skinny little man in his sixties, smiled broadly and said, "Bless your bones, mister! I don't know how to thank you, but if you'll give me your name and address, I'll sure see that Mr. Wilson, the owner of this stageline, finds out what you did. There'll be a handsome reward comin' your way, I'll guarantee you that!"

Before Stranger could reply, the woman, now seated at a window in the coach, said, "You're an angel, mister! A real angel! Those awful men took a brooch that belonged to my great-grandmother. It's priceless to me!"

"You'll have it back in a moment, ma'am," he said with a smile.

The shotgunner stepped around the driver and said, "Boy, am I glad you showed up, stranger! I'm Tad Dunne, and this here's Roy Noble. What's your name?"

"You can call me John."

"John? Just John?"

"That's enough."

"Well, Mr. John, you hold them guns on these scummy dudes while I take back everything they stole."

Stranger nodded, then said to the robbers, "One false move, and it'll be your last."

The shotgunner first removed the masks from the robbers, but did not recognize them. Neither did the driver or the passengers. The outlaws glared at Stranger, but said nothing. While Dunne reclaimed the stolen items and returned them to their owners, Noble hoisted the cash box back on top, then climbed up and placed it once again under the seat.

Stranger then said to Dunne, "If you've got some rope, we'll bind these men up good, put them in their saddles, and tie the reins to the back of the coach. You can deliver them to Sheriff Holden in Prescott."

"We got plenty of rope," Dunne grinned. "C'mon, Roy, help me tie 'em up."

Stranger held his guns on the robbers while driver and shot-gunner bound their hands securely behind their backs. Stranger and Tad then hoisted them into their saddles and secured the reins of their horses to the rear of the coach. Tad would ride atop the coach in the rack and keep an eye on them all the way to Prescott.

Stranger sent a shrill whistle toward the rock ridge, and the big black gelding came through the opening on the run.

"What a beautiful animal!" Roy exclaimed.

"Don't say the word *animal* too loud," chuckled Stranger. "He thinks he's just a large, hairy human."

The driver laughed, then said, "You spoke of Sheriff Holden as though you know him. Do you?"

"Yes, sir. He and I are friends. Just tell him John Stranger said hello, will you?"

"John *Stranger?*"

"Yep."

"Well, I sure will, Mr. Stranger," grinned the driver, wanting to ask more but refraining.

Suddenly the portly woman was out of the coach and heading for the tall man. "Thank you, Mr. Stranger," she said, and she reached up and kissed him on the cheek.

"You're welcome, ma'am," he said, a bit embarrassed.

Roy Noble pulled a stub of a pencil and a slip of paper out of his shirt pocket and said, "Now, Mr. Stranger, if you'll just give me your address, I'll see that Mr. Wilson gets it. He'll definitely want to reward you."

"That really isn't necessary. Besides, my address is a long way off." From his pocket, Stranger produced a silver medallion and placed it in the driver's hand. "This will help you to understand," he said, then turned, mounted Ebony, and rode away.

Tad and the woman moved in close to see what the stranger had placed in Roy's hand. The other passengers climbed out of the coach and joined them.

Noble pushed his hat to the back of his head and made a low whistle, holding the medallion so only he could see it.

"Well, come on," said Tad. "Let us see it. What is it, anyway?"

Noble held the medallion so all could see and said, "Look. It's got a star in the middle, and part of a Scripture verse on it." He turned it so he could see it again. "Says, *THE STRANGER THAT SHALL COME FROM A FAR LAND*. The verse is Deuteronomy 29:22."

"The stranger that shall come from a far land," echoed the woman. "Sure enough—God sent us down an angel to thwart the robbery!"

The four outlaws sat on their horses behind the stagecoach, eyes wide, and exchanged glances.

The sun touched the tips of the Bradshaw peaks as John Stranger guided Ebony due south toward the Aqua Fria River. He watched the yellow sun turn to gold, then to red, and slowly sink behind the mountains. Twilight stole across the desert, lingered for a while, then gradually turned to gloom. The vault of blue-black overhead lightened to the twinkling stars. Then fell the serene, silent, luminous desert night.

Stranger rode on for another hour, listening to the steady sound of Ebony's hooves on the soft desert floor. Soon a large round moon appeared on the eastern horizon and began its rise. Within an hour the moon shone so brightly, it faded the stars in the eastern heavens.

It was then that Stranger heard the gurgle of the Aqua Fria.

Ebony picked it up too and gave a soft whinny. They topped a gentle rise, and the moon-struck river lay before them like a silver ribbon.

Stranger found a spot beside the river to make camp. He removed the saddle from Ebony's back and let him move to the bank and drink. While the horse took his fill, Stranger gathered wood from beneath the mesquite trees that clustered near the bank and built a fire. He took the small coffeepot from his saddlebags and made a strong brew, then sat on the ground next to the fire, leaned against a tree, and ate hardtack and beef jerky. Ebony cropped grass along the bank.

A desert bird sounded a melancholy note from somewhere in the treetops, and a distant coyote howled. Then all was quiet except for the soft murmur of the river.

Stranger finished his meal, washed the tin cup in the river, and put it in the saddlebag. He added more mesquite to the fire. He removed his hat and laid it beside him, leaned back against the tree with a sigh, and closed his eyes.

A face haunted him…a woman's face. Her sky-blue eyes, the breeze blowing her honey-blond hair, her sweet smile, the warmth of her personality…

John Stranger opened his eyes. Breanna's face was there in the red heart of the fire. It hung in the shadows that hovered over the flickering light. It drifted in the darkness beyond. His mind was thronged by memories of Breanna, touched by the sweetness of knowing that she belonged to him.

His thoughts drifted back to that stormy day on the plains of central Kansas when he first laid eyes on her…the day he rescued her from a cattle stampede. John saw a lot of Breanna Baylor in the days that followed, and as those days passed into weeks, he knew he was falling in love.

Then came the blow that shook John to the depths of his soul. Suddenly, unexpectedly, Breanna asked John to remove himself from her life.

John Stranger rose from where he leaned against the tree,

picked up some more mesquite limbs, and tossed them on the fire. He sat back down, laid his head against the rough bark, and recalled the things Breanna had told him when they were recently reunited…

That day in Wichita, Breanna realized she had made a horrible mistake by sending John out of her life. She had called out to him as he rode away, but it was too late. She began praying earnestly that the Lord would bring John back into her life, but even though John rescued her from danger on several occasions, they never spoke to each other.

Breanna began to have a recurring dream in which John came riding to meet her at a cabin in the foothills of the Colorado Rockies. The dream had always ended just as she was asking John's forgiveness and pouring out her heart to him in words of love.

Breanna had been aboard a wagon train in Wyoming, headed for California. Frank Miller was following the train, intending to kill her. Several days previously, Frank's wife Lorraine had been shot accidentally in South Pass City. Breanna was filling in as town physician and had performed surgery on Lorraine, who died on the operating table. Frank believed Breanna could have saved Lorraine, but let her die to get back at him for jilting her. He was trailing the wagon train bent on revenge. At the same time, John Stranger was riding toward the wagon train to look in on the woman he loved.

A serious problem had developed for Breanna. Red Claw, a Snake Indian chief, and his warriors had frequently attacked the wagon train and were still a threat. More than anything, Red Claw wanted to capture Breanna for himself.

Near Fort Bridger, wagon master Rip Clayson directed the wagons into a wooded area where there were high hills and towering rock formations. The wagons were placed in their usual circle in an open spot. They were out of ammunition and could only hope and pray that the cavalry unit they had sent for would find them before Red Claw and his warriors attacked again.

Rip showed Breanna a lofty rock formation some two hundred yards to the east and told her that nature had provided a crude staircase all the way to a cave at the top. He said he wanted her to hide in the cave until the danger was past. He then reached into his pants pocket and pulled out a single .41 caliber bullet for the Derringer Breanna was carrying. It was the only bullet left in the camp.

Rip struggled to find the right words as he told Breanna that should Red Claw find her, she must use the gun on herself. What Red Claw would do to her before he killed her was too horrible to think about. Reluctantly, Breanna promised she would use the bullet on herself before she would allow Red Claw to capture her.

Alone in the shallow cave, Breanna longed for the man she loved and prayed that God would spare her the horror of taking her own life.

A gust of wind fanned the embers of the fire, brightening them. It blew sparks, white ashes, and swirls of smoke into the moonlit night. The Aqua Fria flowed on, undisturbed.

John Stranger let his mind go back to the hurried ride as he pursued Rip Clayson's wagon train...

Stranger had seen fresh graves along the trail and could tell by various signs that the deaths had been caused by Indian attacks. He would not let himself believe Breanna's body was in one of those graves.

It was late afternoon when Ebony suddenly nickered and tossed his head, fighting the bit. There was danger near, and Ebony sensed it. Only seconds had passed when the scream of a cougar split the air.

Then Stranger saw it. There was a man bound to a pine, and the cougar was attacking him!

Stranger quickly pulled his Winchester .44 from its scabbard, took careful aim, and fired. The cat went down with a wild screech, then tried to get up. A second shot put him down for good.

Stranger dashed to the tree and found the man bloodied but still alive. He was shocked to see that it was Frank Miller! Miller recognized Stranger and told him he was following the Clayson wagon train. Snake Indians had surrounded him, tied him to the tree, and smeared him with animal blood, then left him for some wild beast to tear apart.

Miller knew he was dying. He told Stranger that he had been wrong about Breanna and asked him to tell her how very sorry he was. As Stranger was assuring him he would, Miller took his last breath. Stranger cut the body loose and, for lack of a shovel, piled rocks on the body for a grave. He rode hard after the wagon train and prayed for Breanna's safety.

The sun was setting when Stranger entered an area of tall rock formations and saw a man leaning against a boulder along the side of the road. The man told him he was part of the Rip Clayson wagon train and was waiting there to direct a cavalry unit coming from Fort Bridger to the south. When Stranger inquired about Breanna, the man told him that Clayson had hidden her in a cave atop a high rock formation.

Stranger galloped into the camp and asked where Breanna was hidden. Clayson pointed out the cave and said that Red Claw and a band of warriors had just shown up and were making their way up the crude staircase. Somehow they had seen him take her up there. Clayson also told him that Breanna had one bullet in a Derringer and had promised Rip she would use it rather than face what Red Claw had planned for her.

Stranger gouged Ebony's sides, sending him at a gallop into the forest. Stranger glanced up toward the cave and saw the chief in his full headdress in the lead. Breanna appeared at the mouth of the cave, watching Red Claw and the long line of painted warriors climb toward her. Stranger knew there was no way she could see him for the trees.

Suddenly the sound of a bugle cut the air. The Snakes took

one look at the large cavalry unit closing in and hurried down the natural staircase toward the horses they had stashed in the forest below. All but Red Claw—the sound of the bugle had not deterred him from his goal.

Stranger bolted for the staircase, ignoring the warriors still racing down it. He was within fifty feet of it when the last of the Snakes bounded down the sod base. Some were already mounted and galloping away.

Stranger reached the staircase and started climbing with the sound of the bugle blaring behind and below. He caught a glimpse of Red Claw above him dashing toward the cave. A breathless "No-o!" escaped his lips, and he began taking the crude stone steps two and three at a time.

And then it came.

The sharp report of the Derringer slapped the air, spelling death and echoing out of the cave and across the rocky, wooded land.

John Stranger stopped. He went cold inside. Breathing Breanna's name, he charged upward toward the cave. As he reached the top of the rock stairs, his eyes widened and his scalp tingled at what he saw.

Red Claw lay flat on his back, his sightless eyes staring vacantly into space. A blue hole centered his chest, fringed with blood. Breanna Baylor was leaning against the back wall of the cave, her cheeks shining with tears. She held the Derringer loosely in her right hand.

At the sight of the tall figure silhouetted against the purple sky, she let the small weapon slip through her fingers. Breanna found her voice and gasped, "John! Oh, John!"

John Stranger gathered the woman he loved in his arms, his own eyes swimming with tears. "Sorry I was late this time," he said.

"There was nothing I could do but put my bullet in him," Breanna said.

John cupped his hand under her chin and said, "The Lord's

timing is always perfect, darling. That never was *your* bullet. It was meant for Red Claw all the time."

Words long pent-up suddenly burst from Breanna's lips, tumbling one on top of the other. John's forefinger was on her lips. "Hush, darling," he breathed. "You don't have to do this. All that matters is that I know you love me as I love you...that we can have each other. There's nothing to forgive."

John Stranger tossed a few more broken limbs on the fire, and thought of how he had joined the wagon train, wanting to make sure Breanna got through Indian country and over the Sierra Nevada Mountains safely. While they traveled, she told him of her recurring dream and of how she had longed to be in his arms. They prayed together time and again, seeking the Lord's will regarding their relationship. Shortly before the wagon train rolled out of the Sierras into Placerville, California, the Holy Spirit had given direction to both of them. For the time being, they were to continue to fulfill their calling in life—Breanna as a visiting nurse, and John as a traveling preacher, helper of lawmen, nemesis of outlaws, and protector of the helpless.

They would be together from time to time, as God allowed...and one day, in His time, they would marry.

John rolled to his knees, stretched his arms, yawned, and reached for the bedroll, which lay close by, next to his saddle. He unfolded the bedroll and placed the saddle so he could use it as a pillow, then rose to his feet. He went to Ebony, who nickered a soft greeting.

Stranger stroked the gelding's long face, patted his neck, and said, "Well, partner, I guess it's about time to turn in. You get yourself a good night's sleep, okay? We've got a long way to go tomorrow."

Stranger tossed more wood on the fire, removed his gunbelt, then slid into the bedroll. He placed the gunbelt next to his right leg beneath the covers. The mournful cry of a wolf disturbed the soft sounds of the night. Stranger settled his head on the saddle, sighed, and said in a half-whisper, "I understand, ol' boy. I understand."

The soft gurgle of the river and the mild breeze in the trees around him were soothing and conducive to slumber. He was almost asleep when Ebony whinnied in a manner that told him they were not alone. Stranger drew the Colt .45 from its holster beneath the blankets. The big black whinnied again as a sharp clink of metal against stone met Stranger's ears, along with the soft padding of hooves in the sand.

Stranger quickly rolled onto his belly, snapped back the hammer of the Peacemaker, and aimed it at the man who sat astride a gray roan in the glow of the fire.

The rider lifted his hands and called out, "Hey, partner, I mean no harm! I saw your fire when I topped a rise a mile or so back. Just need a little company."

Though the man's face was obscured, Stranger was sure he had heard the voice before. He rose to his feet with the gun still aimed at the rider, then noted the reflection of flame on a badge and lowered the gun. "Come on down, lawman," he said.

Stranger's face was in deep shadow with the fire at his back, but when the rider swung from the saddle, John recognized him. "Avery Stanton!" he exclaimed.

The lawman squinted at the taller man and said, "I know that voice now! Took me a second or two. John Stranger!"

John switched the Peacemaker to his left hand and shook hands with Stanton. Deputy U.S. Marshal Avery Stanton had worked out of the U.S. marshal's office in Denver under Chief Solomon Duvall for four years, then three years ago had been transferred to the office in Phoenix. Stranger and Stanton had ridden together out of Denver nearly five years ago to track down a pair of killers. On the trail—before they caught them—Stranger had led Stanton to Christ.

"So what are you doing out here in the desert at this time of night, my friend?" Stranger asked, tossing more wood on the fire.

"I'm on my way to Flagstaff to pick up a prisoner and bring him to trial in Phoenix. Got a late start, so thought I'd ride till late since the moon's full, then hit the sack till dawn. When I saw the fire, I figured there'd be some trail hands to sleep by. Never dreamed it'd be the man who led me to the Lord."

"I'll never forget that night," Stranger said. "You were a tough nut to crack."

"Yeah, guess I was. But I'm sure glad you kept working on me." He paused, then said, "I'm married now, John."

"Wonderful! What's her name?"

"Melinda. Fine Christian lady. We have a son, too. Avery Lee Stanton, Jr. He's almost two years old. We're very happy. Belong to a good Bible-believing church in Phoenix. Melinda teaches a class of girls in Sunday school. I'd be teaching, myself, if it wasn't that I miss some Sundays because of my work."

"I can understand that."

"You still doing some preaching?"

"Yep. Quite often."

"How about *you*, John. You married yet?"

"Not yet, but the Lord has given me the woman who will one day be my wife."

"Hey, that's great. Tell me about her."

Stranger explained in brief how he had met Breanna Baylor and fallen in love with her. He told Stanton that he had ridden with the wagon train through Indian country and over the Sierra Nevadas to Placerville, where he received a message from Marshal Duvall. The message told of trouble in Apache Junction. Town marshal Ben Clifton was facing greedy miners trying to take over Apache Junction and put their own man in as marshal.

"So that's where I'm headed," Stranger concluded.

Stanton pulled at an ear. "I'm not aware of any such trouble in Apache Junction, John. But I'm well-acquainted with Marshal

Clifton. He's getting along in years. Doesn't have a lot longer to wear a badge. I'm sure sorry to hear he's having that kind of trouble. I suppose this guy the miners are trying to put in is some kind of gunslinger."

"You might say that. It's Hardy Bell."

"Hardy Bell! Oh, man. I hope you get there in time, John. Ben doesn't need to go up against the likes of Bell."

"Be certain death." Stranger gestured toward the fire and said, "I know you've been in the saddle a long time. Want to sit down?"

"Guess the soft sand would be all right. Think I'll take the saddle off my cayuse and let him get a good drink. I see you've still got Ebony."

"Yep. Never saw one I'd trade him for."

"Amen to that."

The lawman loosened the cinch under his saddle and removed it. He led the roan to the water's edge, patted him on the rump, and said, "Take all you want, boy. There's enough for everybody."

As the two friends sat by the fire, Avery asked, "You aware of the Indian trouble in central Arizona?"

"I know the White Mountain, Chiricahua, and Tonto Apaches go on the warpath periodically and kill a lot of white people."

"Yeah. Well, this trouble is different. Right now, it's centered on the Tontos. Most of them are too busy fighting the Zunis to bother with white men. Arizona's governor, Donald Wheeler, is quite happy for the respite, as are the commandants and troops in the forts."

Stranger had piled mesquite branches near the fire. He tossed a few more into the flames and said, "I know the Tontos and the Zunis are bitter enemies, but I've never really known why."

"It's over land."

"I might have guessed."

"The Zunis claim the land that stretches a hundred miles

north and a hundred miles south from Zuni Creek to the Peloncillo Mountains, and all the way west to the Superstition Mountains. They say their people had owned the land for a thousand years. A couple of hundred years ago, the Apaches moved into Arizona, and the Tontos moved onto the land claimed by the Zunis. The most bitter fighting has been over the land the Tonto Apaches have taken over from the New Mexico border to the Superstition Mountains."

"How long has this present trouble been going on?" Stranger asked.

"'Bout five months. There have been some bloody battles, but they got worse about a month ago when the Zunis somehow laid hold on new weapons, including a Gatling gun."

"A Gatling! That'll shed a lot of blood."

"Yes. It already has. They move the thing around, and the Apaches never know which Zuni war party has it. The Apaches do pretty well in spite of the fact they have older and fewer rifles and a thin supply of ammunition. Often they have to take on the new carbines with bows and arrows. But you know how tough those Apaches are. They still hold their own until that Gatling is brought into play. Then they have to hightail it out of there in a hurry."

Stranger rubbed his chin. "I'm trying to remember the Tonto chief's name…"

"Janos."

"That's right. I've been told he's a tough one."

"Plenty tough. He's meaner'n a rattler with a sore throat. Vicious as they come. And hates both whites and Zunis with a purple passion."

"Sounds like a sweetheart."

"Yeah, a real sweetheart. Janos is in a tight spot since the Zunis have become so well armed. Governor Wheeler and the territory's military leaders are on edge, wondering just what Janos might do. They're beefing up their manpower in the forts. New troops are being sent from the East. They expect that Janos might try surprise attacks on the army posts to steal weapons and ammunition.

Nobody knows where the Zunis are getting theirs, but Janos has no other source but the forts."

The two old friends discussed the Indian situation a while longer, then Stanton yawned, shook his head, and said, "Well, John, this here lawman is about tuckered. Guess I better turn in."

"I'm in the same shape. Let's hit the sack."

At dawn the next morning, the two friends ate breakfast together, read Scripture and prayed, then said good-bye and rode in opposite directions.

In the late morning, John Stranger was angling southeasterly across the desert toward Apache Junction when he heard the sound of gunfire off to his left, beyond a range of hills. He galloped that direction.

The gunfire continued as Stranger rode toward the hills, which took about five minutes. When he reached the sandy range, he guided Ebony to a spot near the top of a hill, then dismounted and hurried to the crest on foot. In a sweeping valley below, he saw Apaches and Zunis battling it out.

Stranger hunkered down and watched the battle with keen interest. It was easy to tell the Apaches from the Zunis. The Zunis were bare-chested and wore breechcloths, silver armbands on their biceps, feathered headbands, and crude sandals. The Apaches were fully clothed in long-sleeved shirts of various styles and colors, tan trousers, and the distinctive Apache boots that could be pulled over the knees as protection against cactus. All Apache warriors wore bandannas for headbands, but never adorned them with feathers.

Stranger watched as the Apaches fought against brand new, seven-shot carbines with only a few single-shot rifles. More than half the Apaches were fighting with war lances, bows with iron-tipped arrows, and rawhide slings. Stranger knew if the Apaches had the same firepower as the Zunis, the cliff-dwellers would be vanquished in short order. There were no North American Indians who could fight like Apaches.

A band of Zuni warriors abruptly appeared from behind a

jumble of boulders, wheeling a Gatling gun. When the Apaches saw the "gun with many voices," they hurried to their horses, helping their wounded. They galloped away with the Gatling's .50 caliber bullets chewing up sand and raising dust behind them.

John Stranger eased back down the steep slope of the hill, mounted Ebony, and rode away without the Indians knowing he had been there.

SIX

⟨═◈═⟩

Ten miles east of Apache Junction lay the rugged and mysterious mountains known as the Superstitions. The lower elevations were dotted with towering saguaro cacti amid the smaller prickly pear, cholla, and barrel cacti, and a variety of desert shrubs and colorful wildflowers. A few pockets of ponderosa pine hung onto the highest slopes. The range was replete with steep-sided canyons, rocky apertures, deep caves, and countless jumbled boulders, large and small.

There were springs of water in the shadowed crags of the canyons, along with small streams that flowed plentifully until late summer when the water supply dwindled and some of the streams went dry.

At the northern tip of the Superstitions, the Tonto Apache stronghold was embedded behind massive boulders among the low rocks and open areas that led to the high peaks and the endless maze of canyons.

It was mid-afternoon. Chief Janos was sitting in the shade of a tall rock with several of his warriors. Many young warriors were busily sharpening war knives, making arrows and war lances, or cleaning their rifles.

The young Apache women were busy about their small adobe huts, carrying water buckets from a stream back in the shadowed canyons, tending to the wants and needs of their children, or working on their crafts. The older women sat cross-legged on the ground, mending clothes or working on crafts. The elderly men sat about in groups of two or three, talking about days gone by. The elderly men and the women of all ages took their finished crafts to the Apache Junction merchants to trade for food and other goods. The townspeople in Apache Junction were tolerant of the elderly men and the women and children of the Tontos. The warriors were not welcome.

Chief Janos had some seventy-five or eighty warriors in a half-circle around him. They were discussing the Zuni problem when a sentry cupped his hands around his mouth and called down from a towering rock, "Janos!"

The chief cut off in mid-sentence, looked toward the sentry, and waited for him to proceed.

"Mandano and his war party return! Twenty horses. Sixteen riders."

Janos rose to his feet, and the warriors followed suit. Mandano had ridden out early that morning to patrol the area northeast of the stronghold. As with other subchiefs who were leading patrols, Mandano was searching for Zuni bands to attack. Janos knew that the bulk of the Zuni tribe was still dwelling in cliffs in western New Mexico, and he reasoned that if the Tontos killed enough of them, the survivors would return to their pueblo across the border and give up trying to drive the Tontos from land long claimed by Janos's forefathers.

Mandano, who was not quite twenty-one years of age, was Janos's youngest subchief. He was exceptionally strong and had proven himself courageous in battle, both against the Zunis and the white man's army. He was unmatched amongst the Tonto Apache warriors for his ability with rifle, bow and arrow, lance, sling, and hand-to-hand combat.

The other warriors in the camp joined Janos and the men he

had been talking with as they readied to meet Mandano. The older men, along with the women and children, looked on as Mandano and his mounted warriors threaded their way among the massive boulders that fringed the camp. Mandano rode in the lead, sitting straight and erect atop his painted pony. His face was solemn, as were the faces of the men who followed him.

Mandano's eyes, usually filled with life and luster, were dull and sad as he reined in and looked down at Janos, who ran his dark eyes over the faces of the returning warriors. Janos was larger than the average Apache man, standing five feet ten inches. He was big-chested and muscular, with a fierce countenance. A battle wound received when in his twenties caused the right corner of his mouth to droop in a permanent sneer.

"Chukim, Sergus, Nino, and Santas…all dead?" Janos asked Mandano.

Mandano nodded.

Janos's bronze features were like granite as he watched the other warriors sliding from their mounts. Two were obviously wounded. One had a makeshift bandage on his leg and was being helped down by two others. Another had been hit in the shoulder, and also was being aided.

"Just Kimbro and Larise are wounded?" asked Janos.

"Yes. Both are surface wounds. Shinamo will tend to them."

Janos nodded. "How did it happen?"

"We were fighting a band of Zunis slightly larger than ours. Though they had the new repeater rifles, we were steadily taking charge. If I saw it correctly, we killed six of them and wounded that many."

"Good."

Mandano nodded. "But as with Ono and his warriors—"

"The gun on wheels with many voices."

"Yes. When the Zunis appeared with it, we had to hurry away. They fired it at us, but the Sky Father kept us from being hit in our retreat."

Janos's deep-set eyes were suddenly filled with fire as he recalled the first battle with the Zunis in which his warriors had faced the Gatling gun. His subchief Ono and twenty-two Tonto warriors had been mowed down before they knew what was happening. His entire body shook with wrath.

"Dah-eh-sah! Dah-eh-sah! Dah-eh-sah to the Zunis!"

The warriors took it up in a chant, repeating *dah-eh-sah* wildly over and over, shaking their fists in the air or waving weapons and calling on their sun god to give them strength and wisdom to kill all the Zunis. The rest of the camp—elderly men, women, and children—all joined in. Hatred for the Zunis was almost a tangible thing in the midst of the angry Apaches.

When the warchant had run its course, Janos called the subchiefs to gather around him for a powwow. He sat down in the growing shade of the tall rock with the eleven subchiefs and let his eyes roam over their faces.

"We must find the gun that speaks with many voices," Janos said. "We must take it away from the Zunis and use it on them. They cannot be driven back to their pueblo as long as they have it. We need to steal their new rifles from them, but more than anything, we must stop the Zunis from killing our warriors with the gun on wheels. We must search until—"

Janos's words were cut off by the sentry. "Janos—Kimut and Wundan return! Have Amand, Sierro, and Rimsun with them. The old men have been scalped!"

Amand, Sierro, and Rimsun had walked to Apache Junction to trade their crafts with the merchants for food and clothing and had been seized by white men known as "scalp hunters." Subchiefs Kimut and Wundan were returning to the camp with their warrior bands and had found the old men.

Certain unidentified wealthy white men in Arizona and New Mexico had formed an alliance against the Apaches. Printed flyers had been tacked up in towns all over both territories. The flyers offered ten dollars per scalp for that of an Apache woman, elderly man, or child, and fifty dollars for a warrior's scalp, accompanied by a warrior's headband for proof. The scalps were delivered to specified merchants in the towns, who then turned them over to the wealthy men. The cooperating merchants were paid for their services by the "association," and they delivered the scalp bounty to the men who had turned in the scalps. Arizona and New Mexico were thick with greedy, Indian-hating men who would not hesitate to scalp an Apache for that kind of easy money.

As the two bands filed into the camp between the giant boulders, the three old men were astride horses with whatever cloths the warriors could find to cover their heads. Blood was streaming down their faces.

The wives of the victims rushed to them as the warriors eased them off the horses. Tears ran down the Tonto women's wrinkled cheeks as they wailed and screamed at the gory sight.

Warriors carried Amand, Sierro, and Rimsun to the medicine man's adobe hut. Shinamo laid blankets on the dirt floor of the hut and went to work on the scalped men. The wives helped him, still wailing. All they could do was try to alleviate the suffering and stay the flow of blood. No one ever lived after being scalped.

Janos trembled with wrath as he stood outside Shinamo's hut, staring through the door at the three old men. Rage toward the white men blazed within him. Fists clenched, he vowed vengeance on the scalp hunters and all whites for their atrocities against his people. The word dah-eh-sah came from his lips over and over again. Death to the white scalp hunters! Death to all whites!

Mandano and subchiefs Wundan and Kimut stood closest to their chief, knowing they must allow him to vent his fury before speaking to him. After several minutes, Mandano approached him.

"What is it, Mandano?"

"You were speaking of a plan to steal the gun from the Zunis."

"Yes, we must. But first, I want you to talk to Amand, Sierro, and Rimsun. I want to know how many scalp hunters there were and what they looked like. I want to know how they were dressed and what kind of horses they had. You will give what information you obtain to me and all warriors when we meet to discuss stealing the gun from the Zunis."

Mandano nodded.

"When you have the information, gather the warriors at the rock and send for me at my hut."

Mandano nodded and entered Shinamo's hut.

A quarter-hour later, he called out to all the warriors to gather at the normal meeting place, then sent a warrior to Janos's hut to let him know they were ready. Soon Janos was seated at the base of the large rock, now in full shade, and the warriors were pressed close in a large half-circle, some sitting, some standing. All eyes were on Janos and Mandano, who sat beside him.

Kimut and Wundan were close friends and stood together nearby. Though they admired Mandano for his cleverness and fighting ability, they harbored some jealousy. Both wished for the stature Mandano held in the eyes of their chief.

Janos told the warriors who had just ridden in about Mandano's four men being killed that morning, and that Mandano's band had been forced to ride away, leaving the bodies behind, because the Zunis had wheeled out the Gatling gun. But first he wanted to discuss the scalp hunters. He then asked Mandano to relate what he had learned from Amand, Sierro, and Rimsun.

Mandano rose to his feet, his face solemn. His voice cracked slightly as he said, "I was not able to learn anything from Sierro. Shinamo says—" Mandano choked up.

All eyes went to Janos, who showed displeasure at Mandano's display of compassion. Mandano regained his composure and continued.

"Shinamo says Sierro will die first."

Old men and women of all ages stood a few yards away, looking on. Young mothers with small children stayed farther back, not wanting the cries and fussing of the little ones to disturb the meeting.

"Amand and Rimsun told me there were three scalp hunters. They—"

"Janos!" called the sentry on the rock. "Other bands coming in!"

Janos rose to his feet and stepped up beside Mandano, who was two inches shorter than his chief and not as heavy. "It is time for all war parties to be in. You will wait and give your report to all the warriors."

Mandano nodded.

Five patrol bands converged on the opening to the camp. Only one of the five had found Zunis to fight. The subchief who led that band was happy to report that none of his warriors had been wounded or killed. They had outnumbered the enemy war party and killed two of them. Four others had been wounded.

Janos called for all incoming warriors to gather at the tall rock, then he told them all that had happened that day. Gesturing toward his favorite subchief and warrior, Janos said, "Come, Mandano, and tell us what you have learned about the scalpings. I want all of you to listen closely. Those white devils are probably still in this area. If any of you see them, I want them caught and brought to me. Mandano…"

Mandano stood before the crowd and spoke so all could hear. "Rimsun and Amand say the leader of the three scalpers is a big man. Very tall. Thick-body. Close-set eyes. Heavy beard. Hair long like ours. Brown. Dirty and greasy. Maybe forty years of age. Others called him Gordo. The second scalper is almost as tall. Very slender. Wears thick spectacles. Maybe thirty-five years of age. He has a long scar on his left cheek. Black hair. Not long. No beard or mustache. Gordo called him Tony. The third scalper is a short man. Not as slender as the one called Tony. Has red hair and beard. His hair is long, but not like Gordo's. Very ugly. Other two called him Red. He is maybe thirty years of age."

"What about their horses?" Janos asked.

"The one called Gordo rides a bay gelding with white face

and stockings. Tony's horse is gray with small white spots. Red's is gray with no spots."

Janos ran his dark gaze over the faces of his men. "You will all be alert as you ride the desert. If you see these vermin, you are to capture them and bring them to me. I will make them wish they had never been born…and they will beg to die. I will have the satisfaction of seeing them in pain like they have never imagined!"

The warriors erupted with a loud cheer, raising their fists over their heads. When they grew quiet, Janos said, "Now, we must discuss the gun with many voices. I have formed a plan. Our patrols will ride out with one thing in mind. The Zunis are moving the gun around, but we must locate it, then be prepared to move in quickly and take it from them. We will kill the Zunis with their own death machine!"

One of the warriors cried out, "*Dah-eh-sah! Dah-eh-sah* to the Zunis!"

Immediately he was joined by others. After they had settled down, Mandano turned to Janos.

"Chief, I have been thinking…the gun appears quite heavy and cumbersome. It will be slow and difficult to move to our stronghold. Whatever band finds it will be easy targets for other Zuni war parties. Many warriors' lives could be lost."

"The Zunis move it around," Kimut said. "If they can do it, so can we."

"But the Zunis have warrior bands camped in many places," Mandano said. "They no doubt move it from camp to camp at night."

"Then let us locate it in the day," Wundan said, "and go back at night to attack them and take it."

Mandano set eager eyes on Janos and said, "I have a better idea, Chief."

"And what is that?"

"Let me say first that we do not know where the Zunis laid hands on the gun. Therefore, we would not know where to obtain more ammunition for it. Once we have used up what bullets we steal when taking the gun, it would be of no more use to us."

Janos nodded. "So what is your idea?"

"My idea will endanger only me, not an entire band of warriors. Once we locate the gun, I will go back alone at night, sneak into the camp, and remove the crank that fires the gun. Without the crank, it cannot fire."

"Mandano, have you ever seen a gun like this?" one of the warriors near the front asked. "Do you know how to remove the crank?"

"I have not seen one up close, but I am sure with one blow of a sledgehammer, I could sever the crank from the gun. Before moving into the Zuni camp, I will take the sentries out one at a time. I will disable the gun and be gone by the time the camp has come awake from the noise." Mandano then turned toward Janos.

"I approve of your idea, Mandano," Janos said. "The normal amount of patrols will ride out tomorrow morning in search of the gun…except you. Tomorrow is your regular day for training the young warriors."

Mandano nodded. "I would like to be searching for the gun also, but we must never be slack in training the young men to be great Apache fighters. If the gun is not located tomorrow, my warriors and I will join the search the next day. Do not worry, Chief Janos. We will find the gun that speaks with many voices, and I will render it useless."

Janos dismissed the warriors, and Mandano went to the medicine man's hut. Kimut and Wundan approached Janos, asking if they could speak to him. Janos granted permission.

"We have been talking, Chief," Kimut said. "We have a deep concern and must speak it to you."

"And what is this concern?" Janos asked, studying their dark faces.

"It is regarding Mandano."

"Mandano?"

"Yes. Wundan and I feel he is soft of heart and should not be training the young warriors. We bring to your mind the way he showed a woman's sympathy during the powwow. You have told us many times that this is a weakness."

"We took note of the look on your face when Mandano showed this weakness," Wundan said. "You were very unhappy."

"Yes, I was. I have seen Mandano show a woman's compassion on many occasions."

"Then why does Mandano enjoy your favor so?" Kimut asked. "Why does he train the young warriors and lead the strongest band of warriors?"

"I must remind you that Mandano has done additional training with his own band. He is a fighter like I have never seen. There is none amongst the Tontos who can match him. He is the strongest in body. He is the best with a rifle, sling, bow and arrow, and the fiercest in hand-to-hand fighting."

"But his fierceness ends with fighting Zunis and white soldiers," Wundan said. "You know he does not hate white men enough to kill them like the rest of your warriors do. He will only kill them when they wear a uniform and fight us in battle."

"This is true, Janos," Kimut said. "When you have led us to attack wagon trains, stagecoaches, and farms and ranches, Mandano has refused to take part. This is weakness! All whites are intruders on our land and should die! Mandano should not be a leader of the Tontos. He is soft-hearted toward our enemies."

"By your own words, Janos," Wundan said, "Mandano should not wear the warrior's headband. You have taught us that an Apache warrior should have no compassion whatsoever...that it is a weakness that will affect his fighting power. This is *your* rule."

"So I have taught you," Janos said. "But as chief of the Tontos, I must place in leadership my best men. You two are amongst them. This is why you are subchiefs."

Kimut's features stiffened. "But Mandano is not one of your best men. He refuses to kill whites unless they are soldiers who fight us. Will his weakness not one day affect his fighting power?"

The chief's eyes went blacker than usual. "It is true that Mandano will kill only white men in uniform in battle, Kimut. But he stands as the only exception to my rule. Which of all the Tonto warriors kills as many as Mandano? Or even half as many? You? Wundan?"

Janos drew a deep breath and let it out through his nostrils. "I have learned to tolerate Mandano's woman-like sympathy and compassion because of his skill and courage in battle...and because there is not another warrior amongst the Tontos who can teach the young men how to fight like he does. There will be no change in his position until a warrior rises up in our midst who is better than he."

Wundan and Kimut exchanged furtive glances, then quietly walked away.

SEVEN

———✦———

I t was late afternoon on Thursday, October 17, when John Stranger pulled out of a dry wash, topped its gentle rise, and set his gaze on Apache Junction about two miles to the south.

He put Ebony to a trot, threading amongst towering saguaros, squat cacti, clumps of greasewood, sagebrush, tumbleweeds, and scattered boulders. Within a few minutes, he saw the collection of tents that had been pitched on the north edge of the town. He knew these belonged to some of the gold seekers who had infiltrated the Superstition Mountains some ten miles to the east. Others pitched their tents within the mountains and came out only when they needed supplies or to turn their gold into cash.

As he neared the tent compound, Stranger saw a group of miners heading for town from the mountains. He estimated there were about eight or ten of them. They moved slowly, leading their pack mules and burros, and they were near enough that he could make out three mules with bodies draped over their backs.

Stranger scrubbed a palm across his dusty face and said, "'How much better it is to get wisdom than gold,' and 'Better is little with the fear of the Lord than great treasure and trouble therewith.' Dear Lord, don't the gold seekers live with trouble? Fine, decent men get gold fever and turn into greedy monsters and killers."

Stranger knew the history of the Superstition Mountains. So many men had gone in there hoping to find sudden riches…and never came out alive. Now, here were three more.

He slowed Ebony to a walk as they entered Apache Junction. The shadows of the trees and buildings were growing long as they stretched across the broad main street, which was four blocks long and unnamed, as were its cross streets. It was not an old town, like so many he had passed through in Arizona. The false-fronted clapboard buildings were in good shape, and the paint showed no sign of fading from the wind or the desert sun.

John Stranger ran his gray gaze to the boardwalks on both sides of the street. Something was wrong. Every man, woman, and child seemed somber, listless, as if they had lost the joy of living. Had the gold miners already taken over? He would soon find out.

Many eyes settled on him as he rode slowly along the street. Some of them, especially those of the men, laid a cold scrutiny on him.

Stranger's right hand idly lowered and touched the bone-handled Colt .45 that snugged close to his hip, freeing it from saddle crimp. Then he let his hand hang by his side as he noted a knot of men in front of a saloon. Their hooded eyes took quick appraisal of the stranger on the black horse, their attention lingering for a brief moment on the revolver resting in plain sight on his hip. After he had passed them, they wheeled around and disappeared into the saloon.

Stranger's peripheral vision caught the motion. He felt the beat of his pulse rise a notch, and there was a tingle between his shoulder blades.

He spotted the Desert Rose Hotel just ahead, and across the street from the hotel was a stable. Three doors beyond the hotel was the town marshal's office. Stranger was within a half-block of the hotel as he passed a second saloon. A cluster of men loitered near the saloon entrance and gave him a cool, wary inspection. Stranger nodded to them and gave them a tight smile, but none of them acknowledged the gesture. Passing by them, he felt a current of hostility flow along the street.

He hauled up in front of the marshal's office and noticed that the sign overhead had been freshly painted. It read:

Apache Junction Marshal's Office and Jail
Hardy Bell, Marshal

Stranger swung from the saddle, wrapped the reins around the hitch rail, and headed for the boardwalk. A young couple with two small children passed by in front of him. Both eyed him suspiciously. No doubt they think I'm one of the wicked pack, he thought.

Stranger found the office door ajar about six inches. He pushed it open all the way and stepped in. At the desk was a wiry, hard-looking man. His hat was on a wall hook behind him. His thick head of sandy-colored hair was tousled. He wore a droopy mustache and looked as if he hadn't shaved in three or four days. On his chest was a badge that identified him as Apache Junction's marshal.

Hardy Bell was no more than twenty-five years old. The last report Stranger had heard of him, Bell had killed thirty-one men in stand-up, fast-draw shoot-outs. He wondered how many Bell had killed in cold blood. There were some rumors about that, too.

Bell was hunched over, reading a *Police Gazette* magazine. As Stranger entered, he looked up, then eased back in his chair. Stranger noticed that a chunk of flesh had been chewed out of Bell's left ear and wondered if a bullet had come that close to getting him.

"I'm looking for Marshal Ben Clifton," Stranger said.

"He ain't marshal no more, mister. Can't you read? Or didn't you see that big sign outside?"

Stranger fought the urge to grab the gunslick and slap his insolent mouth.

"I saw the sign, and I can read, but I figured you could tell me where I might find Marshal Clifton."

"Well, I can't. I don't know where he is."

"Well, when did he retire?"

"Retire?" Bell chuckled. "Oh, yeah. Retire. A few days ago."

"Doesn't he own a house here in town? I would assume he'd still be living here, especially since he only retired a few days ago."

Hardy Bell's face tinted. He rose to his feet and said, "I'm busy, mister. I don't have time for this kind of questionin'. All I know is that somebody else is livin' in Clifton's house now. Like I told you…I don't know where he is. Now, if there's nothin' else I can do for you, I'll bid you good day."

Stranger leaned close to Bell and said in a low, level tone, "There is one thing you can do, Hardy. Wipe that impudent sneer off your face."

"Get out of my office! And get out of my town!"

"I'll be glad to get out of the office, *Marshal*, but you can't make me leave Apache Junction unless I break the law. You *do* know the law, don't you? I mean, after all, you *are* wearing a badge."

Bell was about to snap back a reply when sudden activity outside the open door arrested his attention. The group of gold miners Stranger had seen coming from the Superstitions had arrived. People on the street were gathering to look at the bodies.

There were eight miners in the group. Six of them stayed with the corpses while two crossed the boardwalk and entered the marshal's office. One was a grizzled man who had to be pushing eighty. The younger one was a husky, bearded man of about forty. He gave Stranger a quick look up and down, then set his eyes on Bell.

"I'm Hank Smith. Where's Marshal Clifton?"

"He retired. What can I do for you?"

"Retired?"

"Yeah."

"When'd that happen?"

"Few days ago. Looks like you've got some dead men out there."

"Yes. The dead men were our good friends. They were workin' a claim close to ours. We were comin' into town for supplies a while ago and found 'em in an arroyo just outside the mountains. It was murder, Marshal…"

"Bell. Hardy Bell."

Smith's jaw slacked and his eyes widened. "You're *the* Hardy Bell? The gunfighter?"

"In person. You say those men were murdered?"

"Uh…uh, yessir. Somebody tied their hands behind 'em and shot 'em in the back of their heads."

"So why are you tellin' *me* about it?"

"You're the marshal, ain't you? These men were murdered! You need to find out who did it and bring 'em to justice."

Bell shook his head. "Not me, mister. My jurisdiction ends at the edge of this town. There's nothin' I can do about it."

"What? Ben Clifton investigated several murders that had taken place in those mountains. He even caught some of the killers and hanged 'em."

Bell adjusted the gunbelt on his waist. "Well, Ben Clifton ain't marshal here no more. Things have changed. I'll handle the law within Apache Junction's limits, but that's it. Nice talkin' to you."

Bell sat down at the desk and picked up the *Police Gazette*.

Smith looked at Stranger and asked, "Have you ever seen the like?"

"Sure haven't."

"C'mon, Pop," Smith said to the old man and headed out the door.

Stranger gave Bell a stiff glare as he followed the miners outside, but Apache Junction's new lawman didn't bother to look up.

"I'm a stranger in these parts, Mr. Smith, but looks to me like you'll have to take this to the county sheriff in Phoenix."

"Ain't got time," Smith said, pushing his way through the crowd. "We'll just bury 'em and get on back to our claim."

Stranger shook his head and moved down the boardwalk with

people in the crowd watching him. Next to the marshal's office was the town's barbershop. The door stood open, and the barber had a man in the chair with another one waiting. Stranger picked up that their conversation was about the three dead miners. The talk quickly cut off as he stepped through the door.

"Good afternoon, gentlemen," Stranger said. "I came here looking for Marshal Ben Clifton. Your new marshal told me Clifton retired. Would any of you know where I might find him?"

The three men were obviously nervous.

"Nobody seems to know, mister," the barber replied, his voice quavering slightly. "You a lawman?"

"No, but I was sent here by Chief U.S. Marshal Solomon Duvall, whose office is in Denver. Duvall had been contacted by Marshal Clifton, telling him there was trouble brewing here in Apache Junction. Now, I find a no-good gunhawk wearing the marshal's badge, and nobody seems to know what happened to Ben Clifton. You gentlemen know anything about this trouble Clifton had in mind?"

Stranger saw the fear in their eyes.

"We don't know anything about it, mister," the barber said.

"You're sure?"

All three fearfully nodded.

Stranger's brow furrowed. "Seems to me there must be something wrong around here when the town council hires a low-life gunslick like Hardy Bell to wear the marshal's badge."

"We wouldn't know about that, mister," the barber said in a half-whisper. "Now, if you don't mind, I've got to get this man's hair cut."

Stranger nodded, stepped through the doorway, and moved on down the street. He turned into the general store. There were a few customer's moving about, mostly women. The proprietor stood behind a long counter. He watched the stranger warily; fear lived in his eyes.

Stranger smiled, approached the counter, and said, "I'm in

town looking for Marshal Ben Clifton. I've already met your new marshal. He says he has no idea where Clifton is. Would you happen to know?"

The proprietor began shaking his head before Stranger had finished the question. "No, sir. Ben just up and left town. I have no idea where he might've gone."

"Strange. Hasn't he been marshal here quite a while?"

"Ever since the town was established. Soon be eight years."

"And he owns a house here, right?"

"Yes."

The proprietor looked past Stranger at two women carrying goods they had picked up from a shelf.

"Oh, excuse me, ladies," Stranger said, smiling and touching the brim of his hat.

Both women gave him nervous smiles and laid their goods on the counter.

"Sorry I can't help you, mister," the proprietor said, then began writing down the prices of the articles the women were purchasing.

Stranger left the store and returned to Ebony. He led him to the stable, where the hostler was brushing down a cream-colored mare in the corral next to the office, which was actually the front part of the barn.

Stranger approached the split-rail gate and saw the hostler looking at him. "Like to board my horse for a day or two. Maybe a little longer."

The hostler was a beefy middle-aged man with carrot-red hair. "Sure," he said, leaving the mare and moving to the gate. "It'll be a dollar a day for keep and feed. He'll get oats in the mornin' and hay at night. For an extra two-bits per day, I'll give him a good brushin' and a rubdown."

"Sounds like a deal."

Stranger led Ebony through the gate and removed the saddle while the hostler stood admiring the big black.

"Some animal," the hostler said.

"He's the best. I'll pay you for two days, then we'll see if I'm going to be here longer."

"All right. You visitin' someone in town, are you?"

"Well, actually I came here to see Marshal Ben Clifton. I can't find anybody who knows where he went, or when he left town. You wouldn't happen to know, would you?"

"No, sir." The hostler swallowed hard and wiped droplets of sweat from his upper lip.

"Sure seems odd that a man could be marshal of this town for eight years and not have somebody he's close enough to that would know when he left and where he was going."

The hostler shrugged nervously. "You'd think so, wouldn't you? Sorry. I can't tell you who to see, mister. Nobody I've talked to knows anything about where Ben went."

Stranger paid the hostler and carried his saddle to the Desert Rose Hotel, where he found an equally nervous desk clerk who could give him no information about Ben Clifton. He climbed the stairs to his room on the second floor, which faced the street. He laid the saddle in a corner, then went to a small table and poured water from the pitcher into the wash bowl. He washed his face of the thin film of dust he had gathered on the trail. The water felt good and refreshed him.

Then he walked to the window, pulled back the thin curtain, and looked down into the street. The sun was setting, casting a golden hue over the town. He noticed two men standing in front of the Skylark Café across the street. They were looking directly at his window but turned away quickly when they saw him.

Stranger decided he would walk the main street for a while and talk to as many people as he could. Maybe someone would have enough courage to tell him about Ben Clifton.

When he reached the street, the two men in front of the café were gone. He entered the gun shop and the pharmacy and found the same reticence and fear.

He was crossing the first side street, hoping to talk to some more merchants before they closed for the day, when he spotted a white adobe church building with a tall wooden steeple. It was situated on a corner in the residential area, and next to it was a white adobe house.

He hurried down the street and read the small sign in front of the building. This was Apache Junction's First Baptist Church, and the pastor's name was Dale Patrick. Stranger figured the pastor would probably be home this time of day, so he walked toward the house next door. As he approached the front porch, he saw a curtain move, and a small shadow move away from the window. A child?

Stranger knocked on the door and waited. The door swung partially open, and a woman's face appeared. There were two children behind her. The same kind of fear he had seen in everyone else in town was evident in her eyes. "Yes?" she said.

"Ma'am, I was sent to Apache Junction by Chief United States Marshal Solomon Duvall in Denver. Your marshal, Ben Clifton, had contacted him, saying he needed help. Someone was attempting to take over the town, and Marshal Clifton knew he couldn't handle it by himself. I've asked people on the street and in the stores and shops if they know where Marshal Clifton is. Nobody knows, and everybody seems frightened. I spotted the church from the main street and thought I'd check here. Is your husband home?"

The small woman's lower lip was trembling. At first, her eyes had looked like those of some small panicked creature, caught in a trap, the hunter almost upon her, but as Stranger spoke, he watched the fear subside.

"No, he's not, but I know about you. Marshal Clifton told me you would be coming. Your name is John Stranger, isn't it?"

Relief washed over him. Finally, he could get some answers. "Yes, ma'am. I'm John Stranger."

She opened the door wide and stepped back. "Please come in."

"Would you rather I wait and come back when your husband is home, ma'am?"

Her lower lip trembled the more and tears surfaced in her eyes. "He…won't be coming home, Mr. Stranger. Dale was murdered on Monday."

"Oh, ma'am, I'm sorry. If I'd known, I wouldn't have—"

"It's all right, Mr. Stranger," she said, wiping tears from her cheeks. "Please. Come in."

The woman, who was in her late twenties, introduced herself as Diane Patrick, then introduced her eleven-year-old son, Kyle, and her nine-year-old daughter, Trudy.

Kyle extended his hand, and Stranger took it in his own.

"Is your name *really* John Stranger, sir?" he asked.

"Sure is, Kyle. I know you've never heard of anyone with the name *Stranger* before, have you?"

"No, sir."

"But you *have* heard of men named *John.*"

"Yes, sir."

"So I'm only half a mystery, right?"

The boy smiled. "Yes, sir."

"I think Trudy is a pretty name," John said, turning to the girl.

"Well, sir, it's really Gertrude, but I don't like to be called that…or Gertie."

"All right, I'll keep that in mind, Trudy," he said, smiling warmly.

Stranger had caught the aroma of supper when the door first came open. His stomach growled lightly, but only he knew it. He hadn't eaten for a long time.

"Have you eaten, Mr. Stranger?" Diane asked.

"Not since New Year's Day, ma'am."

Diane laughed and said, "I know you want to talk. How about over supper? Would you eat with us?"

"I'd be delighted and honored."

"Good. I was just about to dish it up. I'll just add another plate."

When they had all sat down at the table, Diane was positioned opposite John. She looked at him and said, "We always pray before we eat and thank the Lord for His bountiful blessings, Mr. Stranger."

"So do I, ma'am. I think every child of God should thank the Lord for His bountiful blessings before they eat what He's provided."

A pleasant smile spread over Diane's face. She had chestnut hair, almond-brown eyes, and a porcelain complexion saved from perfection by an appealing spatter of freckles.

"It's wonderful to know you're a Christian, Mr. Stranger," she said. "Would you offer our prayer?"

When John finished the prayer, Diane said, "Eat heartily, Mr. Stranger. I don't ever want a guest at my table to go away hungry."

"I doubt that could happen, ma'am," he said, winking at Trudy. Then he turned solemn. "Ma'am, I'm sure it would be better to tell me about your husband after supper. So let me ask about Ben Clifton. Is he—"

"He's alive and well."

"And you know where he is?"

"I'm the only person in town who knows, except for these children."

"Am I right in assuming that it's the low-handed miners who have taken over the town? The wire Marshal Clifton sent to Chief Duvall indicated this."

"No," Diane said, shaking her head. "At first, Marshal Clifton thought some of the miners wanted control of the town, and this is what he reported to Chief Duvall. But he soon learned that though many of the miners are greedy and will kill anyone who threatens their path to riches, the men who wanted to take over the town were not miners. They are wicked, greedy men who see Apache Junction as a gold mine itself because of its proximity to the

Superstitions and other mountains where gold is being mined."

"I've seen some I think are part of them, but the only one I've met face to face is Hardy Bell."

"He's only one of a bunch of rotten apples. They're led by a man who calls himself Major Vic Coburn. From what I've been able to learn, Coburn was a major in the Union army during the War, then came west with some of his men. They call themselves Coburn's Rangers. They rob and kill for pleasure. Coburn has set himself up as boss of the town and now lives in Marshal Clifton's house. It was Coburn's men who—" Her face pinched, and her throat locked with grief.

"They killed your husband."

She nodded and shed more tears.

"How many men does Coburn have?"

"Eight besides himself and Hardy Bell. He hired Bell because he's fast with his gun. Everyone in town is afraid of him. And they're afraid of what Coburn and his thugs will do to them if they step out of line."

"I've seen that, all right. And let me guess what 'out of line' means—not giving in to extortion, right?"

"Yes. Coburn has set up a tribute system. Every merchant must pay him tribute or suffer the consequences. Harry Buford was owner of the town's clothing store. He bowed his neck, telling Coburn's men he would not pay it nor be intimidated by them. He was found strangled to death in a gully outside of town the next day."

"How long has this been going on?"

"Today is the tenth day. Wally Dothan, who owned the boot and saddle shop, refused also. He was found hanging from the rafters in his own store about two hours after Harry's body was found in the gully. Since then, the only person who refused to meet Coburn's demands was…was my husband. Everybody's scared stiff."

"I could see it in their eyes the moment I rode into town.

Your husband wasn't a merchant, Mrs. Patrick. What kind of pressure did Coburn put on him?"

"He came here last Saturday night with four of his henchmen, including Hardy Bell, and told Dale he wanted 30 percent of the offerings that came in on Sunday…and every Sunday thereafter. Dale told him the money that came in the offerings was God's money, and Coburn wasn't getting it. Coburn laughed and said he would put the money to good use.

"Dale…stood his ground, Mr. Stranger. He looked Coburn in the eye and told him he would never pay the tribute. Coburn told him he wouldn't be allowed to hold church services any longer. Dale told him he couldn't stop him. And the next day, being Sunday, we had our services."

"Did Coburn's men try to stop it?"

"No, but—" Her throat constricted. Tears flooded her eyes again.

Stranger reached across the table and touched her arm. "I'm sorry, ma'am. We weren't going to talk about your husband until after supper."

Diane looked around, and everybody had finished. The children were sitting there, quietly listening in.

"I guess supper *is* over," she said.

"Mama," Kyle said, "you and Mr. Stranger can go talk in the parlor. Trudy and I'll clean up."

"Oh, you don't have to do that, honey."

"Please, Mama. We'll be glad to do it, won't we Trudy?"

The little girl nodded.

Diane pushed her chair back and rose to her feet.

John Stranger stood up. "That was a fine meal, ma'am. Thank you." And to the children, "You two are very special to do the dishes for your mother. I'm sure she wouldn't mind if I reward you." He pulled two twenty-dollar gold pieces from his pocket and handed one to each of them."

"Wow!" Kyle said. "Thank you, sir!"

"Thank you, Mr. Stranger," Trudy said, gazing in wonder at the gold piece in her palm.

"You're both very welcome."

Diane led him to the parlor. "That was very generous of you, Mr. Stranger. Thank you."

"My pleasure."

Diane sat on the couch, and John eased down on an overstuffed chair, facing her.

"You asked me if Coburn's men tried to stop the services on Sunday," Diane said.

"Yes."

"They didn't. But...Dale was murdered in his study over at the church on Monday. I...I found him on the floor with a knife in his heart just before supper."

Diane broke down and wept for several minutes. When she regained control, Stranger told her he would do his best to bring her husband's killers to justice. He then asked her where he would find Ben Clifton.

She explained that he had fled Apache Junction for his life. Diane had hidden him for a short time, then he went to an unoccupied cabin, owned by a deceased friend of his, at the southern tip of the Mazatzal Mountains on the bank of the Salt River. He went there to wait till she sent John Stranger to him. Because of Chief Duvall's confidence in Stranger, Clifton knew he would be of help. He was sure Diane would hear when Stranger showed up in town.

Diane went to a drawer in a small table in the parlor, pulled out a crude map Clifton had drawn, and gave it to Stranger. He looked at it and said he was sure he could find the cabin.

Stranger folded the map and stuck it in his shirt pocket, then said, "Along with everything else I do, Mrs. Patrick, I preach the Word of God. If I offer to preach the services on Sunday, do you think the people will come?"

Diane's eyes lit up. "Why, I'm sure they would pack the building." Then fear etched itself on her face. "But...I'm afraid Coburn will kill you if you try it. Especially if an offering is taken and Coburn doesn't get his tribute."

"I'll handle Coburn, ma'am. You just spread the word tomorrow that there will be a service Sunday morning at ten o'clock, and one Sunday evening at six."

Diane assured him she would get the news out. Stranger said he would come by sometime tomorrow to see how the people were reacting, then told her goodnight.

When he was gone, she leaned her back against the door and sighed. "John Stranger, I don't really know who you are, but I know God sent you to us. Thank You, Lord."

EIGHT

B efore sunrise the next day, John Stranger rode northeast out of Apache Junction toward the Mazatzal Mountains. He was eager to find the cabin on the bank of the Salt River and talk to Marshal Ben Clifton.

It was almost nine o'clock in Apache Junction that morning when two of Major Vic Coburn's rangers skidded their horses to a halt in front of the house owned by Ben Clifton and leaped from their saddles.

Just as they reached the front porch, the door came open. It was filled with a mountain of a man named Mick Holcomb, Coburn's personal bodyguard. He was hatless, and like all of Coburn's men, had short hair. The major believed military men should look masculine, and even during the Civil War, every man under his command wore well-trimmed hair. If they sported a mustache, it could not be drooped or bushy, and they were to shave every day. Coburn had made an exception in Hardy Bell's case, since Bell had not been with him in the War and was not actually one of the rangers.

Holcomb had a mean scowl that seemed permanently etched on his broad, flat face. Coburn liked him that way. It made him all the more intimidating.

Holcomb looked at Dean Ritchie and Elbert Washburn and grunted in his gravelly voice, "You boys look a little excited. Somethin' goin' on?"

"Yeah," Washburn said. "*Trouble* is what's goin' on. We need to see the major."

"What kind of trouble?"

"The kind the major doesn't like to hear about."

"You mean we got another merchant refusin' to pay his dues?"

"No. Worse. There's a new preacher showed up in town, and—"

"You can hear it the same time we tell the major, Mick," Ritchie said. "C'mon. Let us in."

Holcomb nodded and stepped back inside. Ritchie and Washburn followed him into the parlor where Leon Matkins was slouched in an overstuffed chair and Coburn, who had just celebrated his fifty-third birthday, was stretched out on a couch. He had a cigar in his mouth and a nearly empty whiskey bottle in his hand.

"Boys say there's some trouble come up, Major," Holcomb said.

Coburn glanced at Ritchie and Washburn and sat up. "What kind of trouble?"

"You know that guy you had us watchin' yesterday, Major?" Washburn said.

"You mean the dude dressed in black who was asking all kinds of questions of the townsfolk?"

"Yeah."

"Was I right? He's a gunfighter, isn't he?"

"Nope," Ritchie said. "He's a *preacher!*"

Coburn yanked the cigar from his mouth. "A what? A *preacher?*"

"Yep."

"Ah, go on. Preachers don't wear tied-down hog-legs! He's a gunhawk, boys, sure as the world."

"Well," Washburn said, "maybe he's a gunhawk, but he's gonna be preachin' Sunday mornin' and Sunday night at the Baptist church."

Coburn jumped to his feet, slammed the whiskey bottle on the top of a small table next to the couch, and swore. "Where'd you hear this?"

"It's all over town," Ritchie said. "That preacher's widow is tellin' it to everybody."

"And talk is that the whole town is gonna be there to hear him preach, too," Washburn said.

Coburn swore again and threw his smoking cigar across the room. It struck the far wall and bounded to the floor. Matkins left the overstuffed chair to pick the cigar up.

"I tell you, that dude is not a preacher! He's—"

"He's *what?*" Holcomb asked.

Coburn rubbed the back of his neck. "The thought just struck me. Maybe he's a federal marshal or some other kind of law-man. From what you boys have told me about the way he wears his gun, he's either a hot-shot tin star or a gunfighter. Average man doesn't wear his gun slung low and tied down. Now am I right, or am I right?"

"You're right, sir," Washburn said. "So I guess we've got us a preacher who's also a gunslinger or a federal lawman."

"Well, we don't need either!" Coburn said. "He's got to be run out of town…or planted six feet deep. I don't really care which it is."

"Major…?" Holcomb said.

"Yes?"

"Since he's gonna be holdin' services Sunday, why not let him go ahead? Just tell him you're takin' 30 percent off the top of the offerin's. We'll pick up some more money that way. Then run him outta town on Monday. If he won't run, then we'll plant him in the graveyard. Either way, we'll show the people of this town that we can handle anybody comes along and raises hisself up against us."

The major was nodding with a thoughtful look in his eyes. "This dude may be just what we've needed to help us keep these people cowering. Sure, we'll let him hold his services Sunday…long as he agrees to fork over the 30 percent. But he's got to be handled because he knows what's going on here. Since he's talked to that preacher's widow, he's got the whole picture, I'm sure."

"Probably be best if we kill him, Major," Matkins said. "Like you say, if he ain't a gunslinger, he's some kind of lawman. We really don't need either kind movin' on and tellin' what's happenin' here. We need to make it last as long as we can. Pick up all the money possible before we have to pull out."

Coburn rubbed his chin. "Yeah. The dude has to die, but not till Monday. His little preaching escapade'll just put more money in our pockets. Then we'll make a spectacle of him and blow him to kingdom come. That'll rattle everybody just like our killing those two store owners did."

Mick laughed. "*And* that stubborn preacher."

"You're right." Coburn laughed with him. "Seein' that preacher get it took the wind out of their sails. We'll intimidate them some more by killing this second preacher…and whatever else he is." He paused, then rubbed his hands together. "I've got an even better idea. We'll tell this Bible-thumper we're going to take 30 percent, then after the evening service, we'll take it *all!*"

"Now, you're talkin', Major!" Holcomb said. "Won't make no difference to this preacher, anyway. He's gonna be dead!"

Coburn went suddenly sober and turned to Ritchie and Washburn. "Dean…Elbert…you two contact the rest of the boys in town. I'm sure they've heard the announcement about the church services. Tell them what we're planning. I want this preacher brought to me immediately so I can lay down the law to him. Got it?"

"We got it," Washburn said. "C'mon, Dean."

John Stranger waded Ebony across the Salt River at the southern tip of the Mazatzal Mountains. He had followed the map carefully. The cabin where Ben Clifton was hiding out was on the north bank of the river, surrounded on the east, west, and south by tall ponderosa pines and heavy desert brush. Unless a person knew it was there, they could ride by without ever seeing it.

Ebony climbed out of the river and up the steep bank, then carried his master through the dense pines and brush for about a hundred feet before Stranger could make out the cabin. Thin tendrils of smoke rose from the cabin's chimney. There was a small shed next to it, and a tiny corral. Clifton's horse nickered at Ebony as they drew near. Ebony nickered back.

Stranger circled the log structure and started to dismount when he saw the sixty-four-year-old lawman standing in the open door, hitching up his pants. Ben Clifton stood three inches under six feet, and over the last few years had developed a paunch that hung over his belt. His hat was tilted to the back of his head, and he grinned as he said, "Wasn't sure who it might be at first, but when you came into the clearing, I knew it had to be John Stranger."

Stranger grinned and slid from the saddle. "How did you know who I was?"

"By the description Chief Duvall sent me. Now, how many men are there in Arizona who wear all black, stand almost as tall as one of these ponderosas, have a pair of white-ridged scars on their right cheek, a bone-handled Peacemaker in their black holster, and ride a big horse that's as black as midnight?"

"I guess not too many." Stranger walked onto the porch and extended his hand.

The two men shook hands, then Clifton said, "Air's nice out here this mornin'. Kinda stuffy in the cabin. How's about we sit out here for a spell?"

A L   L A C Y

"Fine."

Clifton stepped inside and returned quickly with two straight-backed chairs. He bid Stranger to sit down, then hurried inside to put on a pot of coffee. He returned less than three minutes later and sat down facing Stranger. "Coffee'll be hot in a few minutes. I guess the map I drew was okay?"

"Sure was."

"First thing, Mr. Stranger...how's Diane and the kids? Are they handlin' Dale's death all right?"

"They seem to be. I'm sure with God's help and the passing of time, they'll do better."

"Sorry I had to leave them," Clifton said, shaking his head, "but that major and his cutthroats were out to get me. They wanted me dead. And I would be if I hadn't gotten out of town. Diane hid me until the day after Dale was murdered, but they were closin' in."

"Diane and the children understand that you had to leave."

"I know, but I still hated to go off and leave them. I sure have been prayin' you'd show up real soon. With the confidence Duvall has in you, I figured you'd be the man to handle Coburn and his bunch. How's things in town at the moment?"

"Not good. The people are terrified. It's going to take me some time to rid them of the major and his rodents, but in the meantime, I'm going to do what I can to encourage them. I'm holding church services Sunday morning and evening. Maybe a little encouragement from the Word of God will help."

Clifton cocked his head and squinted. "I know you're an expert at handlin' men crosswise with the law, Mr. Stranger. Are you a preacher, too?"

"I take a stab at it every now and then."

Clifton grinned from ear to ear. "You're gonna be a real help to those people. There's nothin' in this world that can get into your heart like that Bible."

"You mentioned a moment ago that you were praying that I'd show up real soon...and now you make a statement like that about the Bible. Are you a saved man, Ben?"

"I sure am."

"Well, praise the Lord! How long have you been a Christian?"

"Soon be a year."

Stranger's eyebrows arched. "That recently? Tell me how it happened."

"Well, my wife Maisie—who's with the Lord now—got saved about ten years ago. I was marshal over in Santa Fe at that time. She started witnessin' to me, wantin' me to be saved, but I wasn't really interested. But, bless her heart, she prayed for me and just kept lovin' me…and did a little preachin' to me along the way. Dale Patrick and his sweet little wife ganged up on me a little over a year ago and got me to start attendin' services. Some preacher, he was. Plain and pointed. Preached the Word straight at me. Pretty soon that Bible started cuttin' me apart."

"Hebrews 4:12 says it's quick and powerful and sharper than any two-edged sword."

"Well, it sure done its work on me. When I heard Sunday after Sunday how the Lord Jesus went to that cross for ol' Ben Clifton and took ol' Ben Clifton's place and paid his sin debt so's ol' Ben Clifton could miss hell and go to heaven if he'd only repent and receive Jesus into his heart…came one Sunday mornin' when that was all I could take. I walked the aisle when that preacher invited sinners to come to Jesus, and with the help of one of the deacons, I knelt at the altar and got washed in the blood, Mr. Stranger."

Tears were in Clifton's eyes. He thumbed them away and said, "My little Maisie died of heart failure nearly three years ago and was already in heaven when her prayers were answered."

"Well, she knew when it happened, Marshal. When she went to heaven, she joined that great cloud of witnesses who lean over heaven's banisters and watch what's going on down here. Jesus told us there's joy in heaven when a sinner repents. I guarantee you, your Maisie knew when her prayers for your salvation were answered.

And she's waiting to meet you up there some day."

Clifton pulled a bandanna from his hip pocket and wiped tears and blew his nose. "Well, I'm eager to see her again, Mr. Stranger, I'll tell you that. But while I'm still on this earth, I want to return to my job as marshal of Apache Junction. I realize I'll have to step down in a couple more years or so, but I want to serve the town as long as I can."

"I'm going to do all I can to see that you're back on the job real soon, Marshal. But it's best that you stay right here where you're safe until Apache Junction is rid of Coburn and his pals."

"Bothers me to have to do this. It ain't in my nature to back away from trouble. But there's too many of 'em. There's no way an old—ah, I mean a man my age can take 'em on alone."

"We all have our limits."

"Yeah, but at this stage of the game, *my* limits are a whole lot shorter than *yours.*"

"I'm going to need God's help, but Coburn's going down, and his cronies are going with him. You'll be back on the job shortly."

Clifton rose from his chair and tucked the bandanna back in his pocket. "Coffee'll be hot by now. Be right back."

A few minutes later he returned, bearing two steaming tin cups, and handed one to Stranger. "Hope you like it strong."

"The stronger the better. Thank you."

Stranger took a sip. He swallowed it with difficulty and smiled when he saw Clifton's eyes on him."

"Too strong?" Clifton asked.

"Oh, ah…no. Like I said, I like it strong."

"Where you from, Mr. Stranger?"

"Tell you what, Marshal, you can call me John."

"Only if you'll call me Ben."

"It's a deal, Ben."

"Okay, now that we're officially friends, I'll ask it again. Where you from? Originally, I mean."

Stranger looked at him over the steaming coffee cup in his

hand, took another sip, and smiled. He was about to reply when Clifton said, "Another thing...how do you make a livin' doin' what you do? Who pays you? I mean, if you're able to clear Apache Junction of the rats who've taken it over, will you submit an extermination bill to the town?"

Stranger laughed. "No, sir. No bill."

"Well, I don't mean to be a nosy old duffer, but you gotta make a livin' like the rest of us. Where do you get your money? And you haven't answered my first question, either."

Stranger reached in his pocket, took out a silver medallion, and handed it to him. "You wouldn't want a man to give away all his secrets, would you?"

Clifton took the silver disk and extended his arm to full length so he could focus on it. He studied it for a moment, then read it aloud. "The stranger that shall come from a far land. Deuteronomy 29:22." He raised his eyes to meet John's. "I assume that's all I'm gonna get. You're a travelin' man, so you're a stranger wherever you go. Your name's John Stranger, and you're from a far land...but ol' Ben ain't gonna learn what far land. Am I right?"

Stranger smiled. "Like I said, you wouldn't want a man to give away all his secrets, would you?"

"No, I guess not. Main thing about you, my friend, is that Chief Duvall sent you here to rid my town of the vermin that've moved in."

"Let's say *the Lord* and Chief Duvall sent me. With the Lord's help, it'll be done."

Ben Clifton looked at John Stranger with admiration. "Almost sounds like you're some kind of avenging angel to me. My pastor—bless his memory—preached about Christians havin' angels visitin' them here on earth, thinkin' they were men. You know, as the Bible says...angels unawares. That far land ain't heaven, is it?"

Stranger let a slow, reticent grin spread over his face. "I'm mortal, Ben."

"You sure?"

"I ought to know."

"I haven't heard you mention a wife and children."

"No wife or children *yet.*"

"Yet?"

"There is a woman, Ben. A very human, very beautiful, very wonderful woman. And in God's time, I'm going to marry her. You can bank on it."

"Well, tell me about her."

The morning passed as John Stranger told his newfound friend about Breanna Baylor. When it was noon, John said he had better head back for town, but Ben talked him into staying for lunch. When that was over, John mounted Ebony and told Ben he would be back from time to time to let him know how things were going.

Having spent so much time talking about Breanna made John Stranger ache for her as he rode southwestward toward Apache Junction. Soon the afternoon sun began its downward course. Shadows formed on the mesquite and cactus-dotted landscape, creeping into the sandy hollows of the low spots and along the walls of the deep arroyos. Soon the Superstition Mountains came into view, their bold peaks reaching up to claim the southern skyline.

Stranger rode into Apache Junction and headed for the parsonage of the First Baptist Church. As he was dismounting in front of the white adobe house, Kyle and Trudy Patrick darted out the door, welcoming him.

Diane appeared at the front door and watched the tall man bend over and hug both children. Then they began to show him the new clothes and shoes they had bought with their gold pieces. With an arm around each child, John approached the porch, smiling at Diane.

"I think you've found a couple of new friends, Mr. Stranger," she said.

"And I'm the richer for it." He gave them both a big squeeze.

Diane invited him inside. "I assume you found Ben. Is he all right?"

"He's doing just fine, though he's eager to get back to being marshal of Apache Junction. How are the people responding to the news that there'll be services at the church on Sunday?"

"The response has been excellent, Mr. Stranger. There are even people coming who have never darkened the door of the church before."

"Good. This'll show Coburn some strength on the town's part…and of course give me an opportunity to preach the gospel."

A trace of concern showed on the widow's features. "Mr. Stranger, what…what will you do if Coburn's men show up at church to collect tribute? You can be pretty sure they'll come for it."

"I'm not exactly sure what I'll do, ma'am. I'll just have to cross that bridge when I come to it. But don't you worry. Everything's going to be all right."

She studied him for a moment, then said, "Ordinarily I would say things couldn't turn out all right with one man against ten, Mr. Stranger, but there's something about you that tells me you really *can* handle this desperate situation."

"I have the Lord to help me, ma'am. Coburn and his cronies are on their own."

Diane liked the mysterious man more with each minute she spent with him. They talked a few minutes about Marshal Clifton and his desire to be back on the job, then John rode away, saying he would check in with her tomorrow.

Stranger rode Ebony to the stable and led him through the gate. The redheaded hostler came out of the office.

"Howdy, Mr. Stranger. Take a long ride, did you?"

"You might say that." He loosened the cinch to remove the saddle. "Give him a good rubdown, will you?"

"Sure enough. Could...could I ask you a question?"

"Of course."

"Is it really true that you're a preacher, and you're gonna hold services at the church Sunday?"

"It's really true."

"Well, sir, I just want to warn you—that Coburn and his honchos are downright vicious. They don't have a conscience. You know they killed Reverend Patrick and two merchants, don't you?"

"Yes. I'm aware of what they've done."

"Just be careful, will you? I'd hate to see them kill you."

"I'll do that. Will you be coming for the services on Sunday?"

"Wouldn't miss them for the world."

"Good. I may need to take another ride tomorrow. If so, I'll see you then. If not, I'll see you Sunday morning."

Stranger strode down the street to the café across from the hotel. Townspeople smiled at him on the boardwalk, but no one stopped to talk to him. They would feel safer when they were with the crowd at the church on Sunday.

The café was quite busy when Stranger stepped inside. A chubby waitress told him she was sorry, but all the tables were occupied. He would have to wait until the next one became available. Thanking her with a smile, he stood near the door and leaned against the wall.

He noticed people at the tables eyeing him and talking in hushed tones. It took him a few seconds to pick up on it, but they were all glancing at three men who sat at a table near the back of the room. Stranger looked at them, figuring them to be Coburn's men. The three were in deep conversation and occasionally glanced at him as they talked.

H. P. Tobin, who had been a captain under Coburn's command in the Civil War, leaned close to Roy Judd and Roger Tennant and said, "The major's orders are to bring this dude to him. How about we break him first so when we present him to the major, he'll already be inclined to pay the tribute off Sunday's offering?"

"Excellent idea, H. P.," Tennant said. "Don't you agree, Roy?"

Judd grinned evilly. "Yeah. We drag him to Coburn with the starch already outta his britches, I got a feeling the major will fatten our pay envelopes."

"Okay," Tobin said. "Looks like it'll be a while before he gets a table. We can finish eating in five minutes. Soon as we're done, we'll take him outside and work him over a little, then take him to Coburn."

"I can't wait," Judd said.

"Me neither," Tennant said, leering at Stranger.

C H A P T E R

NINE

———◆———

J ohn Stranger was not one for putting off an unpleasant thing.
He caught Roger Tennant's leer and the hard looks of the other
two and decided there was no better time to begin chipping
away at the Coburn bunch than now.

Every eye in the café was on him as he threaded his way
among the tables toward the back of the room. The waitress was
taking an order at a table in his pathway. As he drew near, she whispered, "Reverend, those are bad men. Be careful."

"Thank you, miss."

Coburn's men glared hard at the tall man in black as he drew
up to their table. They kept their seats and waited for him to speak.

Stranger leaned over the table and said, "Do I know you gentlemen? Have we met somewhere before?"

"Don't think so," Tobin said. "Why do you ask?"

"I noticed all three of you staring at me. Figured maybe we
had met somewhere."

Tobin rose to his feet, chewing his last bite of food. "We've
never met you, pal, but we know who you are. We'd like to talk to
you outside."

Stranger looked around at the full house and shrugged. "I
guess I've got time. Nobody's leaving yet."

While the patrons of the café looked on with curious eyes, Stranger led the way to the door. A middle-aged man had just swung the door open and was about to allow his wife to pass through when he saw the four men headed his direction. He touched his wife's arm, telling her to wait.

Stranger saw them and stopped. "Hold it, gentlemen," he said. "Lady coming through." He smiled at the woman and made a half-bow. "Please come in, ma'am."

The woman blinked, smiled, and said, "Thank you, Reverend."

"Yes, thank you, Reverend," her husband said.

"See you in church Sunday?" Stranger asked.

"You sure will," the man said with a smile.

Stranger and Coburn's men stepped out onto the boardwalk. The town's lamplighter was making his way down the street, having passed the café already. There were a few people on the street, and a couple of buckboards rattled by.

Stranger stepped into the dust of the street and turned to face the trio. "What did you gentlemen want to talk to me about?"

Tobin inched a little closer to the man who stood a head taller than he. "We were gonna ask you about the rumor we been hearin', but the question you just asked that fellow confirms that it's no rumor."

"You mean about the church services Sunday?"

"Yeah. That's what I mean."

"There'll be services both morning and evening."

Tobin stepped closer yet, putting himself only inches from Stranger. "They always take collections in church services, don't they?"

"Most of the time."

"Well, I'm officially servin' you notice that you'll be payin' tribute to Major Coburn from your collections. Both mornin' and evenin'."

"We won't be paying Coburn anything, pal. It's God's church, and the money that comes in the plate is God's money. Every dollar and cent of it will go to the widow of the late pastor, who was God's man."

"I don't think you know who you're dealin' with here, Reverend. That kind of attitude could get you into big trouble. Major Coburn has very little patience with people who cross him."

"That so?"

"Yeah, and you better believe it."

"Why, I don't doubt it at all."

"Okay, now you listen to me. If you take a sour attitude about this, Major Coburn'll take *all* the money that comes in the collection. But if you'll cooperate, he'll only take 40 percent."

"Forty percent? Last I heard, all he wanted was thirty."

"Cost has already gone up because you're being stubborn."

"I'll tell you one more time— What's your name?"

"Tobin. H. P. Tobin."

"I'll tell you one more time Mr. Tobin. It's God's church, and the offering money is God's money. It's going to Mrs. Patrick because her husband was God's man. And I mean *all* of it."

People on the street were watching the confrontation, but none from very close.

Tobin shrugged his shoulders, then turned to his friends. "Well, boys, we tried."

Before one of them could move, Stranger struck a quick blow to Tobin's stomach. Breath gushed from his mouth as he doubled over, stunned. He dropped to his knees, groaning, then fell flat, clutching his midsection.

Roy Judd cursed and balled his fists, moving toward Stranger. But he was too slow. Stranger sent a swift kick to his groin. While Judd was going down, Roger Tennant was backing up and clawing for his gun.

Stranger's gun was out, cocked, and leveled on Tennant before the outlaw could clear leather. Tennant froze with his hand on the gun.

"Go ahead," Stranger said.

Tennant pulled his hand away from the gun and said, "Oh, no you don't! I ain't drawin' with you pointin' that gun at me!"

"I didn't mean go ahead and draw against me. I meant go ahead and take it out of the holster and drop it on the ground."

Tennant licked his lips, eased the revolver slowly out of leather, and let it drop to the dust.

"Okay, now kick it over here to me." Tennant kicked it toward him. "Now relieve your pals of their guns. Toss them over here by yours."

Tennant stepped to his friends, who lay on the ground moaning, and slipped the revolvers from their holsters. He kept a wary eye on Stranger's muzzle as he tossed the guns to where his own gun lay in the dust.

Tobin rolled onto his knees, his face slack with pain and nausea. There was a sick look on Judd's blanched features as he rocked back and forth on his back, his legs pulled up against his chest. Then both men began giving up their suppers.

Tennant stood like a statue thinking how angry the major was going to be when he found out the preacher had bested three of his men.

When Tobin and Judd quit vomiting, Stranger stood over them and said, "Get up."

Judd struggled to his feet, wiping his mouth. He remained bent slightly at the waist and his knees were pressed together. He was pale as a ghost. Tobin slowly gained his feet, holding onto his midsection. He too was pale.

Stranger holstered his gun and ran his sharp gray gaze between the three rangers. "You boys go tell your leader there *will* be church services on Sunday as scheduled, and the offering in its entirety will go to Mrs. Patrick."

Stranger's adept handling of Coburn's men gave the people courage. They began to applaud and cheer him. Voices came from the crowd, shouting, "We'll all be in church Sunday, preacher!"

"God bless you, Reverend!" "You sure showed those bullies a thing or two, Reverend Stranger!" "We hope you run them all out of town!"

"You boys may be excused, now," Stranger said.

Tobin ran a sleeve over his mouth. "What about our guns, mister? Can we have 'em back?"

Stranger picked the three revolvers up, broke them open, and dumped the cartridges in the dust. Then he tossed the guns one by one into a water trough near the hitch rail.

"You can pick them up later. Right now, I want you to go tell the major he's not getting any money from the church people, nor is he going to keep us from having our services."

Tobin's eyes were filled with hate. "You're gonna be one sorry dude, mister! Nobody crosses Major Vic Coburn without sufferin' for it."

"Just tell him what I said."

"Who are you, anyway?" Tennant said. "You gotta be a gun-hawk. I ain't never seen a man draw as fast as you. What's this John Stranger stuff? What's your real name? Where you from?"

Stranger reached in a pocket, pulled out a silver medallion, and slapped it into Tennant's hand. He then looked at Tobin and said, "Best thing for you and your major is to find your way out of town." With that, he turned and moved down the street toward the hotel.

Tobin watched Stranger walk away for a moment, then said, "Let's go."

The people glanced at each other in quiet triumph as the outlaws headed down the lantern-lit street. Roy Judd's pigeon-toed, knock-kneed walk brought smiles to several faces.

"You *what?*" bellowed Vic Coburn, his face beet-red. "I'm in a nightmare, right? This can't really be true!"

"Well, sir, you'd have to have been there to understand." H. P. Tobin was stammering. "This guy's—"

"I understand all I have to understand!" Coburn said, pacing back and forth in the parlor of Ben Clifton's house. The other five rangers looked on.

"But, Major," Roger Tennant said, "when I tried to draw on him, it was like the gun leaped out of the holster into his hand. I've never seen a man draw that fast. I—"

"Shut up, Roger! I'm not looking for excuses here! I'm trying to convince myself not to court martial all three of you for letting one man disarm you and make fools of you in front of the townspeople! Find my way out of town, huh?"

The major swore and swung a fist through the air, then opened the fist and glared at the silver medallion in his palm. He swore again and threw the medallion against a wall.

"This is too much for me! I just can't believe you idiots let this man from nowhere get the best of you!"

There was a touch of insanity in Major Vic Coburn that had made him a terror to the Confederates in the Civil War and carried over as he led his rangers across the West, plundering, stealing, robbing, and killing. Coburn's men had learned to kill in the War, and now it was a way of life for them. Though they were tough and hard, they all feared the major. It was the touch of madness in him that fed that fear and made him almost a god to them.

Coburn knew this and relished the power it gave him. He believed he was invincible. Vic Coburn could have anything he set his heart on, and woe to the man who dared stand in his way.

Finally, Coburn turned to Mick Holcomb, who sat on the couch beside Dean Ritchie, and said, "Mick, I want you to go to the hotel and tell this stranger from a far land that I want to see him *right now*. Nobody defies Major Victor Walden Coburn and gets away with it!"

Holcomb rose to his feet. "What if he balks, Major?"

"Then cold-cock the dude. Don't kill him. I want the pleasure of doing that myself later. Right now, I just want him here. Now go!"

"Major, beg your pardon, sir," Tobin said, "but I suggest that Mick not go alone. You should send at least a couple of men with him."

Holcomb glared at Tobin. "So you don't think I can handle this reverend with the gun on his hip, eh, H. P.? Well, let me tell you something, pal. I've never met a man I couldn't handle. You got that? I'm going after him alone, and I'm bringing him back here alone. And when I do, you can apologize in front of the major and the rest of the rangers for saying that I need help!"

Holcomb turned and walked toward the door, then looked over his shoulder at Coburn. "I'll have that scar-faced dude right here in this room in a matter of minutes, Major."

Coburn grinned and pulled a cigar from his shirt pocket. "I'm sure you will, Mick. I remember how you captured that smart-aleck Rebel lieutenant at Wilson's Creek. I don't care whether this stranger from a far land walks through that door or is carried—just bring him to me."

"You can bet Robert E. Lee's boots on it," Holcomb said, and disappeared through the door.

Two sets of stairs led from the lobby of the Desert Rose Hotel up opposite walls to the second floor. Between the staircases was a balcony with a fancy railing that ran in front of John Stranger's room and two others. The balcony turned into hallways in both directions, which led to the other rooms on the second floor.

Inside his room, Stranger was sitting in an overstuffed chair next to a small table, reading his Bible. Two kerosene lanterns burned in the room, one on the small table at his elbow and another across the room on the dresser.

Stranger was engrossed in Psalm 90, marveling at its great

wisdom and at God's admonition for a man to make the best of his short life. He was musing on verse 12 when a sudden loud knock at his door startled him. He jerked, almost dropping the Bible. The knock was repeated as he laid the Bible on the small table and rose from the chair. He crossed the room and opened the door and saw the massive frame and homely face of Mick Holcomb.

"Do I know you?" Stranger said.

"No, but I know you."

"Well, I'm sort of at a disadvantage here. What's your name, pal?"

"Mick Holcomb. I'm here by orders of Major Vic Coburn." Holcomb waited for some kind of response, but Stranger only looked at him blandly. "The major wants to see you at his headquarters immediately. I'm to bring you to him."

"You lumber back to your major and tell him if he wants to see me, he knows where to find me."

Holcomb stepped into the doorway and looked down at Stranger. "I always follow the major's orders, mister. He said to bring you to him *right now*—the easy way or the hard way. Choice is yours."

"Like I said, Coburn knows where to find me. I might add, though, that I'm in the middle of my Bible reading, and when I finish, I'll be retiring for the night. If your major wants to come here between six and six-thirty in the morning, he can see me then."

Stranger saw the muscles under Holcomb's shirt flex and knew a punch was on its way. He beat him to it, sending a quick blow to the man's stomach. The punch backed Holcomb through the doorway. He went to his knees, feeling woozy and shaking his head.

Stranger moved through the door and stood over him. "You may leave now, Mr. Holcomb. Tell your commanding officer not to send a boy to do a man's job next time."

Holcomb scrambled to his feet and lunged at Stranger with a haymaker. Stranger dodged it, and Holcomb's fist smashed into the doorjamb, cracking the wood. He howled and swore.

Stranger unleashed a stinging blow to the big man's meaty jaw. It whipped Holcomb's head to the side, and as he brought it back, Stranger caught him with a like blow with the other fist, whipping Holcomb's head the other way.

Holcomb was off balance, and Stranger moved in and peppered him with repeated jabs to the face. Holcomb tried to fight back, but his eyes were glazed, and he couldn't focus on his target. He made a wild swing and missed by a foot.

Stranger hit him with a sledgehammer blow that sent him backpedaling. He crashed through the balcony railing and slammed the floor on his back, unconscious.

The desk clerk had heard the ruckus on the balcony and was already in the middle of the lobby, watching the action. Two male guests stood beside him. Stranger hastened down the stairs, running his gaze over the faces of the three men, who were staring owl-eyed at him. Before he spoke to the clerk, he paused to check on Holcomb. The man lay on his back, out cold, and there was no sign of him coming to any time soon.

Stranger turned to the clerk. "I'll need you to estimate the cost to have the railing repaired, Mr. Coggins."

"It'll be close to a hundred dollars, Mr. Stranger. As you can see, it's not ordinary railing."

"You sure a hundred dollars is enough?"

"Yes, I believe so."

Stranger knelt beside Holcomb, found his money belt, and opened it. He pulled out a wad of greenbacks and counted out two hundred dollars. He replaced the rest of the money in the belt, stepped to the clerk, and handed him the bills. "There's two hundred, Mr. Coggins. Mr. Holcomb, here, wants to be sure you're covered for the damage he did."

Delbert Coggins and the two hotel guests watched John Stranger pull the limp Mick Holcomb to a sitting position, then bend over and hoist his heavy bulk over his shoulder. They marveled at Stranger's strength as he stood and carried the man toward the door.

Coggins hastened to the door, pulled it open, and said, "Good work, Mr. Stranger. But let me warn you—the major is going to be real upset at what you did to his bodyguard."

Stranger paused, grinned, and said, "Ask me if I care."

Coggins looked puzzled, scratched his head, and said, "Okay. Do you care if Major Coburn gets upset?"

"Does a chicken have lips?"

In the kitchen of the Clifton house, Vic Coburn was playing poker with Dean Ritchie, Elbert Washburn, Lee Litchfield, and Leon Matkins. H. P. Tobin and Roy Judd had gone to bed, still feeling the results of their run-in with John Stranger. Roger Tennant was stretched out on the couch in the parlor, thinking about the speed of Stranger's draw.

Coburn fanned a new hand of cards, glancing at what he had been dealt, then let his eyes stray to the clock on the wall.

"Mick oughtta be back here by now," he said.

Tennant heard the major's words and called, "Maybe that preacher isn't in his room, Major. Could be Mick's waiting for him to show up."

"You're probably right."

Just then Tennant heard a loud *whump* on the front porch. He scrambled off the couch and pulled his gun, shouting, "Major! Something strange out here!"

Within seconds, Coburn and his poker pals were in the parlor, guns drawn. When they saw Tennant at the door, the major asked, "What is it?"

"Big noise on the porch."

"What kind of noise?"

"I'm not sure. Sounded like somebody fell or something."

"Well, open it."

Tennant pulled the door open and saw Mick Holcomb in a heap at his feet.

"It's Mick!" he exclaimed.

There was a rush to the door, and every man swore when he saw Holcomb's face. It was swollen and bloody, and placed carefully between his lips was a silver medallion.

CHAPTER

TEN

<hr />

As the desert sun was lowering toward the west on Friday, October 18, subchief Mandano stood on a flat, elevated rock outside the Apache stronghold just north of the Superstition Mountains. His attention was divided between a group of ten young hopefuls practicing hand-to-hand knife-fighting off to his left and three runners coming in off the desert. Not all young male Apaches made the grade as warrior upon first taking the training course. Some had to go through it several times before winning the title of Tonto Apache Warrior.

It all started when the males were mere lads. They were drilled from early boyhood in the cardinal virtues of cunning and toughness, the twin sources of Apache strength.

To learn how to deal with exhaustion, trainees and warriors were made to stay awake for two and three days at a time while traversing valley and mountain. The Apache warrior trained as a longdistance runner, crossing four-mile courses in blazing heat, carrying a mouthful of water all the way without swallowing it. Trainees had to work up to covering seventy miles a day in the most forbidding terrain. In order to keep warrior status, the mature warriors had to do the same periodically.

Such training in self-discipline made them fighters like no others on earth.

Mandano had sent seven runners in their final stage of training northward about two hours before dawn to run a course Janos had chosen. If they made it back to where Mandano stood by the time the sun cast the shadow of a nearby saguaro on the base of the flat rock beneath his feet, they would earn their warrior's headband. Once they owned the headband, Janos would assign them to a fighting unit under a subchief.

As the three runners drew closer, Mandano saw the other four as tiny figures strung out in the distance. They would fail to pass the course today. Glancing at the saguaro's shadow, he smiled and raised his line of sight back to the first three.

In the lead was young Zareem. He would beat the shadow to the rock. The other two still had a chance, but if they faltered even for a moment, they would go to their beds disappointed tonight.

Mandano had picked Zareem out some two or three years ago, certain that he would make the grade as warrior before he turned nineteen...and his prophecy had all but come true.

A youth approached Mandano from inside the stronghold. He smiled and nodded. It was his younger brother, Casco, who had recently turned thirteen. Mandano had high hopes for Casco's future as a warrior. He could not start his formal training for two more years, but Mandano could see a mighty warrior in Casco.

"Can you see any of the runners, big brother?" the boy asked as he climbed onto the flat rock.

"Yes, I can see all seven, but only three are drawing near."

Casco moved up beside his brother and shaded his eyes against the lowering sun. "Just as you said this morning. Zareem would come in first." He looked at the shadow of the saguaro as it crept toward the base of the rock and said, "He will make it. I think Trindin and Lorendo will make it, too."

Mandano turned and called a halt to the young men using wooden sticks as knives to train in hand-to-hand combat, telling them they had done enough for today's session. He told them the runners were coming in, and invited them to come and watch.

The young hopefuls gathered close to the flat rock, each eyeing the shadow of the saguaro, which was only inches from its base. They could see the distant four, who were now slowed to an exhausted walk, but coming in strong were Zareem, Trindin, and Lorendo. Zareem was just putting on a burst of speed, mouth set in grim determination, leaving the other two behind. The observers went into a chant of encouragement, calling for Zareem to keep up his pace.

Chief Janos appeared, having come from the stronghold. He carried several warrior headbands and craned his neck to see past the shouting young men. He was disappointed to see only three contenders still in the day's race. He checked the position of the shadow and watched Zareem press forward toward the rock, long black hair flying, his face gleaming with sweat and his mouth wide open as he sucked hard for air.

The cheering grew louder as Zareem drew up and knelt at the rock. The edge of the shadow was about the width of his hand from the rock's base. When he laid his hand on the rock, the chant became, "Zareem! Zareem! Zareem!"

Zareem panted and wiped sweat from his brow, and Mandano leaned over, patted him on the back, and said, "Congratulations, my friend. You are about to become a Tonto Apache Warrior!"

Seconds later, Trindin and Lorendo arrived and were able to touch the rock before the shadow did. They were cheered by their comrades also.

When they had caught their breath, they stood shoulder to shoulder before Janos, who congratulated them, pronounced them Tonto Apache Warriors, and placed the headbands on their heads. Again, there was much cheering. Janos did not wait for the other four to arrive. He would show them no consideration because they had failed to accomplish their task. This would make them try harder next time.

The chief led the men around him into the stronghold where

the rest of the people offered their congratulations to the three young warriors.

The sun went down while the celebration was in process, and one by one, Janos's scout patrols began to arrive. Each subchief reported to Janos that they had spotted several Zuni camps, but they had been unable to locate the "gun that speaks with many voices." There had been a couple of skirmishes with the Zunis, but none of the Apaches had been hit.

After the evening meal, Janos met with his subchiefs at the camp's central fire. They sat in a half-circle with the flames casting flickering shadows on their dark faces.

Janos ran his gaze over them and spoke in his deep voice. "I am deeply disturbed. There will be many battles with the Zunis in the days to come, but the Tontos are at a great disadvantage. Our ammunition supply is low. I am planning a raid on the next army wagon train that comes from the East to lay our hands on more rifles and ammunition, but our scouts who camp many miles in that direction have seen no sign of one. We dare not sit and wait. Something must be done. We must drive the Zunis out of Apache territory, but we cannot do so when we must fight their rifles and the gun with bows and arrows and spears."

"Chief Janos, we have more problems," Wundan said.

"Speak."

"Wundan and his warrior band saw many wagons coming across the desert from the East this morning."

"More gold-seekers?"

"Yes. When we passed Apache Junction, we saw more tents had been pitched on the north side of town."

The whites who invaded the Superstition Mountains looking for gold were a source of great irritation to the Tontos. The mysterious mountains belonged to the Tontos, and the white men were trespassers. How dare they blast the mountains with dynamite and dig into the heart of the sacred hills to extract shiny yellow rocks that belonged to the mountains and should be left there?

For many years, Janos had sent war parties into the Superstitions to drive the greedy white men out. Many had been killed by the Apaches; others had been murdered by their own rapacious white brothers. A great number had mysteriously died amongst the maze of canyons and jumbled boulders. The latter, it seemed, had been victims of the mountains themselves.

In spite of the well-publicized deaths, the white men still came in steady streams, driven by the desire for gain. Most who had come out alive had gone home disappointed. But the news of the few who had struck it rich beckoned more like a magnet.

"More white men will die!" Janos said. "I will send many warriors into the mountains to kill them once we have driven the Zunis back to their pueblo, or wiped them out."

"We must hasten to do so," Wundan said.

Janos nodded. "And we will. All of you will take your bands and scout again tomorrow. We must find the gun so Mandano can carry out his plan to render it useless."

The next morning, Janos assigned his three new warriors to their subchiefs. Zareem had hoped to be assigned to Mandano, but was placed in a band led by Krimindo. A new warrior never argued with the chief about his assignment or even tried to persuade him to put him in a band of his choice. Zareem would ride and fight with Krimindo.

Krimindo was not the fighter that Mandano was, but he was fierce and full of hatred for both whites and Zunis. Zareem would learn much while fighting under his leadership.

While the bands were assembling and preparing to ride, Janos climbed to the high rock where a sentry was always posted. He stood beside the sentry in the morning breeze and watched as his scout bands rode out in search of the gun.

Janos had ordered Krimindo to take his party south toward the Gila River. There were twenty-three warriors in Krimindo's unit, and as they left the Superstitions behind, Krimindo hipped around on his horse's back and called to Zareem, who was riding at the rear of the column. Zareem touched his pony's sides with his heels and trotted up beside the subchief.

"Since this is your first ride in a scout party, Zareem, you will ride next to me. Stay alert and listen carefully to my orders if we are attacked."

"I will do whatever you say," Zareem said.

Krimindo and his warriors searched every low spot and behind every hill and rock formation. This was done by dividing into small groups but never allowing much distance to come between them. Hours passed, but there was no sign of the Zunis or their death machine.

The sun was at its apex in the brassy sky when they approached a massive rock formation. It covered better than ten acres of desert floor, with some of its rocky pillars reaching forty to fifty feet high. There were level spots within the formation, but most were hidden behind lofty crags and huge boulders and could not be seen from the desert floor.

Krimindo halted the column. "We will divide into two groups here. Half will go around to the left and half to the right. We will meet on the other side."

There was a rustling noise from the rocks just above them, and they all turned to see a band of Zunis rolling the deadly gun to a stop, its shiny casing glistening in the sun and its ten deadly muzzles trained on them.

There was no time for the Apaches to react. One of the Zuni warriors began turning the crank, and the deep-throated voice of the .50-caliber Gatling echoed across the desert as the Apaches attempted to scatter. Bullets plowed into Apache flesh, dropped screaming horses, and lifted dust puffs where they chewed into the ground. Krimindo took a bullet through the head and peeled off his horse before he could shout any commands to his warriors. The horses who were not hit galloped away in panic, whinnying shrilly.

When the Zuni leader saw that every Apache lay motionless on the ground, he signaled for the warrior who turned the crank to cease firing. The death machine went silent. Thick wisps of smoke lifted from the ten hot muzzles and were carried away by the desert breeze.

The Zunis climbed down from the rocks, rifles ready, and walked among the Apache warriors on the bloody sand. One wounded horse lay breathing hard and ejecting a pained wail. A Zuni warrior took aim and put it out of its misery.

When they were satisfied that all were dead, the Zunis rolled the big gun down out of the rocks and lifted it into the back of a wagon they had stolen from a white rancher. Then they mounted their horses and rode away.

Zareem gritted his teeth and lay still as the warm desert breeze swept over him. He hoped he wasn't bleeding to death from the bullet that had ripped through his left side. He waited several minutes before opening his eyes. Without moving his head, he looked around and listened, but could not see or hear any Zuni warriors.

Cautiously, he lifted his head. He could see the Zunis in the distance, moving north, and he spotted seven Apache horses standing together about fifty yards to the east. Staying low to the ground, he removed the shirt of a dead Apache next to him and secured it around his waist to help stay the flow of blood. He was glad the .50-caliber slug had not lodged in his body.

Zareem waited till the cluster of Zunis was a small dot on the horizon, then struggled to his feet. His heart was heavy as he looked at his Apache brothers. He shuffled across the parched land toward the horses, and with delight, saw that one of them was his. The painted pony nickered at him as Zareem approached.

He spoke softly to the animal and leaned against its side, waiting for the dizziness to clear. Then in a painful leap, he mounted the horse and aimed its nose toward the Superstitions. The other six followed.

At sunrise that same Saturday morning, Marshal Hardy Bell rose from his bed in the small shed at the rear of the Apache Junction jailhouse. Upon Vic Coburn's insistence, a storage shed had been converted into living quarters for Bell. Coburn wanted him close by the office and jail, even at night. Though it was small, the place was comfortable. And with the kind of money he was making from Coburn, he didn't mind what inconveniences he endured.

Bell looked in the mirror and decided it was time to shave. His face hadn't felt a razor for nearly a week. He fired up the small stove and had just put a pan of water over the flame when there was a knock at the door.

"Yeah?"

"Hardy, it's Dean!"

Bell opened the door, letting yellow shafts of sunlight in.

"What is it?"

"The major sent me. He wants to see you *pronto.*"

"What about?" Bell asked, scratching his bare chest.

"That preacher who come into town. Get your shirt on. Coburn's waiting for you."

Five minutes later, Hardy Bell stood before Vic Coburn, who sat at the kitchen table in Ben Clifton's house. Lee Litchfield, Roger Tennant, Elbert Washburn, and Leon Matkins were sitting with him, drinking coffee. Dean Ritchie leaned against the cupboard, his arms folded across his chest. Roy Judd, H. P. Tobin, and Mick Holcomb were conspicuously absent.

While Coburn sipped coffee, he told Bell in detail what John Stranger had done to his men. Judd could barely walk for the pain in his groin. Tobin's midsection was so sore he could hardly stand up straight. Holcomb was seeing double, and his back hurt so bad, he couldn't get out of bed.

Coburn lifted a silver medallion off the table and tossed it to

Bell, who caught it and read the inscription, then shook his head in disbelief.

"What have we got here, Major? Some superhuman from another world? What's this Deuter—Deuteron—"

"Deuteronomy 29:22," Matkins said. "That 'stranger from a far land' is from the Bible."

"The Bible?"

"Yeah."

"What's it mean?"

"Dunno. None of us have a Bible so we can look at it."

Bell eyed the medallion as if it were something poisonous. "That figures, him bein' a preacher and all." He tossed it back to Coburn. "How'd this Stranger dude do this to your boys, Major? I mean…disarm 'em and batter 'em up so bad? Three on him at one time couldn't handle him? And even big Mick couldn't take him?"

"Well, I'm putting *you* on him this time, Hardy," Coburn said. "I want you to bring him to me."

A broad grin spread over Bell's stubbled face. "Bring him to you, nothin'! I'll brace the dude and send him back to his far land!"

"No! You'd be no match for him in a stand-up shootout!"

"I don't cotton to no insults, Major. Have you forgotten why you tracked me for a month so's you could hire me for this marshal's job? Huh? Because I'm faster'n any man alive, that's why!"

Coburn jumped to his feet and pointed a finger at Bell. "Now you listen to me, Hardy! I'm in command here, and you'll do as I say without mouthing off! Ask Roger here about that dude's fast-draw. You couldn't match him, Hardy, much less beat him."

"He's right, Hardy," Tennant saw. "I saw him draw. He's like double greased lightning. There isn't a man in this country who could beat him."

"Look," Bell said, "I've faced some of the biggest names on the roster and took 'em out. If this John Stranger is such a hotshot, how come I've never heard of him?"

"I can't answer that," Roger said, "but take my advice and don't brace him."

"I don't want you to brace him for two reasons, Hardy," Coburn said. "Number one, if he *did* outdraw you, I'd lose my marshal. Number two, I want that lowdown skunk for myself. I want you to sneak up on him and get the drop on him. Understand? He's not as fast as a bullet, that's for sure. Bring him to me. *Alive.*"

"So you can do what?" Bell asked.

"So I can have these boys hold him while I give him a pistol-whipping like nobody's ever had."

"A pistol-whippin'? That's all?"

"Of course not! I'm going to kill him personally after I've taught him that he doesn't mess with me and get away with it."

"Okay, Major. I'll bring him to you."

Coburn smiled and returned to his place at the table. "That's better, Hardy. I want him *today.*"

"You'll have him, but it could take a while. So don't panic if I'm not back right away."

"You've got till sundown. The earlier the better…but the deadline is sundown. I don't want him around to hold church services tomorrow. You *do* remember that this is Saturday, don't you?"

"Yeah. Payday."

"Correct. But you'll lose the whole week's pay if you don't produce."

Bell looked at Coburn with his gunfighter's eyes…cold, hard, intent. "Go ahead and stuff the pay envelope, Major. I didn't like that tall, dark dude the first time I laid eyes on him. He's yours. *Today.*"

CHAPTER

ELEVEN

———◆———

John Stranger left the Desert Rose Hotel and walked across the street to the Skylark Café. As he passed through the door, his eyes ran a check of the café's occupants. It was early, and the place had just opened. There were only five customers...all male. Two men sat at one table and three at a table next to it.

A waitress, who was pouring coffee for all five, saw Stranger enter. She studied him for a moment, then said something to the men. They turned to look, and one of them said, "Yep, Mattie, that's him."

There was a friendly look on every face, and John Stranger felt welcome. All five stood up as he moved their direction.

"Good morning, Mr. Stranger," the waitress said. "I'm Mattie Northrup. We haven't met yet, but I want to tell you how much I appreciate the things I've been hearing about you giving the Coburn bunch a hard time."

"The rest of us feel that way too, Mr. Stranger," an elderly man said. "Please join us. My name's Wilbur Stratton."

Stranger shook hands with Stratton, then was introduced to the others. Stratton invited Stranger to sit with him and his partner, making it three at each table. Stranger sat down and Mattie set a cup before him.

"Coffee?"

"Yes, please."

While she poured, Mattie said, "Everybody here just ordered our special—scrambled eggs, bacon, fried potatoes, and biscuits."

"Sounds good to me, ma'am…long as you keep my coffee hot." He gave her a wink and a smile.

"Will do."

"And give Mr. Stranger's ticket to me, Mattie," said Bill Crawford, the man who sat across the table from him.

Stranger threw up a palm. "Oh, no, Mr. Crawford. That isn't necessary."

"Oh, but it is. After what I saw you do to those three birds yesterday evening, I'd buy your breakfast every day for the next hundred years."

"We were just talkin' about what happened at the hotel last night," Marlon Kramer said. "The way we heard it, Coburn's bodyguard tried to drag you out of your room, and you knocked him off the balcony, then carried him away unconscious. Is that the way it was?"

"Yep. That's about it."

"What did you do with him?"

"I carried him over to Ben Clifton's house and dumped him on the front porch, still unconscious."

Kramer chuckled. "I'll bet Coburn had himself one big conniption when they found Mick like that. The man's about half crazy."

"Only half?" Stranger said, and everyone laughed.

"Well, we just want to commend you," Nick Farr said. "Aren't any of us qualified to take on Coburn and his bunch of killers. We don't know anything about you, but you sure know how to handle their kind. I didn't think there was one man anywhere who could put Mick Holcomb down."

"I just caught him off guard," Stranger said with a grin.

"What do you suppose the major will do now, Mr. Stranger?" Don Abel said.

"Hard to say, since I don't really know him. But my guess is he'll lash out at me, maybe try to shoot me in the back. Anything to get me out of the picture."

"What are you gonna do?" Crawford asked.

"Bide my time. Cross the next bridge when I come to it."

"Are you gonna stick around till Coburn's been run off?"

"Yep. Run off or disposed of in whatever way he makes necessary."

"What about Hardy Bell, Mr. Stranger?" Abel asked. "Can you handle him?"

"I can take care of him. Probably have to kill him, though. He's not the kind to surrender. I'll try to take him alive. I hate having to kill a man."

"You bein' a preacher, must be extra hard," Stratton said.

"Being a *Christian* makes it hard, but sometimes the bad guys don't give me any choice. I always try to take them alive, but so often they choose to shoot it out. Any honest man who wears a badge faces the same thing, and whether he's a Christian or not, I've never found a lawman who enjoyed killing men. But I'm afraid it's just necessary to protect society."

"But you're not a lawman, are you?" Crawford asked.

"I've worn a badge a few times, but only when I had a special need for its authority. I'm on an assignment right now for Chief U. S. Marshal Solomon Duvall in Denver. He wired me and asked that I come here and see if I could help Marshal Clifton. Said some miners were trying to rid the town of Clifton and put in their own man as marshal. I've since learned that it's not miners, but Coburn and his rangers."

"You won't need a badge to arrest Coburn and his bunch?" Stratton asked.

"Not really. I can't take the whole gang on at once, so I'll have to find a way to capture them one by one and lock them up where the major can't find them. Then I'll call in the marshal from Phoenix to come and take them into custody."

"If you could overpower Bell first, you could lock them up in the jail," Kramer said.

"Good thought. I'll have to do some more thinking on it, come up with a plan, then put it into action."

"Well, if you capture some before Bell," Abel said, "I'm sure there are enough of us with barns and sheds around town to give you a place to keep them tied up till the jail's available."

"I just might take you up on it."

"So you're going ahead with the church services tomorrow?" Stratton asked.

"Sure am."

"Good!" Kramer said. "Every one of us will be there with our families."

"Yes, and my husband and I will be there, too," Mattie said, drawing up with a full coffeepot in her hand.

"Wonderful!" Stranger said.

An hour later, John Stranger left a packed café, elated at the response he received from every customer who had come in while he ate his breakfast. He would have a large crowd to preach to on Sunday. He wondered how they would all fit inside the church building.

He walked to the church grounds and knocked on the parsonage door, but there was no response. He went next door to the church building and found the front door propped open. Stepping inside, he saw Kyle and Trudy dusting the pulpit.

They both looked up at the same time. Eyes wide, they gasped in chorus, "Mr. Stranger!" and hopped off the platform. They ran to him, and he put an arm around each one and hugged them close.

Diane appeared, holding a broom and dustpan. Her head was wrapped in a bandanna, and a wisp of hair lay on her forehead. She smiled at him.

"Hello."

John smiled back. "Hello, ma'am. I see you and the kids do

the janitorial work around here."

"Just sometimes."

John moved down the center aisle with the children in his arms.

"What can I do to help?"

"Oh, nothing. We're almost finished." She took a quick breath and said, "We heard about your run-in with Coburn's men at the café last night."

"News travels fast in a small town."

"Mm-hmm. And we heard about Mick Holcomb taking flight off the hotel balcony. With a little help from you, I might add."

"I suppose I helped him a little."

"What do you think the major will do now?"

"Oh, I look for him to retaliate. But in what way remains to be seen."

"You're…you're still going ahead with the services tomorrow?"

"I am. From what I'm able to pick up around town, we're going to have just about everybody here. I'm not sure where we're going to put them all, but we'll jam them in till the walls bow if we have to."

"Sounds wonderful." Diane pushed the loose wisp under the bandanna. "Do you suppose Coburn and his bunch will show up?"

"Hard to say, but if they do, they'll get their ears full of gospel."

"What if they try to disrupt the services?"

"We'll just have to take that as it comes. I won't be wearing my gun while I'm preaching, but I'll have it in the pulpit. I've had to preach with a gun in the pulpit before."

Diane smiled. "You amaze me, Mr. Stranger."

"In what way?"

"A preacher with a gun."

"I'm not the first preacher to wear a gun, I'm sure. And I'm probably not the first one to take a gun to the pulpit, either."

"I suppose not. But I doubt there's been one who could match you with either the Bible or the gun."

"Now, ma'am, how can you say that? You've never heard me preach, and you've never seen me use my gun."

"No, but I heard about how fast you drew on one of Coburn's men. And there's just something about you that tells me you're just as good with the Scriptures."

"Well, I guess you'll find out for sure in the morning." He gave the children a tight squeeze, then released them. "I'm heading out to see Marshal Clifton. I told him I'd keep him posted on what's happening in town. Thought I'd let him know about my clash with Coburn's men last night and how things are looking for the services tomorrow. Besides, he's pretty lonely out there. Figure he'd like some company."

"I'm sure he'll welcome it. Would you take him something for me?"

"Certainly."

"I've got some newspapers over at the house. I'm sure it'd help him if he could keep up with what's going on."

Diane led Stranger to the house, the children crowding close to him as they walked. He again put his arms around them. When they entered the house, Diane went to a small table in the parlor and picked up three editions of the *Phoenix Sun*. She folded them and handed them to Stranger.

Stranger's eyes fell on the front page of the paper on top. The headline for an article at the bottom of the page caught his eye. He put the other papers under his arm and unfolded the paper to read the article.

"What is it?" Diane asked.

"This headline about Governor Wheeler's son."

"Oh, the wedding?"

"Yes." He read a couple of lines. "I know your governor and his family. Wedding's the twenty-sixth…next Saturday. Hardly seems possible that Dan's old enough to be getting married. His

bride-to-be is Rebecca Ann Wilson. Oh, I see—she's daughter of
Gunther Wilson, owner of the Arizona Stagelines."

"That's him. Very wealthy, I understand. How do you know
Governor Wheeler and his son?"

"I got to know Donald Wheeler about five years ago, when he
was in business up in Flagstaff and chairman of the town council.
Flagstaff's bank was robbed, and I came riding into town only minutes after it happened. The town marshal and I jumped on our
horses and went after them. Every dollar was returned to the bank,
and the robbers went to prison.

"When the marshal told the town council that I had actually
caught the robbers by myself, Wheeler put on a special dinner in
my honor, and that's where I got to know his family. Dan would
have been about sixteen then. They had me for dinner in their own
home the next evening. I was impressed with Dan. He's a fine
young man."

"I'm sure he is," Diane said. "All that's ever been said about
him in the papers has been good."

Diane and her children walked Stranger to the door. "Mr.
Stranger, please tell Ben that I'm praying for him…and praying that
the Lord will use you to rid this town of Coburn and his henchmen. We're going to see Ben back in his office real soon, I just know
it. You tell him, won't you?"

"I sure will, ma'am. See you at church in the morning. You
too, kids."

Kyle and Trudy said good-bye and waved as he walked away.

An hour later, there was a knock at the parsonage door. Diane
was in the kitchen kneading dough. Kyle and Trudy were playing
with friends in the backyard.

Diane picked up a dishtowel and wiped her hands as she went
to the door. When she pulled it open, she felt a sudden revulsion. It
was Hardy Bell.

"Yes?" she said, eyeing the badge he had no right to wear.

"I want to know where that John Stranger is. Since he's

plannin' to preach in your church tomorrow, I figured you'd know his whereabouts. I've been lookin' all over town for him. Desk clerk at the hotel said he left real early this mornin'. Hostler said he picked up his horse and rode away little over an hour ago. Where'd he go?"

"He's preaching here tomorrow, yes, but that doesn't mean he has to report to me where he's going to spend his day. Since he saddled up, I'd say he was going out of town, wouldn't you? Besides, what do you want him for?"

"My own business!" He wheeled and stepped off the porch, then mounted his horse and rode away, muttering to himself.

It was late morning on the same day at the Tonto Apache stronghold in the Superstitions. Chief Janos emerged from the medicine man's hut with his face drawn. He looked around at the faces of the old men, the women, and the children who were gathered close.

"Shinamo is dead," he said.

The aged medicine man had been training a warrior named Clumban, who was nearing fifty, to become the Tonto medicine man upon his passing. Clumban had been riding with Krimindo for the past two years and had ridden out in Krimindo's search party that morning. Janos told himself they would have the ceremony inducting Clumban as the new medicine man that night.

Two elderly men entered Shinamo's hut to begin preparing the body for burial. The crowd was dispersing when the sentry atop the tall rock shouted, "Janos! A wounded warrior is riding in alone, with six riderless horses!"

Janos and several of the elderly men made their way to the spot between two giant boulders which served as the stronghold's gate. The wounded warrior was bent over his horse's neck, barely hanging on. The other horses trailed a few paces behind. As the wounded rider drew near, the men could make out the face. One of them exclaimed, "Zareem!"

There was a rush to help the bleeding warrior from his horse. Others took the reins of the riderless horses and noted the blood on their backs. They feared the worst.

Zareem was conscious, but very weak. Several men carried him to the shade of a boulder and began giving him water. Janos knelt beside him, wishing Shinamo was there to help. When he examined the wound, he called for two women to do what they could to clean it and put on a fresh bandage.

As the women began their work, Janos asked, "What happened, Zareem?"

Zareem licked his lips and asked for more water. When he had received it, he choked momentarily, then said, "The gun. Ambush at a field of rocks…near the big spring. All dead…except me."

The news was like a blow to Janos's chest. He was filled with a mixture of grief and wrath. His hatred toward the Zunis was stronger than ever, and he cursed the man who had invented the "gun that speaks with many voices." Janos left Zareem in the women's care and went to his hut in mourning.

A short time later, three elderly Apache men returned to the stronghold from Apache Junction, where they had been doing some trading. They had new tin plates and cups wrapped in newspapers by the proprietor of the general store. Several people gathered around to tell the old men of Shinamo's death and of the Zuni ambush. They were stunned at the news.

Janos left his hut and drew up as the old men were unwrapping the cups and plates. One of them dropped a crumpled newspaper page, and it fell at Janos's feet. The chief picked it up, and his eyes fell on an article about a wedding for the governor's son. He opened the page fully, and as he read, a plan began to form in the Apache chief's mind.

———

"Hey! John Stranger!" Ben Clifton exclaimed as he stepped off the porch of the cabin, smiling warmly. "I didn't expect you back so soon!"

Stranger dismounted, gave Ebony a loving pat on the neck, and shook hands with Clifton. "Well, some things have happened in town that I thought you ought to know about. Besides, I figured maybe you'd like a little company."

"Well, you've got that right, my friend. It's pretty lonely out here. And on top of that, it's kind of tough sittin' out here wonderin' what's goin' on in my town…and in the rest of the territory, for that matter."

"Oh!" said Stranger, snapping his fingers. "Speaking of what's going on, I've got some newspapers for you. The *Phoenix Sun*. Diane asked me to bring them to you."

Stranger fished the newspapers out of the saddlebag and handed them to Clifton, who thanked him and bid him sit down with him on the porch.

"So, how are Diane and the children?"

"They seem to be handling things pretty well, considering what they've been through. I sure am getting attached to those two kids."

"Yeah, they're special, all right. Be easy for most anyone to get attached to the likes of those two."

Stranger then told Clifton of his run-in with Vic Coburn's men. Clifton was elated to hear that Stranger had shown three of them up in front of the townspeople, and just as elated to learn what he had done to Mick Holcomb.

"So how you plannin' to get rid of Coburn?" Clifton asked. "Got any plans?"

"I'm going ahead with the services tomorrow, Marshal. That could bring it all to a head. I'll just have to take things as they come.

But I assure you, Apache Junction is soon going to be rid of those no-good crooks. And by the way, Diane said to tell you that she's praying for you…and praying that the Lord will soon have you back on the job."

Clifton smiled and blinked at the moisture gathering at the corners of his eyes. "God bless her."

"Why don't we just have us a prayer meeting about this whole thing right here and now, Ben?"

"I'll vote for that."

The two men prayed for some time, then Clifton invited Stranger to have lunch with him. Stranger stayed with him till late afternoon, then headed back to town.

As the sun lowered toward the western horizon, Hardy Bell moved nervously about town, keeping an eye out for John Stranger. He watched the main street, especially the stable and the hotel.

His insides were twisted tight as he watched the shadows grow longer. The sun was now touching the western horizon. He was passing the Desert Rose Hotel when he saw Lee Litchfield and Elbert Washburn angling across the street toward him. Bell stopped, and as the two men drew up, Litchfield said, "We're heading for the house. The rest of the boys are too. Looks like your deadline's drawing close, Hardy."

"Yeah. That stinkin' preacher's got to be here to hold those services tomorrow. I don't know why he isn't in town."

"Oh, he'll show up," Washburn said. "But it's not looking too good for him to do it before sundown."

Bell removed his hat, wiped sweat from his brow, and said, "I wish the major had given me a little more time."

"Well, you know the major," Litchfield said. "There'll be no changing his mind on that. See you later."

As the two men walked away, Bell saw other rangers moving

toward the side street that led to the Clifton house. He cursed under his breath. He was going to face Vic Coburn's wrath…and he was going to lose a week's pay. What had happened to John Stranger? Where could he possibly be?

Bell's heart took a sudden leap in his chest. There was John Stranger astride his black horse, coming down the street from the north toward the stable.

Bell's pulse pounded in the side of his neck. The sun wouldn't be completely down for at least a half hour. It would take some doing, but Hardy Bell would get the drop on John Stranger and have him in Vic Coburn's hands before the last rays of the sun disappeared.

C H A P T E R

TWELVE

———◆———

Hardy Bell hurried down the boardwalk, darting between buildings to keep from being seen by John Stranger. People on the street saw Bell acting strange, but had no idea what he was doing.

Bell drew up between the apothecary and the hardware store and watched Stranger dismount and lead Ebony into the stable. Some three minutes passed, and Bell saw Stranger coming out of the stable office. The gunfighter tensed, ready to make his move, then swore under his breath when he saw Nick Farr and Bill Crawford come out of the hardware store. They saw Stranger and approached him. The tall man smiled and greeted them.

The two men stayed and chatted. The sun slipped downward. It seemed to Bell that it was setting faster than it ever had in his lifetime.

Then Stranger started to walk away, and the two men walked with him. Bell swore under his breath and followed them. When they reached the hotel, both townsmen told Stranger they would see him in church the next morning, then moved on down the street.

Bell waited until Stranger went inside the hotel, then ran up and peered through the lobby window. The clerk was nowhere to be seen. Stranger mounted the stairs and disappeared.

Bell hurried through the hotel door and looked around. There was no one in sight. A small sign on the desk announced that the clerk would be back shortly. Bell pulled his gun and bounded up the stairs.

John Stranger entered his room, thinking about Ben Clifton. The man had dedicated himself to keeping the peace in Apache Junction, and now the likes of Vic Coburn would dare to rob Clifton of closing out his career with dignity. Somehow, Coburn had to be stopped, and stopped soon. Stranger had been praying all the way in from the cabin. He felt that the Lord was going to bring things to a head very soon. It just might come tomorrow at the church services.

John tossed his hat on the dresser and sat on the edge of the bed. He was about to take off one of his boots when he heard rapid footsteps on the stairs. Then came a knock at the door.

"Yes?"

A muffled voice said, "Mr. Stranger, it's Marshal Bell. I need to talk to you."

John Stranger pulled his gun, placed it in his left hand, and cocked it quietly. Then he opened the door a few inches with his right hand.

He found himself looking down the muzzle of Bell's Colt .45. The hammer was in firing position, and behind the gun were the bulging eyes of Bell. The gunslick grinned and said, "This gun has a hair trigger, mister, and my trigger finger is itchy. Major Coburn is very upset with you and wants to see you immediately. If you're wearing your gunbelt, I want it removed."

"Looks like we've got us a Mexican standoff here, Hardy."

"What do you mean?"

"Well, the gun I'm holding behind the door is cocked and aimed straight at your heart. It too has a hair trigger. Now, you can drop your hammer and put a bullet into my face, but reflex will put a .45 slug through your heart."

Bell held his features tight, but a slight tinge of fear showed in his eyes. He wanted to look down and see if Stranger was wearing his gunbelt and if the holster was empty, but he dared not take his gaze off the man's face. He let a few seconds pass, trying to think of what to do next.

"Well, señor, what do we do? One of us is going to have to back down."

"Well, it ain't gonna be me!"

"Seems the standoff holds. It's not going to be me, either."

There was dead silence for several seconds, then Bell said, "Maybe you're bluffin'. Maybe you're not even wearin' your gun."

"All you have to do is take a look. Go ahead. You'll see an empty holster."

"Oh, no you don't! You ain't distractin' me so you can win this standoff."

"Well, mister, you'll just have to take my word for it. I've got my muzzle aimed at your heart, and I'm feeling a bit impatient. So either drop the hammer or drop the gun."

Sweat began to bead on Bell's forehead. "You willin' to die, Stranger?"

"If that's the way it has to be, yes. Are you?"

Hardy Bell had faced death in the eyes of many a gunslinger in his young and violent life, and had cheated death by drawing faster and shooting straighter than his opponents. But this was something new. The look in John Stranger's iron-gray eyes gave him a chill. For a long, silent interval, he weighed his options.

"Okay, mister," Bell said, biting his lower lip, "I'm gonna back away from the door and leave."

Even as he spoke, Bell raised the muzzle of his revolver and eased down the hammer. Before he could take a backward step, Stranger swung the door wide and leveled the Peacemaker on his belly.

"Stay right where you are, Bell." Stranger extended his free hand. "And give me the gun."

Bell's heart leaped in his chest and his face lost color. He started backing up.

"No, sir, mister! You ain't gettin' my gun!"

The railing behind Bell had not yet been repaired. The wide gap left when Mick Holcomb had crashed through it was directly in Bell's path.

"Give me the gun, Hardy."

Bell continued to back up, shaking his head. "Not on your life, Stranger! I'm not givin' my gun—"

There was a sharp gasp, and then he was falling. He hit the floor with a thud, landing solidly on his back. It knocked the wind out of him and jarred the revolver from his fingers, sending it sliding across the lobby floor. Stranger bounded down the stairs, holstering his gun. He picked up Bell's weapon, stuck it under his belt, and lifted him to his feet. Bell was gasping for air.

"All right, let's go."

Bell stiffened. "Go where?"

"Where you belong. To jail."

"What are you talkin' about?"

Stranger pointed toward the back of the hotel. "That way. We'll go down the alley."

Bell bristled and set his jaw. "I ain't goin' to no jail!"

Stranger lashed out with a punch that would have jarred a Brahman bull. The blow knocked Bell off his feet and left him lying once again on the floor. This time, he was out cold.

Stranger hoisted the gunfighter over his shoulder, looked to see if there were any observers, then carried Bell out into the alley. Cautiously, he made his way down the alley to the rear door of the marshal's office, where he relieved Bell of his keys and opened the door.

Bell was coming to as Stranger dropped him on a bunk in the first cell. He looked up at the tall man, blinked glassy eyes, and said with a thick tongue, "What're you doin'?"

"Leaving you where you can't cause any more trouble."
Stranger turned toward the cell door. "Sit tight. I'll be back."

"Wait a minute! You can't leave me in here!"

"Watch me."

Stranger grinned and swung the barred door shut. As the key
rattled in the lock, Bell rolled off the bunk, swearing and shouting.

"Scream all you want, Hardy. Back here, nobody can hear
you. And even if they could, they can't help you."

Stranger walked away and entered the office, with Bell's angry
voice hurling profanities at him.

It was growing dark. Stranger lit a lantern and found the key
ring for the cell doors. He removed the key and pocketed it, along
with the key Bell had been carrying. He searched through the desk
and found two more keys and pocketed them, also.

Stranger found a small sign Ben Clifton had used when he
had to leave the office for an extended time. It read: *Marshal Out of
Office. Will Return as Soon as Possible.* He placed it in the window
of the door, blew out the lantern, and exited through the back door
into the alley. Within minutes, he entered the hotel the back way
and moved down the hall to the lobby. Clerk Delbert Coggins was
on the front porch of the hotel in conversation with a couple of
townsmen, and did not notice Stranger's entrance. The tall man
crossed the lobby, stepped out onto the porch, and greeted the men.
The three of them watched Stranger cross the street and enter the
Skylark Café. He had been the subject of their discussion before
appearing from the interior of the hotel, and still was after he had
entered the café.

It was the same all over town. The people of Apache Junction
were looking to John Stranger to deliver them from the Coburn
bondage.

Later in the evening, at the Clifton house, Coburn paced the floor
of the parlor and chewed on a dead cigar. There was fire in his eyes.
It had been dark for two hours, and Hardy Bell still had not
returned with John Stranger.

Fuming and swearing, Coburn continued to pace in front of
his seven men. The only ranger not in the room was Mick
Holcomb, who was still laid up in bed.

Finally, Coburn swore and threw the cigar across the room.
"Lee! Roger! Take Elbert and Leon and go find that lame-brain. He
may be a hotshot gunfighter, but he isn't much at carrying out
orders. He's probably ashamed to show up here because he failed to
lay hold on that preacher. I want him here immediately. Go find
him!"

The four men leaped to their feet, donned their hats, and
bowled through the front door. The major followed them as far as
the edge of the porch, shouting after them as they hurried down the
street, "Make it quick, men! I want Bell here pronto!"

Coburn moved back inside and looked at H. P. Tobin, Roy
Judd, and Dean Ritchie.

"Let's play some poker. I've got to have something to occupy
my mind."

The major was still muttering to himself and his mood was
getting blacker as they sat down at the kitchen table. Tobin, Judd,
and Ritchie eyed each other furtively. They had best let the major
win tonight. It might keep him from going completely over the
edge. They had seen a few of his tantrums and didn't care to see
another.

The poker game dragged on for two hours, with Coburn
showing no enjoyment though he was winning every hand. His
mind was on Hardy Bell in spite of the game...Hardy Bell and
John Stranger.

The game was interrupted with the sound of voices and heavy footsteps at the front of the house. Coburn's head came up. He laid his cards face-down and said, "They better have found him."

When the four men filed into the kitchen without Bell, Coburn looked up at them and said, "Well?"

Litchfield cleared his throat. "Major, we've scoured this town. Hardy just isn't here."

Coburn banged the table with his fist.

"Don't tell me that! Of course he's in this town! Where else would he be?"

"Well, sir—"

"Did you think to check the barn to see if his horse is there?"

"Yes, sir. And it is. But Hardy has flat disappeared."

Coburn jumped to his feet and gripped the edge of the table. Tobin, Judd, and Ritchie quickly scooted their chairs back and jumped out of the way as Coburn hurled the table against the back wall. Cards fluttered in the air and poker chips clattered on the floor.

"Are you telling me you've literally looked this town over?"

"Yes, sir," Tennant said. "No one in the saloons, the cafés, or on the streets has seen him. We checked his shack, and we looked through the back windows of the marshal's office. No lights. No Hardy. Nothing."

"You check the hotel?"

"We looked through the big window of the lobby," Matkins said.

"What about Stranger's room?"

The foursome looked at each other blankly.

"We never thought of that, Major," Washburn said.

"Well, what am I paying you guys for? You've got brains—use them! Maybe Hardy went to Stranger's room and got himself clobbered."

"That could be it, all right," Litchfield said.

"Well, get over there and check it out! If you find him in

Stranger's room, I want both of them brought to me. If I can get my hands on that tall dude tonight, there won't be any church services tomorrow. Now get going!"

John Stranger sat on the bed in his hotel room. He had eaten supper at the Skylark and was now going over his sermons for tomorrow. His big black Bible lay open before him. Suddenly his attention was drawn to the sound of voices in the lobby.

He left the bed and moved to the door, turned the knob and opened it quietly. He could see Roger Tennant standing near the desk, which was out of his view. It took only a few seconds for him to determine that Tennant had others with him, though he couldn't see them. A male voice was pressing clerk Delbert Coggins, asking if he had seen Hardy Bell during the evening.

Coggins's high-pitched voice trailed up to Stranger's ears. "No, sir, Mr. Litchfield. I haven't seen the marshal tonight at all. Why would he be coming into the hotel?"

"He was wanting to see that preacher. We figured he might've come here looking for him."

"Well, I was out for a spell. He could've come in during that time. Reverend Stranger is in his room. Possibly Marshal Bell is up there with him. You can go up and knock on the door. It's number two, right up there in the center of the balcony."

"Let's go, boys," Litchfield said.

Stranger saw Leon Matkins and Elbert Washburn step into view, followed by Litchfield and Tennant. When they reached the bottom of the staircase, Litchfield signaled for them to stop.

"I'll knock on his door. You guys flatten yourselves against the wall beside the door. Elbert and Roger on the far side, Leon on the near side. I'll simply ask Stranger if he's seen Marshal Bell. When you hear me say 'Bell,' swing out where he can see you with your guns on him. We'll make him turn Hardy over to us, then we'll take both of them to the major. Got it?"

"Got it," all three responded.

As they started up the stairs, Litchfield noticed Coggins watching them with fearful eyes from behind the desk. Litchfield put a finger to his lips and scowled. The clerk swallowed hard, blinked, and gave an intimidated nod.

Each man went up the stairs on his toes, doing all he could to make the ascent in silence. The stairs squeaked a few times, making them wince.

When they reached the balcony, Washburn, Matkins, and Tennant took their assigned places against the wall. Litchfield looked down both hallways to the other rooms on the second floor. There was no one in sight. He stepped in front of the door and banged it with his knuckles five or six times.

There was no response.

He knocked again.

Silence.

"He ain't in there!" Tennant whispered. "That stinkin' clerk lied to us!"

"Well, bust the door down!" Washburn said in a loud, croaking whisper. "He's probably got Hardy bound and gagged in there. Let's get him out!"

Suddenly, a harsh voice cut the air from the corner of the hallway to their left.

"No need to break the door down, boys. He's not in there!"

The rangers jumped with a start, their heads whipping around, eyes bulging. John Stranger had them cold, a cocked revolver in each hand.

"First guy to flinch takes a bullet! Now I want you to ease the hammers down on those guns—real slow-like—and drop them on the floor. You there at the door. Unbuckle your gunbelt and let it drop."

Washburn, Matkins, and Tennant gave Litchfield a helpless look. He gave them a slight nod.

When Stranger's instructions had been obeyed, he moved closer and said, "So you boys want to see Mr. Bell? All right. Let's go see him."

"Where is he?" Litchfield asked.

"You'll see. Now all of you put your hands behind your heads and lace your fingers together. If I see so much as a twitch, you've seen your last sunrise. Understand?" No one responded. "You boys deaf? I asked if you understand."

"We understand," Tennant said.

"Good. Now, move down the stairs. I want to say something to Mr. Coggins, then we're going out the back way."

When the rangers reached the lobby floor, Stranger held his guns on them and spoke to the clerk, who stood behind the desk, eyes bulging.

"Mr. Coggins, you trust me, don't you?"

"Yes, sir, Mr. Reverend Stranger, sir."

"If any other rodents show up looking for these boys, you just tell them they were here and knocked on my door, but you didn't see them leave. Got that?"

"Yes, sir."

"Now, so I don't make a liar out of you, Mr. Coggins, I want you to turn your back so you don't see them leave. We're going out the back way."

Delbert Coggins managed a weak grin and turned his back. "Whatever you say, Mr. Stranger. Where are you taking them?"

"They're going to go see their pal, Hardy Bell. Right now I've got him in jail, but I think it might be prudent to move him and these four someplace else till Coburn's out of the picture. Their guns are on the balcony, Mr. Coggins."

"I'll pick them up."

"Appreciate it," Stranger said, then urged the outlaws down the hall with his guns at their backs.

—◆—

It was ten o'clock, and Vic Coburn was in a frenzy. He paced the kitchen floor like a caged beast, and his hands trembled with anger.

"What's happening? Why haven't they come back?"

"They must not've found Hardy at the hotel, sir," Ritchie said. "They're probably leaving no stone unturned. Who knows? They may be searching every house, barn, and shed in town."

"That would take a week. I don't think that's what they're doing. There's something fishy going on, and we're going to find out what it is. Come on."

Ten minutes later, the major and Judd, Tobin, and Ritchie filed into the lobby of the Desert Rose Hotel. When Delbert Coggins saw Coburn, his face blanched.

"I want to know something, little man," Coburn said.

"Yes, sir?"

"Is John Stranger in his room?"

"Uh…no, Mister Major, he ain't. He went out a while ago and hasn't come back."

"Did you see some of my men come in here tonight?"

"Well, I…uh—"

"Come on, man! Did you or didn't you?"

"Well, sir, I did. They, uh, went upstairs and knocked on Reverend Stranger's door." He pointed toward the balcony. "It's the middle door right up there."

"Okay, so they knocked on his door. Then what? Did they go inside his room?"

"Not that I know of, sir."

"Well, did you see them leave?"

"No, sir."

"If you didn't see them leave, they must still be up there. Come on, men, let's go and see for ourselves."

Coggins watched the four men ascend the stairs. They had

their guns out by the time they reached the door of room number two.

Coburn pounded on the door, holding his revolver ready. When there was no response, he pounded again, yelling at the top of his voice, "Open up, Stranger! It's Major Coburn! Open the door, or we'll break it down!"

"No! Please don't break it down, Major!" Coggins called from the lobby floor. "If Reverend Stranger isn't answering the door, it's because he isn't in there! Neither are your men, or they would open up."

"I want to see for myself. Come up here and unlock this door!"

Coggins pulled a skeleton key from his pocket and headed for the staircase closest to him. When he unlocked the door and stepped back, the four men plunged inside. Seeing no one, Coburn turned and stormed past Coggins and down the stairs with his three men on his heels.

"I know where they are," Coburn said. "Stranger somehow got the drop on them. What better place to lock them up than the jail!"

The foursome hurried down the dimly lit street toward the marshal's office and jail.

"Why didn't I think of it before! Since Stranger got the upper hand on Hardy first, he'd have Hardy's key to the office. Once in the office, he'd have access to the cell keys."

They found the office door locked and saw the sign Stranger had placed in the window. Coburn told Ritchie to break the door open, which he quickly did. They flared a lantern and went into the jail, but found it empty. Coburn swore and his face went beet-red.

"What has he done with my men? Well...one thing for sure. He ain't gonna have a church to preach in tomorrow. C'mon, men. We've got some important business to take care of."

CHAPTER

THIRTEEN

———◆———

Major Vic Coburn stormed out of the marshal's office with Dean Ritchie, H. P. Tobin, and Roy Judd beside him. As they moved through the dark streets, heading for the Clifton house, Coburn said, "We'll wait till three in the morning to set the fire. That way it'll be a full blaze before it wakes the neighbors. And when Stranger sees the church going up in smoke, he'll be sorry he ever messed with Vic Coburn!" They turned onto the street where the Clifton house was located. "We'll pick the right time to throw guns on him and make him tell us where our guys are. Once we have them with us again, Stranger will die!"

"I can't wait to watch you kill him an inch at a time!" Tobin said. "After what he did to me, I'll enjoy watching him suffer."

"Yeah, me too," Judd said. "He deserves everything you're going to give him!"

"I'd like to administer a little torture myself, Major," Ritchie said.

"Sorry, my friend, he's all mine. But I assure you, you'll enjoy watching me make him squirm and beg for his life. And when he's dead, we'll milk this town dry!"

The four men had a good laugh as they drew up to the dark house.

Coburn paused at the porch and said, "H. P., you and Roy go
to the tool shed behind the house and bring those two cans of
kerosene Clifton so conveniently left for us. Set them here on the
porch."

Tobin and Judd headed for the back of the house. Coburn
and Ritchie stepped inside, and feeling their way in the dark, soon
had two lanterns burning in the parlor. Coburn headed for the
kitchen to fire up a lantern there.

"I'll go check on Mick," Ritchie said.

He felt his way along the dark hall to the bedroom Mick
Holcomb shared with three other men. He slipped into the room
and groped along the wall to the dresser and found the lantern. He
took a match from a box near the lantern, struck it, and lifted the
glass chimney. The flare of the match lit up the room. He touched
flame to the wick and looked toward Holcomb's bed. Mick
Holcomb was not there. The covers were thrown aside and one of
the pillows was on the floor.

Ritchie hurried to the rear of the house, carrying the lantern,
and stepped out onto the back porch, looking toward the privy.
Tobin and Judd were coming out of the tool shed, carrying the cans
of kerosene.

"You guys see Mick?" Ritchie asked.

"No," Tobin said. "You know he can't get out of bed."

"Well, he did."

"You mean he's not in his bed?" Judd asked.

"Nope. I figured he might have managed to get up and gone
out to the privy."

"Well, let me look." Judd set his can of kerosene down and
walked to the privy, which was some thirty yards from the back of
the house.

"If Mick's gone, Dean, it isn't because he walked away," Tobin
said. "Somebody *took* him! Bad off as he is, he couldn't even make it
to the privy…let alone somewhere else."

Judd banged the privy door shut and called from the darkness, "He isn't here!"

"That's it," Ritchie said. "John Stranger's got Mick, too."

Coburn came out the back door. "What's going on?"

"It's Mick," Ritchie said. "He's gone."

"What? What do you mean gone?"

"He's not in his bed, and he's not in the privy neither."

"Stranger!" Coburn said. "Stranger got him!"

"That's the way I figure it, Major," Ritchie said. "You know as well as I do Mick's in no shape to just up and walk away from the house."

Coburn swung a fist through the air. "Everything was going just fine till John Stranger showed up in Apache Junction."

Breanna Baylor's arms were flung wide as John Stranger drew Ebony to a halt in front of Dr. Lyle Goodwin's office in Denver. There were tears in her sky-blue eyes and a sweet smile graced her face. Stranger slid from the saddle, and they embraced for a long moment, then kissed tenderly.

"O John, I've missed you so!" she said as he held her tight.

"I've missed you, too," he said softly. "When we're apart, it's like half of me is missing. You're my very heartbeat, my—"

"Mr. Reverend Stranger! Mr. Reverend Stranger!" came Delbert Coggins's voice rudely into his dream, along with a loud banging on his hotel room door.

Breanna was gone like a wisp of smoke, and John sat up in bed, rubbing his eyes.

"Mr. Reverend Stranger!" the desk clerk repeated, still pounding on the door.

"Yes, what is it?"

"The church is burning down, Mr. Stranger!"

"Oh, no! I'll be right there! Just take a minute!"

"I'll wait for you!"

A bright-red flare in the sky over Apache Junction filled John

Stranger's room with a dull, pinkish light. It took him only a minute to dress, pull on his boots, and strap on his gunbelt. He noted by the clock on the wall that it was almost 3:30 A.M.

Delbert Coggins was waiting for him when he opened the door. He could hear excited voices on the street.

"I thought you'd want to know about it, sir, or I wouldn't have awakened you."

"You did the right thing."

Stranger dashed down the stairs, leaving the clerk behind, and out onto the boardwalk. Many people were in their night clothes leading sleepy-eyed children toward the church building engulfed in flame. Stranger feared that the parsonage, too, might have been set on fire, and he breathed a prayer that Diane and her children would not be harmed.

He was relieved when he rounded the last corner and saw that the parsonage was intact. It was far enough from the blazing building that it was not in danger. Soon he could make out Diane and her children standing on the parsonage porch. Several men and women were gathered around them, watching the fire with tears in their eyes. Kyle and Trudy clung to their mother, who was weeping also.

"Oh, Mr. Stranger!" Diane said as he came running up.

"I'm so glad you three are all right," he said, breathing a bit hard from his run. He laid his hands on the heads of Kyle and Trudy, and both smiled at him.

The wind caused smoke to whirl and spiral overhead, and ashes fell in a steady dry rain. Flames shot fifty feet into the night air.

Stranger bent close to Diane and spoke one word. "Coburn."

She blinked against her tears and nodded.

"The fool has no idea what he's done," John said.

Diane wiped tears again and said, "'Whoso diggeth a pit shall fall therein: and he that rolleth a stone, it will return upon him.'"

"Proverbs 26:27, isn't it?"

"Yes."

"Couldn't be more accurate," he said.

Wilbur Stratton and Bill Crawford approached, and Stranger gave them a grim smile. "Arson, gentlemen."

"Yeah," Crawford said. "Coburn arson."

"We just wanted to tell you that this doesn't cancel the services tomorrow, Mr. Stranger," Stratton said. "Looks like the weather's going to be all right. We'll just have open-air meetings morning and evening. People can sit in their buggies, surreys, and wagons."

"Great! I'll go for that!"

"The devil won't put a stop to your preaching the Word after all, Mr. Stranger," Diane said.

John smiled at her, then spoke to the two men. "Spread the word. Services will be held as scheduled. We'll gather right here in front of the parsonage at ten o'clock in the morning and again at the regular service time tomorrow evening."

"We'll do it!" Crawford said.

The two men began moving through the still-growing crowd, announcing that the preaching services would be held in spite of the fire. The people were elated at the news.

"Praise the Lord!" one man shouted. "We'll still have the victory!"

Those around him emphatically agreed.

On the fringe of the crowd beneath a stand of Palo Verde trees, Major Coburn huddled with his three cronies. As the crowd began to disperse, Coburn and his men eased back into the shadows.

"We'll crash their little open-air party in the morning, boys. About the time the Reverend Mr. Stranger starts preaching, we'll move in with double-barreled shotguns and drag him away right in front of their eyes. Major Vic Coburn is going to make a laughingstock of John Stranger." Coburn chuckled, then added, "Right now, I want to meet that scar-faced dude eye to eye."

The trio looked at him askance.

"What for?" Tobin said. "Let's save it all for tomorrow."

"Oh, we'll save plenty for tomorrow," Coburn said, "but I've just got to look him in the eye and tell him who set the church on fire."

"He already knows, Major," Judd said. "Everybody in town knows."

"Yeah, but I'm going to tell him to his face. I'm not scared of him, and I want him to know it. He's going to tell me where he's got our boys stashed, too. I'm sick of his little game."

On the front porch of the parsonage, John Stranger told Diane and the people who stood close by that they should return to their beds.

"You two take your mother back in the house," he said to Kyle and Trudy. "Get some rest so you'll be fresh for church in the morning."

"Yes, sir," Kyle said. "I'll see that these two ladies get some more sleep before the sun comes up."

"Good boy," Stranger said with a grin. Then to Diane, "I'll be here about a quarter till ten."

"Why don't you come at eight for breakfast?" she asked.

"I'd love to, but that means you'll have to get up earlier."

"No it doesn't. I still have to fix breakfast for the three of us. It won't be any effort to add enough food for one more."

"Okay," he said, smiling broadly. "See you at eight."

He started across the yard toward the street and could feel the heat of the fire on his back as he walked. His path took him close to a stand of Palo Verde trees, and movement in the shadows caught his eye. He tensed and slowed his pace when he saw the four dark figures emerge from the shadows. He recognized Judd and Tobin and figured that one of the other two would be the major himself. His gun hand hovered over the butt of the Peacemaker on his hip.

"Hold it, preacher!" Coburn said.

Stranger came to a halt. Coburn took a step ahead of his men, putting about twenty feet between him and the man he hated with a passion. His right hand dangled close to his gun. Stranger waited for him to speak, watching the gun hands of all four.

"I'm Major Vic Coburn."

"Am I supposed to be impressed...or frightened?"

"I just want you to know who set the fire."

"I already know."

"You know why I did it?"

"Probably several reasons. But whatever they were, you're going to be sorry."

"Oh, really?" Coburn cocked his head and raised his eyebrows. "And how's that?"

"You set fire to God's house. He won't be pleased."

Coburn laughed and said, "I *am* God, mister! And I'm here to serve notice that I own Apache Junction and you're trespassing. So get out of my town!"

"If you're God, why don't you throw me out?"

"I will in good time. But when I do, I'll be throwing you *down*... to your grave."

"Tell you what, pal. Do it, then talk about it."

"Like I said...in good time."

"Well, you better hurry, because your ownership of Apache Junction is going to be short-lived."

Coburn laughed hollowly. "We'll see about that. Now, something else, Mr. Reverend. I want my six men...and I want them *now!* Where are they?"

Stranger held Coburn's gaze and pointed toward the inferno. "They're right over there. You burned them to death."

"What do you mean?"

"I had Bell locked up in jail, but when I collected your other no-goods, I decided you'd probably look there for them, so I moved them. I placed all six of your boys, all bound and gagged—including big Mick—in a storage room at the back of the church. You saved me and the hangman a lot of trouble, Coburn."

Coburn stared at Stranger in open-mouthed astonishment. This "man from nowhere" had blocked him at every turn and out-smarted him completely. The realization was too much. It drove a fiery bolt of rage through him. The hand above his gun began to twitch.

"Don't try it, Coburn," Stranger said. "You're really not God."

But the major's rage overrode his good sense. He clawed for his gun, ejecting a wild, wordless yell. He had yet to clear leather when Stranger's gun roared. The .45 slug drilled Coburn's heart, driving him backward and dropping him on his back.

Before the major was down, Tobin's hand dropped. He had barely cleared leather when Stranger's gun roared again. The bullet hit him in the chest like a sledgehammer, knocking the wind out of him and toppling him like a rotted fence post in a high wind. He drew one ragged breath...and died.

Stranger was glaring at Judd and Ritchie, but neither one went for his weapon. They stared wide-eyed at their dead leader, then threw up their hands, lifting them as high as they could above their heads.

"Don't shoot!" Ritchie cried. "Please don't shoot!"

Just then the entire framework of the burning building groaned and collapsed within itself in a giant roar, sending great balls of flame and billows of smoke skyward.

Judd and Ritchie looked at the flaming heap and thought of their cohorts. It was all over. They would face a judge and jury in Phoenix, and then the hangman.

"Let your hands down easy, and drop those gunbelts," Stranger said.

While they were doing so, several townsmen came out of the shadows. They had watched the whole thing. They thanked John Stranger for ridding the town of Vic Coburn and his gang, and tagged along as Stranger escorted Judd and Ritchie to the jail and locked them up. He would wire the U.S. marshal's office in

Phoenix on Monday, asking for someone to come and take them for trial.

Stranger left the solemn outlaws in a cell together, then returned to the street. The group of men bid him goodnight and said they would pick up the bodies of Vic Coburn and H. P. Tobin and take them to the town's undertaker.

On Sunday morning, nearly the whole town showed up in their buggies, surreys, and wagons for the service. Neighbors close to the church grounds simply carried chairs from their homes to sit on.

The church building had been reduced to smoldering rubble, but the crowd paid it little mind as they jubilantly sang hymns from memory. They were relieved that their bondage was over, and their singing showed it.

Every eye was on John Stranger as he stood before them and preached a sermon on God's deliverance of the children of Israel from Egyptian bondage, relating it to the experience the town had just gone through. He then linked the deliverance of Israel to God's deliverance from the bondage of sin and Satan through the Lord Jesus Christ.

Stranger gave an invitation at the close of the message, and several adults, teenagers, and children filed forward to open their hearts to Christ for salvation. There was great rejoicing on the part of the church members.

Before dismissing the service, Stranger ran his gaze over the crowd and said, "Now, we have to talk about a very important matter, folks. Apache Junction needs this church as a lighthouse of the gospel, and this church must have a new building. You all need to band together and build it."

There was an immediate response to Stranger's words. Businessmen—even those who were not members—offered financial gifts. Within a matter of minutes more than enough money to cover the cost of building materials was promised. The man in black commended them for their good response, then asked for volunteers who could donate their time and labor to erect the new building. Men, women, and teenagers raised their hands, saying they would help.

They decided that lumber and materials would be purchased immediately in Phoenix, and construction would begin within a couple of days.

Stranger reminded them of the service that evening and started to close in prayer when Bill Crawford said, "Mr. Stranger, before we close the service, could I say something?"

"Of course."

Crawford took a few steps forward and stood beside Stranger. "Folks, we owe an awful lot to this man. We need to express our appreciation for what he did to rid us of the Coburn gang."

"That's right!" shouted Nick Farr. "God bless you, Mr. Stranger!"

There was an immediate uproar of joyous, spirited voices, cheering and applauding John Stranger as their hero.

"You're our Moses, John Stranger!" Marlon Kramer shouted. "You led us out of bondage!"

The happy hubbub gained even more volume, and Stranger's face flushed in embarrassment. He raised his hands for quiet and waited till it came.

"I appreciate your feelings, folks, but give your praise to the Lord. I was only His instrument. All the praise goes to Him."

"The Lord needed a willing instrument, Mr. Stranger!" an elderly man shouted. "God bless you for being that willing instrument!"

There was more cheering and applause.

Stranger quieted the crowd once more and told them that Ben Clifton was alive and well and eager to come back to his town and his job. There was elation over the news. Stranger then called on Wilbur Stratton to close the service in prayer.

After Sunday dinner with Diane and her children, John Stranger rode Ebony out to the cabin on the Salt River. Ben Clifton had heard Ebony blow as John guided him through the trees, and he was waiting beside the cabin to greet him.

"Howdy, John. Glad to see you."

John slid from the saddle, returned Ben's smile, and said, "I'm here as a messenger for the people of Apache Junction, Ben. They want you back on the job as soon as you can get there."

Clifton's wrinkled face lit up. "You...you mean—"

"It's all over, Ben. Pack up your stuff while I saddle your horse. I'll tell you all about it while we ride for town."

The silver-haired lawman let out a wild whoop and dashed into the house.

When Marshal Clifton appeared at the preaching service that evening, he was given a warm welcome by the people. After the sermon, Wilbur Stratton stood up and said the church not only needed a new building, it needed a new pastor. He asked John Stranger if he would consider the position.

The crowd applauded and cheered, but John explained his special calling from God. He must move on.

"However," he added, "I will stay and help on the construction of the new building." He then closed the service in prayer, asking the Lord to give the church the new pastor of His choice.

Twilight was on the land as the people dispersed and headed for their homes.

Nick Farr, Don Abel, Marlon Kramer, and a couple of men Stranger had not met approached him.

"Mr. Stranger," Farr said, "could we talk to you a moment?"

"Of course."

"Well, sir, the five of us came over here this afternoon, and we found five charred skeletons. But we couldn't locate the sixth."

"I tied six of them up in there. You must've overlooked the other one."

"Could be, but I don't think so."

"I told him what it was, Mr. Stranger," Abel said. "One of them must've been in such a hot spot that the fire totally burned up his bones."

"Enough heat will do it," Stranger said. "You all saw the fire. There was plenty of heat in that blaze. No doubt that's what happened."

Farr rubbed the back of his neck and said, "I guess that had to be it. Well, thanks again, Mr. Stranger, for what you did. We'll never forget it."

"My pleasure."

CHAPTER

FOURTEEN

O n Sunday afternoon, while John Stranger and Marshal Ben
Clifton rode toward Apache Junction, Tonto Apache Chief
Janos gathered his warriors around him in the shade of the
big rock.

When they were all present, Janos ran his dark gaze over their
bronzed faces and said in his deep, guttural voice, "You are the very
best warriors in the world. You are far superior fighters than the
Zunis. You have done well in warring against them, although you
have had to battle against *besh-e-gars* mostly with bows and arrows.
And then the Zunis laid hold on the gun that speaks with many
voices. But I have made a plan that will bring about the defeat of
the Zunis."

Janos turned to Mandano, who stood at arm's length beside
him, and extended his hand. All eyes noted the folded newspaper
Mandano gave to the chief. Janos opened the paper and showed
them the article announcing Dan Wheeler's marriage to Rebecca
Ann Wilson.

"The wedding is to take place next Saturday at the First
Methodist Church in Phoenix. The ceremony will be held out of
doors in the churchyard. This will be a perfect opportunity for a band
of Tontos to make a surprise move. They will ride in and capture

155

Dan Wheeler, the governor's son, while he and the bride are taking their vows. Dan Wheeler will be brought to the mountains. We will hold him captive.

"All of you know we are desperate for weapons. Our only sources for weapons are the army forts. They are too well-manned for us to attack, but with Governor Donald Wheeler's son in our hands, I will demand fifty new *besh-e-gars* and a good supply of ammunition. I will also demand three of the guns that speak with many voices.

"Governor Donald Wheeler will be given a limited amount of time to meet my demands. If he fails to do so, his son will be killed!"

Janos's words were packed with power. There was an eruption of shouts and whoops that evolved into a blood-curdling war cry that went on for several minutes. The warriors waved bows, arrows, war lances, knives, and war clubs. The clamor reached its climax with the warriors shouting out a death chant in haunting repetition.

"*Dah-eh-sah* to the Zunis! *Dah-eh-sah* to the white-eyes!"

When the noise died down, Janos dismissed the warriors. Mandano started to walk away, but Janos called to him.

"Mandano. I wish to speak with you." The chief led his favorite warrior to a private spot. "Mandano does not show excitement about my plan."

"The plan is excellent, Chief Janos. It is my desire to see it be successful. But it displeases me when you plan to murder Dan Wheeler if his father fails to produce the weapons and ammunition demanded."

"You are a mystery to me, Mandano!"

"A mystery?"

"You are the finest warrior and the greatest fighter I have ever known. You are fierce in combat. Few men have such intelligence and few men have the strength you possess. You make me proud that you are a Tonto Apache. But...I cannot understand this soft spot in your heart for white men. They are trespassers on our land.

They come and steal from us. They send their army to conquer us. What is it? Why do you not hate white eyes as I do…and as your Apache brothers do?"

Mandano looked squarely into his chief's eyes. "This soft spot you speak of, Chief Janos, is not toward white men only. It is a soft spot for human life and its sacredness. You have seen me kill our enemies, both red and white, in battle, and you have seen me kill in self-defense. To kill in battle or to kill in self-defense is one thing, but to murder a helpless person is another."

Janos started to speak, but Mandano cut him off.

"I remind you, my chief, that your father held all human life as very sacred. Numkena called the yellow rocks over which white men kill each other the tears of the sun. The Sky Father, who fills the heavens in the day, looked into the future when he created the earth and saw how greedy white men would be. He saw that they would kill each other to satisfy their greed…and he wept.

"The Sky Father's weeping was well-founded, Chief. White men murder each other over the very tears of the sun, more than over anything else. Certainly the Sky Father holds human life as sacred or he would not have wept as he did over the senseless murders that take place among white men, even in our holy Superstition Mountains."

Janos was at a loss for words. He stared blankly at the ground beneath his feet.

"I remind you, Chief Janos, that today *all* Apaches call gold the tears of the sun, even as your father Numkena had, because they believe the Sky Father values human life."

Janos lifted a hand to keep Mandano from cutting him off.

"Apaches do not kill white men because of greed, Mandano, but to drive the intruders from our land. If we must kill Dan Wheeler because his father refuses to meet my demands, it is not greed. It is retribution on the white-eyes governor for refusing weapons and ammunition that we might defend ourselves against our mortal enemies."

"If it should happen that the governor refuses," Mandano said, "it will not be Dan Wheeler's fault. Why should he have to die?"

"You do not listen when your chief speaks, Mandano! I said it is *retribution!* If the governor refuses, he must be punished! The punishment will be the death of his son! If you hated the vile white men as any Apache should, you would agree that I should kill Dan Wheeler if his father denies us the weapons!"

Mandano set cool eyes on Janos. "If the Sky Father hates white men like you do, why did he cry the golden tears over them? I will capture Dan Wheeler as you have planned, my chief. And I will deliver your demands to his father. I will even go along with threatening to kill the governor's son if the demands are not met. But I will not go along with killing him. I will not!"

Janos looked toward his god in the brassy sky, then set his gaze on his favored warrior.

"All right, Mandano. I will not kill Dan Wheeler if his father refuses to meet my demands. He will, however, remain our captive."

"That is fine. I am ready to do your bidding to capture him."

Janos's face brightened. *"Enjuh!"* he exclaimed, laying a hand on Mandano's shoulder. "I will work on the plan so it will be executed with precision. I will have it worked out by tomorrow morning. You will have several days to prepare your warriors."

On Monday morning, the people of Apache Junction were enjoying their new freedom and finding life once again worth living. Marshal Ben Clifton was back in his office, and business in the commercial district was back to normal.

Several men took wagons and headed for Phoenix to purchase lumber and materials for the construction of the new church building. Work would begin as soon as the rubble could be removed.

John Stranger was the first customer at the Western Union office. He sent a wire to the U.S. marshal in Phoenix, explaining what had happened and that Marshal Clifton had two outlaws in his jail that must face murder charges. He requested that someone be sent to pick them up and take them to Phoenix. Ten minutes later, a return wire informed him that two deputies would be there Wednesday morning.

Marshal Clifton was sweeping the office when he heard John Stranger's voice through the open door that led to the boardwalk. He paused to look that direction and saw three young women looking at Stranger with adoring eyes and praising his adept handling of the Coburn gang.

Clifton noted Stranger's discomfort and chuckled to himself. Stranger tipped his hat and thanked them for their kind words, then escaped into the marshal's office. Clifton laughed aloud.

"You're a pretty popular feller in this town, my boy! Those little gals just about had you backed up against the wall. Lotta men in this town would give a month's pay to have those three flirtin' with 'em like that!"

"They weren't flirting, Ben. They were just expressing their appreciation for my having a hand in ridding the town of those rodents."

Clifton laughed heartily. "I ain't *that* old, John! I know flirtin' when I see it."

"I came over here to tell you that I wired the U.S. marshal in Phoenix. There'll be a couple of deputies here with a wagon to pick up Judd and Ritchie Wednesday morning.

"Good. I'll be glad to get rid of 'em." There was a brief silence, then the marshal said, "John, I'll never be able to thank you properly for cleanin' up my town for me. If I was a mite younger, I maybe could've handled that bunch myself."

Stranger grinned. "I'm sure you could have. Now if you'll excuse me, I want to pay a little visit to Mrs. Patrick and her children."

"It's nice of you to be concerned about 'em, John. I'm wonderin' what's gonna happen to 'em when the church calls a new pastor."

"That's what I want to see her about. I hate to think that she and those sweet kids will be without a place to live when that happens."

"Well, I would think the church oughtta do somethin' for 'em, but I don't know if we'll be able to afford it."

"I understand. Who was to know a thing like this would happen, anyhow? The church will probably have all it can handle, taking care of the new pastor and his family...if he has one."

"Well, I've got a few bucks in the bank. I'll do my part to help if they need it."

"I'm sure you would, Ben, but I don't think that'll be necessary. Anyway, I'm going to look into it."

Suddenly the attention of both men was drawn to the open door as Wilbur Stratton stepped in from the boardwalk, bracing himself on the door frame. His mouth was working, but he couldn't seem to form the words he wanted. John noted the terror in Wilbur's eyes.

"Wilbur, what is it?" John said.

"It's...it's Hardy Bell! He just left the hotel, and he's looking for *you*, John!"

"Wilbur, what are you talkin' about?" Ben said. "Bell died in the fire!"

"Then it's his ghost, 'cause he's out there on the street!"

John looked past Wilbur and saw the slender form of Hardy Bell standing in the middle of the street, looking straight at him.

"Stranger!" Bell yelled. "I'm callin' you! Come out here!"

"John, don't!" Clifton said, but a wave of Stranger's hand cut him off.

Stranger moved past Wilbur Stratton and stepped out onto the boardwalk. There were people on both sides of the street, gawking in disbelief, as if they were looking at a ghastly apparition.

As Stranger moved calmly to the edge of the boardwalk, Bell studied him with a surly regard.

"We're squarin' off, you and me, Stranger! I've got a score to settle with you! You killed the major, didn't you?"

"He forced me to."

"Well, if you hadn't shown up in this town, stickin' your nose in where it don't belong, things would still be goin' good. I hate your guts, Stranger. Besides, I gotta prove to you and all these goggle-eyed people that I'm faster'n you. I wish the major was here to see this. He thought I was too slow to brace you. Well, I ain't! And now I'm gonna prove it!"

Stranger kept his eyes on Bell as he stepped off the boardwalk into the dust of the street. People scattered from the line of fire. He caught a glimpse of Diane Patrick in the crowd, fear pinching her pretty face. Mattie Northrup stood beside her. Since the door of his office was in the line of fire, Marshal Clifton took Wilbur Stratton by the arm and led him a few steps down the boardwalk.

When Stranger was some forty feet from Bell, he stopped and said, "I guess you know who set fire to the church building."

"Yeah, but Major Coburn didn't know we were in there, I'm sure of that."

"How'd you escape?"

A sneer curled Bell's upper lip. "What does it matter. I'm here, and I'm gonna kill you!"

"The major was right, Hardy. You're too slow. Take my word for it. You can live a little longer if you just unbuckle the gunbelt and let it fall."

"Live a little longer? What do you mean by that?"

"I'm turning you over to Marshal Clifton. You'll stay in his jail with Judd and Ritchie till the federal marshals come on Wednesday. They'll take you to Phoenix where you'll face a judge and jury.

Then, of course, the three of you will hang for murder."

"I ain't dyin' at the end of no rope, Stranger!"

"If you go for that gun, you'll die where you stand."

Bell stared at Stranger, his unshaven face rigid.

"Big talk! I'm gonna kill you and leave this stinkin' town, Stranger! That feeble old marshal over there ain't gonna stop me, neither! He tries it, they'll bury him right beside you!"

Even as he spoke, Hardy Bell's gun hand snaked downward.

C H A P T E R
FIFTEEN

———◆———

The crowd stood amazed at the scene that had just been played out before them. The speed of the tall man's draw left them slack-jawed and speechless.

While the morning breeze carried the small cloud of blue-white smoke away, John Stranger holstered his Peacemaker and walked toward the man who had been so sure he could outdraw him. He stood over a dead Hardy Bell and hooked his thumbs in his belt.

Bell's right hand was frozen on the butt of his Colt .44, which was only partially out of its holster. His sightless eyes stared vacantly toward the Arizona sky, fixed in a glare of shock. He had lived long enough to know the major was right.

Stranger shook his head and sighed. "Sorry, Hardy. I warned you."

The crowd pressed close, almost hypnotized by the sight of the dead gunfighter lying in the dust.

"Well, John," Marshal Ben Clifton said, "I guess word will spread that you took out one of the top guns. You'll be challenged by a bunch of 'em now."

"Won't be the first time. I've had to put some other top guns in their graves."

"Mr. Stranger," one of the townsmen said, "I've never seen such gunhandling in all my born days. Were you taught by some famous gunfighter?"

"No, sir. Just picked it up naturally."

One man in the crowd said to a friend next to him, "Tell you what, Jim, when I first saw Bell standin' here in the street, I thought sure enough he'd come back from the dead."

"I guarantee you he won't be back this time. Mr. Stranger put that bullet straight through his heart. He's dead, and he's gonna stay dead."

Marshal Clifton looked around and said, "Couple of men carry Bell's body over to the funeral parlor, will you?"

Two husky men pushed to the front and lifted the corpse by the wrists and ankles.

"Tell Thaddeus to go ahead and bury him," Clifton said. "Town'll pick up the tab."

The men nodded and carried Hardy Bell away.

Stranger saw Diane Patrick pushing her way through the crowd with Kyle and Trudy following. "Oh, Mr. Stranger," she said as she drew up, "I'm so glad you're all right."

"Thank you, ma'am," he said, touching the brim of his hat.

"You tried to make him listen."

"Yes, ma'am. Like most of them…he turned a deaf ear."

"Wow, Mr. Stranger!" Kyle said. "You're really fast with your gun! I hope someday I can be that good!"

Stranger laid a hand on the boy's head. "Tell you what, Kyle. Unless you plan on being a lawman, just leave the guns alone."

"I'm gonna be a preacher like my daddy was."

"That's wonderful. Then you just concentrate on being fast on the draw with your Bible. Forget the guns."

"But you're a preacher, and you carry a gun."

"I'm not a pastor like your daddy was. God's given me a special job to do, and I often have to do the work of a lawman. Men like Vic Coburn and Hardy Bell make it necessary at times. I didn't want to kill Bell. You heard me try to talk him out of drawing against me, didn't you?"

"Yes, sir."

"Wouldn't it have been a good thing if there'd been a preacher back when Hardy Bell was your age who would've told him about Jesus?"

"Yes, sir. Then he wouldn't have been a gunfighter and a bad guy and died like that, would he?"

"Right. You just set your mind on being that preacher who'll take the gospel to a lot of young men so they won't turn out like him."

"Yes, sir. That's what I'll do!"

"Thank you," Diane said.

"My pleasure. You know, I was about to head for your house when Bell showed up. I wanted to talk to you."

"Well, the children and I were about to head home when all this happened. Would you like to go with us now?"

"Sure. Give me your grocery sack. I'll carry it for you."

"Remember what I told you, John," Ben Clifton said. "If my help is needed..."

"I won't forget."

John Stranger set the grocery sack on the kitchen cupboard of the parsonage. Diane sent Kyle and Trudy out to play, then turned to John and asked, "Will our chat take long enough for you to drink a cup of coffee?"

"Oh, I'm sure it will."

"All right. You sit down there at the table. It'll only take me a minute to get the fire going. It hasn't been that long since breakfast."

"How about letting me do it for you? While you're filling the coffeepot."

Diane agreed. When the coffeepot was heating up, they sat opposite each other at the kitchen table. John thought the young widow looked a bit weary. There were gray circles under her eyes.

"All right," Diane said. "What did you want to talk to me about?"

"I've been wondering what you and the children are going to do for a place to live when the church calls a new pastor. Do you have any plans?"

"Well, not exactly. I know that when the time comes, we'll have to move out. There are relatives back East—both mine and Dale's—but I don't want to be a burden to them. Besides, Apache Junction is our home. I've talked to Kyle and Trudy about it. We want to stay here if it's at all possible."

"Of course. You have friends here, and your church is here. What about income?"

"The proprietor of the general store's offered me a job as clerk. And this morning on the street, Mattie Northrup...she's the main waitress at the Skylark Café—"

"Yes, I know her."

"Well, Mattie's brother-in-law Clark Fortin owns the café. He and his wife are also members of the church. Mattie told me that Clark wants me to take over one shift as cook...either daytime or nighttime. From what Mattie says, the choice will be mine. I think the pay at the café will be a little higher than at the store."

"Is there someone to care for the children while you're at work?"

"I've had four families in the church offer to keep them for no charge. By spreading it among that many, it won't be a big load on any of them."

"Do you think you can provide for yourself and the children on what you would make at either job?"

"Well...not really. If I took the job at the store, I'd be free to work as night cook at the café. It'll take what I make at the store to pay the rent on a house, if I can find one. I hate the thought of being away from Kyle and Trudy so much, but there really isn't much choice. Without a husband to provide—"

Diane's features reddened and tears filmed her eyes. She rose from the table.

"I think the coffee's about ready," she said, choking on her words. She set a cup in front of Stranger and poured coffee into it.

"Do you know of any houses in town for rent?" John asked.

"There are none at the moment. All four of those families who offered to care for the children have also offered to let us move in with them until something opens up. As hard as that would be, that may be our only choice. At least we'd have a roof over our heads."

"Yes, but you're right. It would be hard. Two households under one roof make for strained relations and can cause some real problems. Too bad there isn't a house for sale that you could buy making payments about the same size as rent would be."

"There is one for sale on the southeast corner of this block. The owners are getting up in years and are moving to Santa Fe where they have a married daughter and a married son and six grandchildren. I talked to Ralph about renting the house, but they have to sell it so they can buy one when they get to Santa Fe."

Stranger took a swallow of his coffee and set the cup down. "Is the Smith house large enough for you and the kids?"

"Oh, yes. It's much more spacious than this one."

"What are they asking for it?"

"Twenty-five hundred. It's a fair price, but he has to have it all when the house is sold." She sighed. "So…that's out. One thing about it, Mr. Stranger. The Lord knows our situation. He's a great big wonderful God. He'll provide a house for us in His own way and His own time."

Stranger downed the last of his coffee, set the cup down, and stood up.

"Well, little lady, I must be going. Thank you for the coffee."

Diane shoved her chair back and went to the back door.

"The children will want to tell you good-bye."

Kyle and Trudy were called in, and both gave their newfound friend a big hug. Mother and children walked him to the front porch, where he said good-bye and walked away.

"He's such a nice man, Mommy," Trudy said. "He really loves us, doesn't he?"

"Yes, honey. Mr. Stranger is a kind, loving man."

"He's also tough on bad guys," Kyle said. "I like him."

Nearly an hour had passed since John Stranger left the parsonage when Trudy ran into the kitchen where her mother was cleaning cupboard shelves.

"Mommy! Mr. Smith is coming into the yard!"

"Oh?" She wiped her hands on her apron and moved toward the door that led to the parlor. "I wonder what he wants?"

Ralph Smith was almost to the porch when Diane opened the front door and smiled at him.

"Hello, Ralph."

"Good morning, Diane. And good morning to you, Miss Trudy."

"Good morning, Mr. Smith," Trudy said.

"Where's Kyle?"

"He's playing with Bobby Roberts down the street," Diane said.

"Nice boy, Bobby." He stepped up on the porch and extended a large brown envelope toward her. "This is for you."

"For me? What is it?"

"Take a look inside. It's self-explanatory."

Diane noted that the envelope was marked "Apache Junction Land Office" in the upper left-hand corner. She slipped her fingers inside and pulled out an important-looking document. It was the deed to the house on the southeast corner of her street, and the owner's name was listed as Diane Louise Patrick.

Her eyes widened and her mouth fell open. "What is this?"

"Bessie and I have deeded our house over to you. It's all legal and proper, as you can see."

"But...but...but how? I...I don't understand."

"The explanation is simple, my dear. John Stranger."

"J—? Wh-what do you mean?"

"I mean, Diane, that John Stranger bought our house. Gave us our asking price. He had me deed the house to you."

Diane Patrick's knees went weak. Smith reached out and took hold of an arm, steadying her.

"Are you all right?"

"Yes, I'm fine. I'm just...overwhelmed. Why would Mr. Stranger do this for us?"

"Well, I expect because he wanted to."

"But where would he get that kind of money? Certainly not from preaching here and there. And not from taking assignments from the U.S. marshal in Denver."

"That I can't tell you, Diane, but what's that old saying? Don't look a gift horse—"

"Oh, I'm not. It's just that...I feel so guilty."

"Guilty?"

"Mr. Stranger might be needing that money for himself."

Smith smiled. "I'm sure he knows what he's doing." ·

Diane's lower lip began to quiver and tears welled up in her eyes.

"I must thank him. Do you know where he is?"

"No, I don't. When we finished our business at the land office, he went one way, and I went the other."

"Well, I'll find him." She paused, then asked, "How soon will you be moving?"

"In about a week. If you want the house sooner..."

"Oh, no! That's fine. We can stay here until the church calls a new pastor. If you need longer, that's all right."

"I would say at the longest it would be no more than ten days. In the meantime, you can come and look the place over anytime you want. We...ah...we're leaving all the furniture, so you can keep what you want and sell the rest. But we can talk about all of that later."

"Fine. I'll bring the children and come over in a day or two."

When Smith was gone, Diane turned to Trudy.

"Honey, do you understand what you just heard?"

"Yes, Mommy. Mr. Stranger bought Mr. Smith's house and gave it to us for a present. Other than Daddy—other than Daddy, Mr. Stranger is the nicest man I've ever known."

"He sure is, honey. Would you run down to Bobby's house and tell Kyle to come home?"

"Sure."

"Don't tell him about the house. I want to do that. Just tell him I have a surprise for him."

"Okay."

Trudy bounded off the porch and ran down the street. Diane hurried inside the house, fell on her knees at the couch in the parlor, and wept as she poured out her heart in praise and gratitude to the Lord.

When Kyle came in moments later with his sister on his heels, Diane told him what John Stranger had done for them. Kyle was surprised and amazed. Then together, Diane and the children knelt at the couch. Each one prayed aloud, thanking God for their new house...and for John Stranger.

When John Stranger left Ralph Smith at the Apache Junction Land Office, he decided to take Ebony for a ride. He walked to the stable, saddled up, and trotted the big black eastward toward the Superstition Mountains. He was about a half-mile out of town when he saw a man stumbling toward him across the desert.

He quickly put Ebony to a full gallop. The man fell, struggled to his feet, took a few steps, and fell again. Stranger skidded Ebony to a stop and slid from the saddle, noting that the front of the man's shirt was soaked with blood. Just as he knelt beside him, the man fell flat on his face. Stranger turned him over and saw that he had been shot twice in the chest. One of the bullets had to be close to his heart. He was glassy-eyed and his face was flour-white as he tried to focus on Stranger while working his jaw.

"Don't try to talk," Stranger said. "I'll put you on my horse and take you to the doctor."

Stranger was about to pick the man up when he gasped a clear word three times. "Jacob…Jacob…Jacob…" Then he coughed once, closed his eyes, and went limp. His breathing stopped.

Stranger felt for a pulse in his neck, but there was none. He went ahead and picked the lifeless form up and carried it to Ebony.

People stopped and stared as John Stranger rode down the main street with the corpse draped behind the saddle.

"Where'd you find him, Mr. Stranger?" somebody called out.

"Just outside of town to the east."

Someone alerted Ben Clifton that Stranger was riding in with a dead man on his horse. Clifton was on the office porch as the tall man veered toward the boardwalk and drew rein.

"You know him, Ben?"

Clifton stepped into the street and leaned low so he could see the man's face.

"Name's Jacob Weiser. He and his partner, Jacob Waltz, came to the Superstitions several months ago hoping to find the lost Sombrero Mine. Waltz is called 'the Dutchman' by the other miners. I have no idea why—he's a full-blooded German. Where'd you find him?"

Stranger dismounted to the squeak of saddle leather.

"Little less than a mile east of town. When I first caught sight of him, he was stumbling and clutching his chest. By the time I got to him, he had fallen flat on his face. He said the name 'Jacob' three times before he died. What can you tell me about this lost Sombrero Mine, Ben?"

Clifton was toying with his mustache and finally looked up at Stranger.

"What was that?"

"I said, tell me about this lost Sombrero Mine."

"Oh. Well, some twenty-five years ago a Mexican prospector named Don Miguel Peralta discovered a rich vein of gold somewhere in the Superstitions. He had nine men working with him. Peralta named the mine the Sombrero. He and his partners were pulling vast amounts of gold out of the Sombrero, and one day they were ambushed by Apaches. The Indians dragged their bodies to the top of one of the Superstition peaks and left them for the vultures to pick clean.

"One of Peralta's men, Pablo Garcia, was miraculously still alive, and the Apaches didn't know it. He managed to crawl to a spring and wash and dress his wounds. Weeks later, he showed up in a little town south of the Superstitions called Florence.

"He's been around these parts ever since, but has refused to tell anyone the location of the mine. When Waltz and his partner showed up here to begin prospecting, they heard about the lost mine and offered Garcia a large amount of money to take them to it. The story is that Garcia's desire for that much money was greater than his fear of the Apaches, so he took Waltz and Weiser far into the Superstitions and showed them the mine."

Stranger eyed him with speculation. "You say 'the story is.' What do you mean by that?"

"Well, it's the story the Germans have told...that they paid Garcia, then he hightailed it out of there. Garcia has never been seen since. That was nigh on to five months ago."

"Any idea what might have happened to him?"

"I have an idea, all right, but I can't prove it."

"Waltz?"

"If I was a bettin' man, John, I'd bet my bottom dollar that Waltz and Weiser killed Garcia once he had led them to the mine. Getting rid of a body back in those crags and canyons would be no problem."

"But why kill him?"

"Best reason I can think of is so he could never lead anyone else to the mine. Those two had greed written all over their faces, John, and there was always the possibility that somebody else would come along and offer the Mexican even more money to lead *them* to the Sombrero. Gold fever makes men do weird things."

"Isn't that the truth."

"So anyway, Waltz and Weiser kill Garcia, and now Weiser comes out of the Superstitions with two bullets in him and dies, croaking out the name *Jacob* three times. What else do I need to make me believe Jacob Waltz shot him?"

"Couldn't he simply have been trying to tell me his own name?"

Clifton grinned. "Maybe. But for my money, the Dutchman has done his partner in so he can keep all the gold for himself."

"That's right, Marshal," said a man who stood nearby. "Jacob Waltz is bad medicine. We all know that."

There was general agreement among the gathered crowd.

"See what I mean, John?" Clifton said. "These people have all had ample time to observe Waltz. They know a bad character when they see one. Weiser wouldn't have won any popularity contest around here either, but Waltz is worse. Much worse. He's rude and caustic and displays a real mean streak. Whenever the Germans came to town, Waltz usually started trouble in the saloons."

"So nobody but Jacob Waltz knows the location of the mine?"

"That's right. They've kept it a closely guarded secret. I know of several men who tried to follow them to the mine. They either became lost or they were murdered by the Germans. At any rate, they never came out."

"Did you ever talk to the Germans about the strange disappearances?"

"Yep. Every time. They always denied they knew anything about men followin' 'em. There was no way of provin' any different. And it'll be the same way this time. When Waltz shows up in town and I question him about Weiser's death, he'll say he knows nothin' about it."

"So there's really nothing you can do?"

"Oh, I could contact the county sheriff in Phoenix and tell him about it. He'd come and look at the body, but I guarantee you he'd never go into those creepy mountains or even send a passel of deputies in there to find Waltz and bring him out so he could be questioned."

"So what are you going to do?"

"Wait."

"For what?"

"For Waltz to show up in town. I'll ask him if he knows who shot his partner. He'll say he doesn't know or come up with some fictitious name I can't follow up. Like I said, I'd bet my bottom dollar that Waltz did his partner in, but he'll get away with it for lack of evidence."

"Looks like you're gonna get your chance to talk to Waltz, Marshal," someone called out. "Here he comes now!"

CHAPTER
SIXTEEN

———◆◆◆———

All eyes turned toward the rider on a large piebald. He was recognizable not only by the familiar horse but also by the small-brimmed hat that resembled a derby.

Jacob Waltz ran his blue-eyed gaze over the crowd gathered in the street in front of Marshal Clifton's office, then focused on the body draped over Ebony's back. The people cleared a path for the German, whose features reflected both anguish and fury. Ben Clifton saw it, and told himself the man was a good actor.

Waltz, a short, stocky man of fifty, slid from his saddle, glanced at Clifton, and moved up to the lifeless form of his partner. He stood like a statue, looking at Weiser and shaking his head in apparent disbelief. Clifton moved up beside him with Stranger a step behind.

"What do you know about this, Jacob?" the marshal asked.

"I know nothing except that to get water at a small stream in an adjacent canyon, Jacob leave the mine but never return. I become worried. After an hour or so, I go looking for him. I find blood spots on the rocks beside the stream where we dip our buckets always. The spots trail out of the mountains toward town. I saddle my horse and follow to where the blood trail stop. I assume someone pick Jacob up. A moment ago, as I ride in, a man tells me he has seen a rider come into town with a body lying over the back of his horse." He took a deep breath, and his features went beet-red. "Marshal, you must find whoever kill my partner and bring them to justice!"

Clifton did not comment, but glanced at Stranger, then the crowd.

Waltz was looking back at the body when Clifton asked, "You didn't hear any shots?"

"No, but our mine is deep. I was working where I wouldn't have heard shots from another canyon."

"Why would someone have shot your partner, Jacob? If they were trying to find your mine, all they would have had to do was follow him when he returned with the water."

"Who knows? Many strange things happen in those canyons." He paused, then asked, "May I take the body and bury it? I feel this loss much. Jacob was not my partner only, but a good friend."

"All right. Go ahead and take it."

Waltz transferred his partner's body to his own horse, then mounted and rode eastward out of town without saying another word. Clifton and Stranger watched him ride away.

"He murdered the man sure as we're standin' here, John," Clifton said. "Now the gold is all his."

"And there's nothing you can do about it," Stranger said.

"Yeah. Nothin'."

The crowd broke up. Stranger headed for the hotel. Marshal Clifton returned to his office.

Stranger entered the Desert Rose and saw a tall ladder in front of the balcony. There was a man atop the ladder repairing the railing with the help of a partner who was on his knees on the balcony floor. Delbert Coggins stood next to the ladder, talking to the men. When he saw Stranger, he smiled and headed toward him.

"Howdy, Reverend. I've got a message for you from Mrs. Patrick. She came here to see you, but when I told her you weren't in, she asked me to tell you to please come to the parsonage whenever it's convenient."

"All right. Thank you for relaying the message." He turned and left the hotel.

Five minutes later, Stranger was walking across the church grounds toward the parsonage. He saw a crew of men loading charred debris into wagons. They all greeted him warmly, then went back to work.

Diane Patrick appeared at the door just as he stepped up on the porch. There were tears in her eyes.

"Hello, Mr. Stranger. I'm so glad you got my message. Please come in."

John removed his hat and stooped as he stepped past her to keep from hitting his head on the lintel. He saw Kyle and Trudy looking up at him with broad smiles.

"Hi, kids!" he said, opening his arms.

They both dashed to him, wrapping their arms around his waist, and in chorus, thanked him for giving them the house.

"Well, Uncle John couldn't let you and your mother have to pitch a tent when the new pastor comes and wants this house."

"Uncle John!" Kyle exclaimed. "Can we call him Uncle John, Mother?"

Diane smiled. "Well, since Mr. Stranger called himself Uncle John to you, you may."

"I love you, Uncle John," Trudy said, hugging his waist harder.

"I do too!" Kyle said. "You're the nicest man in all the world!"

Stranger chuckled. "Well, there are some people who might argue that point with you."

"Yes," Diane said, dabbing at her tears with the corner of her apron. "Like those men locked up over at the jail." She looked into his eyes and with a quaver in her voice, said, "How can I ever express my gratitude for what you did? There's no way to—"

"You don't need to, ma'am. Jesus said it's more blessed to give than to receive. It was my pleasure to do it, and believe me, just seeing the look on your face right now and the joy on the faces of these children is thanks enough."

"But you hardly know us. I mean…twenty-five hundred dollars!"

"Ma'am, I have a rich heavenly Father. The money I used to buy the house was His money, not mine. Since He's your Father too, just give Him the thanks and the praise."

"Oh, believe me, I've been doing so ever since Mr. Smith walked away from that door!"

"Then everything is as it should be."

"Mr. Stranger…?"

"Tell you what. Since I'm now Kyle and Trudy's uncle, you can call me John."

"All right, John. I'm…curious."

"About what?"

"Is there a Mrs. John Stranger?"

"Not yet, ma'am. But a certain Breanna Baylor will one day be my wife."

"Well, all I can say is that Miss Baylor is a very fortunate woman."

"You're very kind, ma'am. But the fortunate person is me. Breanna is the most wonderful woman God ever created."

"That's beautiful. I'm sure the two of you will be very, very happy."

"Thank you, ma'am. Only the Lord knows what He has planned for *your* life, but I'm sure there are happy days ahead."

"Yeah!" Kyle said. "And we have our own house to be happy in!"

The next day, construction began on the new church building. John Stranger bought work clothes at the clothier in town and pitched in to do his part. While the day passed, he thought often of Breanna, missing her and praying the Lord's protection on her.

There were passing moments when he also thought of Jacob Waltz. Marshal Clifton was sure the man was a murderer, and Stranger had a feeling down deep that he was right. But try as he may, he could think of no way to bring the man to justice.

Out on the desert north of the Apache stronghold, subchief Mandano was training ten young warriors in the art of horsemanship. He taught them how to mount and dismount quickly, and how to ride at a gallop and use the horse's body as a shield while firing at the enemy from under the animal's neck. When he was satisfied that they had mastered the techniques, he impressed upon them that they must practice until every move was second nature to them.

He was walking to his horse to demonstrate how to use a horse's size and strength in close combat when one of the young Apaches pointed past a massive cluster of boulders some seventy or eighty yards away and shouted, "Mandano! Zunis!"

More than a dozen mounted Zunis were bearing down on them at a full gallop. When they knew the Apaches had seen them, they raised their feathered carbines over their heads and gave a blood-curdling war whoop.

The training ground skirted an area covered with small boulders large enough for a man to take cover behind. Mandano knew there were only three carbines in his group. One was his. The two oldest youths had the others. The rest of them were armed only with bows, arrows, knives, and war clubs.

"Quick!" Mandano shouted. "Get to the rocks!"

The Apache ponies were clustered nearby, and they raised their heads, eyes bulging, when the galloping Zunis began firing. When one of them released a shrill whinny and began to trot away, the others followed.

Mandano led the youths among the rocks, shouting for them to take cover and to remember all the things he had taught them. What they had practiced for many long months must now be put into practice. They must wait until the Zunis were well within arrow range before they started shooting. The two young warriors with carbines were to cut loose when he did.

The Zunis came charging in, rifles blazing. When they were within thirty yards, Mandano fired his carbine, knocking one of the screeching Zunis off his horse. The Zunis quickly left their horses and began charging the Apaches, firing their weapons. Soon the Zunis were also using the rocks for shelter and taking pot shots at the Apaches.

Mandano saw two of his men go down. A second Zuni was hit, but at the same instant, another Apache went down. Then another.

Mandano was down to two cartridges. The whooping Zunis kept working their way among the rocks, pressing closer and closer to the Tonto positions. He was forced to use both cartridges. One of them dropped a Zuni, but the other struck a boulder and whined away angrily.

Amid the dust and smoke, Mandano caught a glimpse of Red Feather, a noted warrior and subchief who was the son of Hawk Wing, a venerable Zuni chief. Mandano knew that unlike the Apaches, the Zunis would make a hasty retreat if they lost their leader.

He called to his nearest warrior and told him he was going after Red Feather. The warrior was to pass the message on to the others. They must keep the Zunis occupied while he crawled among the rocks and took out their leader.

Mandano pulled his knife from its sheath, went to his belly, and began crawling amid the boulders toward Red Feather. It took him only a few minutes to work his way behind him.

The Zuni subchief was hunkered low behind a boulder,

reloading his carbine, when Mandano seemed to come from out of nowhere, eyes wild, long-bladed knife in hand. Red Feather dropped the rifle and the cartridges, and his hand darted to his waist for his knife. That was as far as he got. The determined Mandano drove his blade full-haft into Red Feather's heart.

Mandano sheathed his knife and picked up Red Feather's carbine. He gathered the cartridges and finished loading the magazine, then jacked a cartridge into the chamber. He crawled again amid the boulders, heading back to his young warriors who were gallantly fending off the Zuni attack. He had barely left Red Feather's body when he heard one of the Zunis scream to the others that the subchief was dead.

Suddenly the Zunis were running toward their horses and firing their rifles aimlessly in the direction of the Apaches. Mandano raised up and fired a shot at them as they swung aboard their mounts. They galloped away, and the Apaches rose to their feet. The two with carbines were out of ammunition, and only three Tontos had any arrows left. The death of Red Feather had come none too soon.

Six of the Tontos were dead, and two had flesh wounds. The wounded ones were bandaged with shirts from their dead companions, and the bodies of the dead were draped over the backs of their horses. A quick count showed that five Zunis had been killed. Mandano commended the youthful fighters for a job well done and told them they were now full-fledged Tonto warriors. They had experienced combat and were alive to tell it.

When Mandano and his weary warriors entered the Apache stronghold, there was grief over the loss of the six young men. The wounded ones were cared for by the same women who were nursing Zareem, who was still barely holding on to life. The men prepared the bodies of the dead for burial.

Chief Janos had been perfecting his plan for abducting Dan Wheeler, and when he looked at the bodies draped over the horses' backs, he was more determined than ever to get his hands on U.S. army weapons—including the Gatling guns—and take the fight to the Zunis. Saturday could not come soon enough for him.

By Friday, the new church building in Apache Junction was taking shape. So great had been the number of volunteers that the framework was up and part of the roof was already on.

In Phoenix the wedding rehearsal took place late Friday afternoon, then Governor and Mrs. Donald Wheeler treated the members of the wedding party to a meal in the First Methodist Chruch fellowship hall. Gunther and Martha Wilson were close friends of the Wheelers and were pleased that their daughter was marrying into the Wheeler family. Dan was already a partner with his future father-in-law in the stagecoach and shipping business.

At twenty-one, Dan was two years older than his bride. Like his father, he was blond, blue-eyed, and stood just over six feet tall. Brunette Rebecca Ann was tall and slender and quite pretty. Everyone agreed that they made a handsone couple.

The hall was well-lighted with kerosene lanterns that hung from the ceiling, and the tables were decorated with candles. Happy chatter filled the place, punctuated from time to time with laughter.

The bride and bridegroom were seated at the same table with their parents, along with the bride's younger sister Susan, who was the maid of honor, and the groom's best man and best friend, Gordon Bailey. Also at the main table were Reverend Martin Clouse and his wife, Sadie.

Dan and Rebecca Ann sat side by side, and though they conversed with everyone at the table, they often grew quiet and just looked into each other's eyes. Abigail Wheeler smiled at her son from across the table and said, "Danny, you're not eating, and neither is Rebecca Ann. You two are going to be hungry later if you don't eat now."

"Mom, I'd rather look at Rebecca Ann than eat."

Abigail reached across the table and patted his hand. "Honey, you've got the rest of your life to look at her, but if you don't eat, that won't be very long."

Dan sighed, looked into his bride's dark-brown eyes, and said, "Yeah, Mom, but what a way to go!"

Abigail smiled and shook her head. "You've really got it bad for her, haven't you, son?"

"God just might have to expand the universe, or my love for Rebecca Ann is going to start knocking stars out of the sky."

"I'm glad you love her that much, Danny."

"And I love him the same, Mom Wheeler," Rebecca Ann said.

The governor had caught part of the conversation, though he had been talking to Gunther Wilson. He laid down his fork and put his arm around Abigail's shoulder, then turned to his son.

"Tell you what, my boy—you'll have to go some to love Rebecca Ann as much as I love your mother."

Reverend Clouse set his coffee cup down and said, "But you go ahead and give your father a run for his money, Dan. The Bible says a man should love his wife as Christ loves the church, and that gives every one of us husbands a lot to live up to."

Dan took hold of Rebecca Ann's hand and said, "Well, I'm going to do my dead-level best to love her that much, Pastor." Then he turned to his wife-to-be and said, "Looks like a beautiful night out. How about you and me taking a little stroll? After all, this will be your last chance to take a walk with me as a single man. By this time tomorrow, I'll be a married man."

"Oh, you!" Rebecca Ann said and gave him a playful punch on the shoulder.

The happy couple left the churchyard holding hands and slowly made their way along the dusty streets until they reached the bank of the Gila River. They stood together, hands clasped, and marveled at the beauty of the moonlight as it danced on the surface of the rippling water. After a few moments, Rebecca Ann stared down at the stream and said, "Dan, it feels like it's the bank that's moving, not the water."

"Yeah, it seems that way, doesn't it? It's what they call an optical illusion."

Neither spoke for a moment, then Dan said, "My love for you is no illusion, Rebecca Ann. It's real. And it always will be."

She looked up at him dreamy-eyed, and he folded her into his arms. They kissed tenderly, then he led her to a large rock, and they sat down together. Dan took both of her hands in his.

"Sweetheart," he said, "tomorrow I'll take my vows publicly, but right here, tonight, I want to tell you that I will love, honor, and cherish you till the day I die."

Tears surfaced in her eyes. "And I vow the same to you, my darling Dan."

They kissed again, then embraced.

"O Rebecca Ann, tomorrow will be the happiest day of our lives!"

"Yes. I can hardly wait!"

C H A P T E R

SEVENTEEN

———◆———

The wedding on the First Methodist Church grounds was set for two o'clock on Saturday afternoon. Guests began to arrive shortly after 1:30, among them several dignitaries and their wives, including members of the Arizona Territory legislature, Phoenix city councilmen, Chief U.S. Marshal Harvey Claxton, and Colonel Bradley Munford, commandant of Fort McDowell, the army's nearest post. A captain and a lieutenant accompanied the colonel and his wife.

Some two hundred chairs and over a dozen benches had been set up in an area at the rear of the church, which was partially shaded by a stand of mesquite and Palo Verde trees. A white-latticed arbor, covered with stringy vines and Palo Verde branches, had been placed in front of the seats and in line with an aisle which divided the seating into two sections. A pump organ was next to the arbor.

Rebecca Ann and her mother, along with the bridal attendants and the maid of honor, were in the parsonage close by, getting dressed. Sadie Clouse was busy doing what she could to help.

In the pastor's office inside the church building, Dan Wheeler paced the floor. His groomsmen, both single as yet, were joking with him.

"No wonder you're nervous," Wiley Aultman said. "When a man mounts the steps of the gallows, he knows it's all over. Things will never be the same, Dan ol' boy. You're about to take the final plunge."

"Yeah, Danny," Ned Rogers said, "you've had your last day of freedom. Of course, at this point you can still back out. My horse is saddled, watered, fed, and burped. He'll take you to safety at a gallop if you'll just run out there and hop in the saddle. Ride, man, ride!"

Dan stopped pacing and took a playful clip at Ned's chin. "That's enough, you two! I can't wait till the time comes when you're in my shoes!"

"Maybe Ned'll get trapped by some gal and dragged to the altar, but not me!" Wiley said. "No, sir!"

Dan looked at the clock on the office wall. The pendulum appeared to be swinging very slowly, and it seemed the hands were stuck. He looked in the mirror and straightened his tie for the dozenth time in the twenty minutes they had been in the office. Gordon Bailey stepped close to his best friend and clamped a steady hand on his shoulder.

"It'll be over soon, Danny. You'll be all hitched up before you know it."

Dan let a weak grin spread across his face. "I don't remember you being this nervous when I was your best man, Gordie."

"Well, I was. You've just forgotten the way I acted." He sighed. "I'd go through it all over again a million times, though... happy as I've been with Marianne. I know you and Rebecca Ann are going to be just as happy."

The sound of the pump organ came suddenly from outside, playing a hymn. Martin Clouse looked at the clock and smiled.

"Bertha's right on time. It's ten minutes till two."

Dan's friends kept his mind occupied for the next ten minutes, then the pump organ went silent. Dan's knees went watery and his palms turned clammy. When the wedding march began, he preceded the pastor, the groomsmen, and the best man through the door and headed for the lattice arbor. When he saw the size of the crowd, he swallowed hard. Hundreds of people had gathered.

The groom was flanked by his three friends, and the preacher took his position beneath the arbor. All four faced the audience, looking toward the parsonage. Gunther Wilson waited at the rear of the audience next to the aisle, ready to escort his daughter to the altar.

Dan's heart leaped within him when he saw the door of the house come open. The bride's attendants filed out one at a time, followed by the maid of honor. Then Dan saw Rebecca Ann step out into the sunlight, and the sight of her took his breath away.

The organ continued playing softly as the attendants reached the aisle. The bride drew abreast of her father, and when he gave her his arm, the organist raised the volume for, "Here Comes the Bride."

Martha Wilson rose to her feet and turned to look at her daughter. All eyes were on the beautiful young woman in white as she and her father moved slowly down the aisle. Women were weeping and men were swallowing lumps in their throats.

Daniel Louis Wheeler thought his heart was going to rip through his chest as Rebecca Ann drew near and he could see her smiling at him through the veil. When she and her father came to a stop, he could see tears in her eyes.

The organ went silent, and the preacher asked, "Who gives this woman to be married to this man?"

"Her mother and I," Gunther Wilson said.

He placed Rebecca Ann's hand in Dan's, and she turned and kissed her father's cheek through the veil, then took her place beside the groom. The preacher nodded for them to move to the arbor, and as they were doing so, the groomsmen and attendants closed in behind them.

The ceremony proceeded, the vows were taken, and soon Reverend Clouse pronounced them husband and wife and said to Dan, "You may kiss your bride."

Susan Wilson raised the veil for her sister, carefully placing it at the back of her head and on her shoulders. The happy couple looked lovingly into each other's eyes, then Dan took Rebecca Ann into his arms.

Just as their lips met, a loud war whoop sounded accompanied by thundering hooves. Two dozen mounted Tonto Apaches surrounded the area and held arrows and rifles on the crowd.

Martha Wilson and Abigail Wheeler gripped their husbands' arms, frozen in terror. Throats tightened and eyes bulged. Hands began to tremble.

The preacher stood in slack-jawed astonishment. Groomsmen and attendants' features turned white with dread. Colonel Munford looked at the two officers with him and found them as stunned as he was. Though they were wearing sidearms, they knew they dared not try to use them.

A tiny gasp escaped Rebecca Ann's lips when Mandano came riding up the aisle, leading a riderless horse. His black eyes were fixed on the bride and groom, his mouth set in a grim line. The rifle in his hand was leveled on Dan.

"No one move!" Mandano said.

And no one did.

"Oh Dan, I'm scared!" Rebecca Ann said.

Dan's gaze was fixed on the rugged Apache riding toward them. He squeezed his bride tight and whispered, "He's not taking you, honey! I'll—"

"Dan Wheeler," Mandano said, pointing the muzzle of his rifle at the groom's heart, "you will mount this horse and come with us!"

Governor Wheeler rose to his feet. "What is this? Where are you taking my son?"

Mandano ignored him, and holding his rifle on Dan, said, "You will obey me now!"

The governor's face was beet-red. He started in Mandano's direction, but checked himself when one of the warriors raised his rifle and aimed it at his chest.

"You will sit down!" the warrior said.

Wheeler gave him a hard look and sat down. Tears brimmed Abigail's eyes. She clutched her husband's arm and in a tremulous whisper, said, "What are they going to do with our son?"

"I have no idea. They've got us in a helpless position. There's nothing we can do!"

Dan looked at Rebecca Ann, thankful it was not her they were taking. She swung her fear-filled eyes on the subchief.

"Please, sir, this man is my husband. He's done nothing to you! Why are you taking him?"

Mandano fixed Dan with fierce eyes. "You will mount the horse, or my warriors will shoot your father!"

"I must do as he says," Dan said to his bride. He let go of her reluctantly and swung aboard the Indian pony. Rebecca Ann burst into tears.

Mandano set heavy eyes on the governor and said, "If anyone follows, your son will die."

Colonel Munford and his two officers were in the same section as the governor, a few rows back. Mandano glared at the colonel and said, "If the soldiers appear at the Tonto camp, Dan Wheeler will be killed. Governor, you will hear from Chief Janos tomorrow at your house."

Mandano led Dan's horse between the front row of chairs and the arbor and headed toward the street. The mounted warriors also moved that direction, keeping their attention and their weapons on the crowd.

Dan looked back at Rebecca Ann, telling her with his eyes that he loved her. Through a wall of tears she watched him go.

When the Apaches vanished from sight with their captive, there was bedlam in the First Methodist churchyard. Some women fainted; others screamed. Men shouted curses at the Indians. There was mass confusion as the guests collided with each other in an attempt to get to their buggies, surreys, and wagons.

Rebecca Ann was gasping for air, ready to faint. The preacher and the best man went to her to keep her from falling. Martha struggled toward her terrified daughter, weeping, with Gunther supporting her. Abigail Wheeler headed for Rebecca Ann also, leaving her husband, who was talking with Marshal Claxton.

Claxton was asking the governor if he had any idea why the Tontos had taken Dan when Colonel Munford drew up with his officers flanking him.

"Excuse me, Marshal." Munford said. Then to Wheeler, "What do you want me to do, Governor? It's too late to have my men ready before sundown, but I sure can have them ready at sunrise."

"We can't be hasty, Colonel. You heard what the man said. If I send the army against their camp, they'll kill Dan."

"But, sir—"

"The only thing we can do, Colonel, is wait till I hear from Janos tomorrow. When I know what he wants, we'll decide on a course of action."

"Do you want protection for your family and the bride's family, Governor?" Claxton asked. "I'm a little short on deputies at the moment, but—"

"We can provide that, Marshal," Munford said. "I know that most of your men are out on assignments, and I have the manpower at my disposal. If the governor wants protection, the army can and will provide it."

"I think it would be good, Colonel," Wheeler said. "Until this…this horror is over, it might be best if the Wilsons stay at our house where your troops can protect us all in one place. I'll talk to Gunther once we've got everyone settled down. You send in as many men as you think necessary."

"I'll not *send* them, sir, I'll *bring* them. I'm staying close to this situation until it's over."

"I appreciate that. And thank you for the offer, Marshal. No reason to spread your ranks thin when Colonel Munford has his troops available."

Claxton smiled and nodded. "If you think of anything else I can do, Governor, please let me know."

"I will."

Claxton walked away, and the colonel noted that several people were gathered around the bride, who was sobbing her heart out.

"I know you need to be with your daughter-in-law, Governor. I'll see you at your house as soon as I can assemble my men and ride back to town. Probably be about six o'clock."

Governor Wheeler thanked Munford and moved to the front row of chairs where Rebecca Ann was seated with her mother on one side and her mother-in-law on the other. Susan was next to Abigail. Gunther Wilson, Reverend Clouse, and most of the attendants stood close by.

Rebecca Ann was bent over, her face buried in her hands as she sobbed Dan's name over and over. The governor knelt down in front of her, took hold of her wrists, and said, "Honey, listen to me. We're going to get Dan back. You'll see."

Rebecca Ann lifted her head and looked into her father-in-law's eyes.

"How do you know that? You don't know that!"

Reverend Clouse leaned over the governor's shoulder. "Rebecca Ann, we have a wonderful God. He is able to bring Dan back to you."

"I don't mean to be disrespectful to God, Pastor, but why did He let those awful heathens come and take Dan at all? Couldn't He have prevented that too?"

"Yes, He could have, dear, but He didn't. So He has a purpose for allowing this. Please don't despair. Listen to your father-in-law, now."

"Honey, listen to me," the governor said. "If all the Apaches wanted was to kill Dan, they wouldn't have had to go to the trouble they did to interrupt the wedding ceremony. Simply killing him would have been easy. Are you listening?"

"Yes." She sniffed and dabbed at her tears with a hanky someone had put in her hand.

"Chief Janos has done this because he wants something of me.

I have no idea what, but when I find out tomorrow, we'll go from there. Don't despair, Rebecca Ann. Dan is my son, and I love him with all my heart. I'm not going to let Janos harm him."

She looked deep into his eyes. "You mean, whatever it is Janos wants, you'll see that he gets it?"

"If it's humanly possible, yes. You can count on that."

Her face twisted and her eyes brimmed with tears. "But why did it have to be Dan? Why couldn't they have taken someone else? We…we were barely even married—" She bit down hard as the tears spilled down her cheeks. "Last night…when Dan and I took our walk down to the river…we both agreed that this was going to be the happiest day of our lives. But it's turned out to be the most awful day I have ever lived! Oh, I want Dan back! I want my husband!"

She buried her face in her hands and sobbed.

Governor Wheeler told Gunther that Colonel Munford was bringing a cavalry unit to the governor's house that evening to provide protection until the situation was resolved. He invited Gunther and his family to join them, and Gunther accepted. He wanted to be at the Wheeler home when the Apaches came back to reveal what it was Chief Janos wanted.

Dawn was just a hint of gray on the eastern horizon when Governor Donald Wheeler threw back the covers and sat up. Abigail turned toward him on her side and placed her hand on his back.

"Did you sleep at all, darling?" she asked.

He leaned over and kissed her cheek. "No more than you did."

"I hope Janos doesn't wait all day to make contact with you."

"I hope so too," he said, rising from the bed and walking to the window.

Their bedroom was on the third floor of the large house. He pulled the curtain back and looked down at the tents in the large open area next to the yard. The soldiers—one hundred and thirteen of them—had arrived just before six on Saturday evening and set up camp.

Governor Wheeler could see Colonel Munford in conversation with a small group of men. He turned from the window and said, "Why don't you stay in bed for a while, honey? I'm sure the Wilsons didn't sleep, either. I'll go downstairs and tell Amanda to hold off starting breakfast till later."

Abigail threw back the covers and sat up. "No, I think I better get up now and make myself presentable while you're shaving. I certainly don't want my guests to be up before I am."

"Okay, but I think I should tell Amanda to delay starting breakfast till we know the Wilsons are stirring."

"That'll be fine," she said, yawning. "Go on down and tell her."

Amanda was in the kitchen about to start a fire in the cookstove when the governor entered in his robe. He was surprised to find all three of the Wilsons and Rebecca Ann dressed and sitting at the table.

"Good mornin', Gov'nor," Amanda said. "These folks didn't get no sleep last night on account of Mister Dan bein' in the hands of them 'Paches. I was about to get the fire goin' so's I could make 'em some coffee."

"Fine, Amanda. I guess none of us got any sleep. If you folks will excuse me, I'll go shave off this stubble. Abigail and I will be down in time for breakfast."

"You don't suppose Janos will make us wait all day before he contacts you, do you, Donald?" Gunther asked.

"I sure hope not. But I wouldn't put it past him to stretch our nerves good before we hear anything. See you all in a few minutes."

The morning passed without any contact from the Tonto chief. The two families sat in the parlor and talked, trying to keep up their morale. Rebecca Ann was having the hardest time staying in the conversation, and from time to time, she broke down and wept.

It was high noon when a sentry stationed at the entrance to the driveway called to the colonel and told him three Apaches were riding their way under a white flag. Munford called for his men to show themselves, weapon in hand. When the Apaches drew up to the sentry, he stepped in front of them.

"State your business," he said.

"We are here to bring a message from Chief Janos to Governor Wheeler," Mandano said.

"Send them in, corporal," Munford called. He turned to his captain and said, "Go tell the governor the Apaches are here."

The colonel stood tall and straight with several men flanking him as Mandano drew near the porch. The warrior on his left held a rifle with the muzzle pointing skyward. The white flag attached to its barrel flapped in the breeze.

"Governor Wheeler will be here in a moment," Munford said.

It took only seconds for Donald Wheeler to emerge from the house into the brilliant midday sunlight. Behind him, Abigail, Rebecca Ann, the Wilsons, and Amanda watched and listened from the open double doors. Wheeler moved up beside Colonel Munford and set his eyes on the Indian on the middle horse.

"Before we go any further, I'd like to know just who I'm dealing with here."

"My name is Mandano. I am a Tonto subchief. I speak for the honorable Janos, chief of the Tontos."

"I assume my son is all right."

"He is."

"I'll take your word for that since I have no choice. Now, what is it Janos wants?"

Mandano laid out Janos's demands for rifles, Gatlings, and ammunition. And he told the governor his son would be executed Apache-style if the demands were not met within seven days.

When he heard these words, Wheeler turned to Munford and asked in a whisper that only the colonel could hear, "Is this possible?"

Even as the governor was asking the question, Mandano spoke again.

"The guns and ammunition are to be delivered to the rock gateway of our stronghold in the Superstition Mountains by high sun one week from today. The colonel knows where the stronghold is located."

"Why does Janos want these weapons, Mandano?" Wheeler asked.

"Because the Tontos need them to fight the Zunis, who have many new rifles and a Gatling gun." Mandano wheeled his horse around abruptly and looked over his shoulder. "At high sun one week from today, Governor. Your son will die if you fail to meet Chief Janos's demand."

"Wait!" Wheeler called. "Do I get my son back at the same time?"

"Yes!" Mandano called back, already putting his horse to a trot. The other two Apaches followed, and soon they were gone.

The onlookers met Donald Wheeler when he mounted the porch steps, followed by Colonel Munford. Rebecca was already tearful as she dashed to her father-in-law.

"Dad Wheeler, you *will* send the guns and ammunition to Janos, won't you? You said you would do whatever it takes to save Dan's life."

The governor pulled a handkerchief from his hip pocket and mopped his brow.

"Rebecca Ann, I've got to think this thing through before I make any moves. If I don't act wisely, I could set a precedent that would be disastrous in dealing with the Apaches from now on."

Abigail moved up beside her daughter-in-law, who was staring at the governor in disbelief at what she had just heard him say.

"Donald," Abigail said, "can Colonel Munford supply these demands by this time next Sunday?"

"Yes, I can," Munford said.

"Then what is there to think through? Donald, you heard that heathen—if Janos doesn't have his guns and ammunition by this time next Sunday, Dan will be tortured and killed. There's no alternative. You must see that the demands are met!"

"Don't you care about Dan?" Rebecca Ann said, tears already running down her cheeks.

"Of course I care about Dan!" Wheeler said. "But I've got to have a little time to work on this. Maybe there's some way to rescue Dan without giving the Apaches those guns."

"How? If you send the army charging in there, they'll kill Dan before the soldiers can possibly rescue him."

"She's right, Donald," Abigail said. "There's no other—"

"Just a minute! There's more involved here than just Dan's life. If I give Colonel Munford the order to take the guns and ammunition to Janos, the Apaches will eventually use them against white men. I'll have the deaths of who knows how many white folks on my conscience."

"And if you don't," Abigail said, "you'll have the death of your son on your conscience. Will you be able to live with that?"

"Dad Wheeler," Rebecca Ann said, "you *must* meet Janos's demands! You can't let him kill Dan! You—"

Donald Wheeler snapped his fingers. "That's it! That's it!"

"What's it?" Gunther Wilson asked, stepping closer.

"Gunther, there may be another way out of this!"

"*What* way?" Abigail asked.

"Honey, you remember John Stranger, don't you?"

"How could I ever forget him?"

"I heard Friday afternoon that John is in Apache Junction. Some kind of trouble he's there helping the local marshal handle. I forgot to mention it to you. The wedding and all, you know."

"So you think John can help us?"

"I'm sure of it! He's the most resourceful man I've ever known. He can go into the Superstitions and rescue Dan, I know he can! I'll wire him tomorrow and ask him to come to Phoenix immediately."

"But you said he's there to help the marshal," Abigail said. "Maybe he's too busy to try to rescue Dan."

"He'll take time off to save Dan's life, honey. I guarantee it."

"Just who is this John Stranger, Governor?" Gunther asked. "I've heard that name somewhere recently."

While everyone listened, Wheeler told how John Stranger had brought a gang of outlaws to justice some five years previously in Flagstaff. He had a reputation for successfully handling seemingly impossible situations.

"I've heard of him, Governor," Colonel Munford said. "If anyone can go in there and bring Dan out unharmed, it's him."

"But what if he can't?" Gunther said. "The Apaches could have Dan so well-hidden in those mountains, your man could search for him for years and never find him. And even if by some miracle he did find him, getting the two of them out of there alive would take a greater miracle."

"I know lots of stories about John Stranger, Gunther, besides what I've seen with my own eyes," Wheeler said. "If I can talk him into going in there after Dan, I'm confident the rescue will be accomplished. Janos can just whistle for his guns."

"Governor, I'll have the guns and ammunition ready for delivery by Thursday," Colonel Munford said. "But if this John Stranger will take a shot at rescuing Dan, I think it's worth a try."

Wheeler turned to his wife and daughter-in-law. "How about it, ladies? Will you go along with me on this? Let me see if John Stranger will make the rescue attempt?"

Rebecca Ann and Abigail looked at each other, then nodded their assent.

EIGHTEEN

I t was early morning on Monday. John Stranger was in his work clothes on the roof of the new church building, nailing down wooden shingles. Four other men were working on the roof also, and while they pounded nails, they discussed the two sermons Stranger had preached the day before.

"I learned so much in just those two sermons, John," one of them said. "I sure wish the Lord would let you be our pastor."

"I have different orders, but I'm sure God will give you a good man."

Stranger's attention was drawn to the street, where Marshal Ben Clifton was hurrying into the churchyard.

"John," he called, "a wire just came for you. Come on down."

Stranger grinned at the other men. "Sorry to leave you fellas, but it sounds important."

"Yeah, we know!" one of them said. "That ol' hammer's gettin' heavy!"

"Aw, you figured me out!" Stranger said.

The others laughed and returned to their task.

"So who sent me a wire, Ben?" Stranger asked when he reached the ground. "Duvall?"

"No, sir. The governor."

"Of Arizona? Donald Wheeler?"

"Yeah. He needs you in Phoenix as fast as you can get there. Said it's extremely important—a matter of life and death. He heard you'd come here to help me, but didn't know when you might leave. He wants you to let him know if you're comin', and if so, when he might expect you."

"I'm going, of course. Would you wire him back for me and tell him I'll be there in little more than an hour?"

"Will do."

Stranger thanked him and broke into a run, heading for the hotel. He quickly changed clothes, left with his saddlebags over his shoulder, and ran to the stable. Moments later, he led Ebony through the gate onto the street and headed west.

When Ebony was warmed up, Stranger gave him his head. The big black loved to run, and the tall man loved to ride him at a full gallop. The warm wind kissed Stranger's face and plucked at his hatbrim while he wondered what Governor Wheeler might need him for.

By the time Phoenix came into view, Ebony wore a sheen of sweat, and foam from his mouth flecked his chest. When they were within a few hundred yards of the town's edge, Stranger slowed the magnificent animal to a trot.

Stranger had been in the saddle exactly forty-nine minutes when he guided Ebony around a corner onto the street where the governor's house was located. He saw the tents and the uniformed men and wondered even more what was going on.

A sentry took a couple of steps into the street when he saw horse and rider coming. Drawing up, Stranger spoke before the soldier did.

"John Stranger here by request of Governor Wheeler."

"Yes, sir. The governor is eagerly waiting your arrival." He turned and cupped a hand beside his mouth. "Colonel Munford, sir! Mr. John Stranger has arrived!"

The commandant of Fort McDowell rose from a bench on

the broad front porch and motioned for Stranger to ride on in. Smiling warmly, he bid the tall man to dismount, introduced himself, and offered his hand. Stranger met it with a firm grip.

"I'm mighty glad to meet you, Mr. Stranger. I've heard some very good things about you. *Before* the governor brought your name up yesterday, I mean."

"Well, you can't believe everything you hear, Colonel."

"Perhaps not, but I have no reason to doubt what I've heard about you. Governor Wheeler wants to be the one to tell you what this is all about, sir. Let's get you to him."

Stranger flanked the colonel as they walked briskly down a marble-floored hallway toward the library. The click of their heels seemed to echo throughout the house. They were almost to the library when the door came open and Donald Wheeler stepped out to meet them.

"John!" Wheeler said, extending his hand. "So good to see you! It's been a long time."

"It sure has, sir," Stranger said, shaking his hand. "Too long. You were merely council chairman in Flagstaff then. Please accept a belated congratulations on becoming governor of this great territory."

"Thank you. I assume you and Colonel Munford have introduced yourselves."

"Yes, sir."

"Well, come into the library, John. There's a lady here who's eager to see you again…and some folks who want to meet you."

The three men entered the library, and Abigail Wheeler stepped forward from the rest of the group.

"John," she said sweetly, extending her hand, "it's so nice to see you again."

Stranger bowed, took her hand in his, and kissed it lightly.

"The pleasure is mine, ma'am."

"Always the gentleman, aren't you?"

"Well, I try," he said.

"John," the governor said, "I want you to meet Gunther Wilson, owner of Arizona Stagelines. Gunther...John Stranger."

Suddenly Gunther's eyes widened and his mouth popped open.

"Wait a minute—John Stranger! Now I remember why that name rings a bell. You thwarted a robbery of one of my coaches a few days ago south of Alexandra."

"Yes, sir, I did."

"You gave the driver a silver medallion...had some Scripture on it."

"Yes, sir."

Wilson pumped Stranger's hand.

"Well, sir, I want to thank you for what you did. You come and see me when this is all over. I want to give you a reward."

"Thank you, Mr. Wilson, but that really isn't necessary. I'm just glad I came along at the right time."

Donald Wheeler introduced Martha and Susan Wilson to Stranger, then said, "And now, John, I want you to meet the Wilsons' other daughter, Rebecca Ann, who is also our daughter-in-law."

Stranger smiled broadly as Rebecca Ann moved toward him.

"Daughter-in-law...so this is Dan's wife."

"Yes," the governor said.

Stranger noted the sadness in the young woman's eyes as she extended her hand.

"It's a pleasure to meet you, Mr. Stranger. Mom and Dad Wheeler have been telling us all about you."

"Thank you," he said, taking her hand and looking around. "Where's Dan? You just got married Saturday, didn't you? I remember seeing an article about the wedding in the *Phoenix Sun* last week."

Rebecca Ann's face pinched and tears welled up in her eyes. Stranger looked at the governor.

"What is it, sir? Has something happened to Dan?"

"Let's all sit down," Wheeler said.

When everyone was seated, the governor cleared his throat and said, "John, I've asked you to come because Dan has been abducted by the Tonto Apaches. They have him in the Superstitions and are threatening his life."

Stranger raised his eyebrows and took a deep breath. "I see. And why have they done this?"

Wheeler told Stranger how the Apaches had disrupted the wedding ceremony and taken Dan, then returned the next day with their demands for guns and ammunition. Rebecca Ann began to weep as her father-in-law told Stranger that Dan would be killed if the weapons were not delivered by noon on Sunday.

Stranger leaned forward on the chair and met Wheeler's gaze.

"But you really don't want to give those guns to Janos, right? That's why I'm here."

Wheeler sighed. "If we arm the Apaches, there'll be a lot of white people die by those guns. Among the Apache chiefs, Janos is one of the bloodiest. He carries a burning hatred toward white people, and he can kill a white man, woman, or child as easy as you or I would kill a bug."

"So you want me to go into the Superstitions and rescue Dan before noon next Sunday, correct?"

Wheeler's face reddened and his eyes showed a hint of tears just beneath the surface.

"Yes, John. You're the only man I know who can do it. Will you?"

Rebecca Ann jumped off the couch, tears flowing down her cheeks, and fell on her knees before John Stranger.

"Please, Mr. Stranger! Please bring my husband home to me!"

John Stranger took hold of her arms and stood up, gently lifting her to her feet.

"I'll do my best, Rebecca Ann."

"Oh, God bless you!" she cried. "God bless you!"

Stranger turned and looked at the governor. "I'm sure you're aware, sir, that finding Dan and getting both of us out would be very difficult even if there were no Apaches."

"Yes," the governor said, rising to his feet. "But if it's possible to get Dan out of there alive, you're the man to do it, John."

Rebecca Ann took hold of his arm and said with a shaky voice, "We all know that by going in there, you're risking your own life, Mr. Stranger. I want you to know that I don't take this lightly. You have my utmost gratitude."

"That goes for all of us, Mr. Stranger," Gunther said.

"I'm glad to do it, sir," John said.

Rebecca Ann looked with admiration into Stranger's face. "I'm amazed, sir, that you would so readily risk your life for someone you met only once."

Stranger smiled at her. "I have a special calling from the Lord, little lady, and He's equipped me for my calling. If I felt the situation was absolutely impossible, I wouldn't try it...that would be foolish. But what I face here is not impossible, so I promise you I'll give it everything I've got to make this mission a success. With the Lord's help, it can be done."

"Thank you," Rebecca Ann said and wrapped her arms around Stranger. She held on for a few seconds, then let go and backed away.

Stranger looked at Colonel Munford, then back at Wheeler, and said, "May I make a suggestion?"

"Of course," the governor said.

"I suggest that you order the army posts all over this part of Arizona to keep patrol units moving about to hold the Zunis at bay. If the Zunis are not attacking the Tontos, Janos will be a bit more relaxed about getting his hands on the weapons. We don't want him too antsy. From what I know of him, he's quite high-strung, anyway."

"That makes good sense, John," Wheeler said. "I'll order it done."

"Good." He looked around at everyone. "Well, nice to meet

all of you. You understand that I'll have no way of communicating with you once I'm in the Superstitions. But the Lord willing, I'll have Rebecca's husband back in her arms before noon next Sunday."

There were appreciative words from the group as John Stranger left the library. Governor Wheeler and Colonel Munford walked him to the front porch and bid him Godspeed as he mounted and rode away.

John Stranger rode hard for Apache Junction and prayed that the Lord would give him wisdom and safety and help him to rescue Dan Wheeler.

Arriving at Apache Junction, he stopped at the general store and loaded up on beef jerky and hardtack. He also bought an additional canteen and filled it, along with his other one, with water. He then went to the marshal's office to let Ben Clifton know where he was going and why. Clifton was out of the office, so he jotted the marshal a quick note that he would be gone for a few days and would see him upon his return.

It was early afternoon when he rode out of Apache Junction and headed due east for the Superstitions. He knew the Tonto stronghold was located at the northern tip of the Superstitions on the east side, so he planned to enter the mountains a couple of miles south of the stronghold on the east side. He would stash Ebony at the first stream he came to and go in the rest of the way on foot.

Soon Stranger was riding the undulating land that skirted the rugged Superstitions, moving from the south along the eastern foothills. He continued to pray for help and guidance as he let his eyes take in the desert shrubs, plants, and cacti that fringed the range. He rode around a massive rock formation and started down into a draw.

Suddenly he pulled rein and said, "Whoa, boy!"

What he saw at the bottom of the draw made him move quickly. He slid from the saddle, led Ebony behind a huge boulder and looped the reins over the limb of a scrub oak, then hurried back to the crest of the draw.

Three white men had a teenage Apache boy on the ground in a brush thicket. They were laughing and having a good time, telling the boy they were going to take his scalp. The largest of the three straddled the Indian and waved a knife in his face. The young Apache struggled to free himself, but would not shame himself by crying out or begging for mercy. Three saddled horses stood close by, with the Indian's painted pony standing aloof, looking on.

"Go ahead, Gordo," one of the men said. "Cut his nose off before you scalp him. Cut his tongue out, too."

The laughing scalp hunters were so intent on the youthful Apache that they were unaware of John Stranger running toward them in the soft sand.

"Yeah, let's take the tongue first," Gordo said. "Open your mouth, kid!" As he spoke, he reached for the Indian's jaw to force his mouth open.

The boy squirmed and twisted his head and struck Gordo square on the mouth with his fist, cutting his lip. Gordo backhanded the boy hard, stunning him, then put fingertips to his lip. When he saw the blood, his eyes bulged with fury and he roared like a wild beast.

"Kill him, Gordo!" one of them yelled. "Kill him!"

"Not till I pay him back for this! I'm gonna beat his face in, then scalp him!"

Gordo struck the boy in the face three times and was about to hit him again when a sharp voice cut the air.

"Hold it! Hit him again, and you'll lose your fist!"

All three heads whipped around to see John Stranger standing not more than twenty feet from them. His Peacemaker was in his hand and the hammer was in firing position.

Gordo, still astride the Indian, glowered at the intruder.

"Mind your own business, mister!"

"I am minding my own business. My business is to keep this kind of thing from happening."

"You're a scum-bucket Indian-lover, mister! As a white man, you should hate the dirty savages!"

"Nobody called them savages before white men came in here and took their land from them. When they dared fight back, now suddenly they're savages, even *dirty* savages. All they're doing is fighting to protect what's theirs, the same as you men would do if you were in their place."

"You sound like a preacher to me," one of them, a skinny man with spectacles, said.

"Maybe. Might do you some good to listen to some good Bible preaching when you get the chance."

While the skinny one had Stranger's attention, the third man went for his gun. The Peacemaker roared, and the man went down.

Gordo raised the knife to plunge it into the Apache's heart. Stranger's gun boomed again. Gordo stiffened when the slug hit him, dropped the knife in the sand, and toppled over.

The skinny one had his gun up and was bringing to bear when Stranger fired again. The slug exploded his heart, but his finger squeezed the trigger. His gun roared and the bullet tore at Stranger's left sleeve. He felt it, but knew it had missed flesh when there was no pain.

He breathed a prayer of thanks and looked to see if there was any movement among the scalp hunters. There was none. All three were dead.

Stranger holstered his gun and knelt beside the boy. His face was bloody, and he was beginning to swell around the eyes.

"I've got some water on my horse, son," Stranger said. "I'll get it and wash you up."

"Thank you for saving my life, mister."

"What's your name, son?" Stranger asked as he rose to his feet.

"Casco."

"You Tonto?"

"Yes. I live in the mountains. Janos is my chief."

There was a sound of thundering hooves from somewhere over the crest of the draw. Suddenly a swarm of Apaches appeared atop the crest to the north and charged down the sandy slope whooping and yapping.

Casco struggled to his feet. "Do not worry, mister. These are Tontos. I will tell them that you saved me from the scalp hunters. They will not harm you."

The Apaches thundered to a dusty halt. Two had rifles, which they already had aimed at the man in black. The others had bows and arrows, with war clubs tied to their waists. The leader signaled for his warriors to dismount, and did so himself. They kept Stranger covered as they slid from their horses.

Casco staggered to the subchief, who was looking at the three dead men, and said, "Wundan, this man saved my life. I was riding back from Apache Junction when these men you see lying dead came at me from behind some boulders. They caught me and threw me off my horse. They were going to scalp me and kill me. But this man came along and killed them instead."

Wundan looked at Stranger and spoke to Casco in Apache.

"Casco, you understand that even though this white man saved your life, he is still our enemy. And he is our captive. He must be taken to Janos."

"But Janos will kill him!"

"This I cannot help," Wundan said. "Any white man captured on Apache soil must stand before Janos. This is Janos's command. If I do not take him and Janos should find out—"

"Then send a warrior for my brother first. Let me tell Mandano what happened here. Mandano can talk Janos out of killing this man."

The name Mandano rang a bell in Stranger's mind—the subchief who abducted Dan Wheeler and returned the next day to issue Janos's demand for guns and ammunition.

"I must remind you that Janos's hatred for white eyes sometimes drives him beyond reason," Wundan said. "Even your brother may not be able to keep him from killing this man."

"But we must try. I would be dead now if this man had not killed the scalp hunters. Mandano will be very grateful to him for saving my life. He will convince Janos to spare him."

"I will do as you say, Casco," Wundan said. "I will send a warrior to bring Mandano. But do not lean too heavily on your brother. Even he has limited influence on our chief."

Lord, John Stranger prayed, You allowed this to happen for a reason. You knew I wouldn't let those scalp hunters harm the boy. I'm trusting You to not only keep Janos from killing me, but to let it result in Dan Wheeler's release.

CHAPTER

NINETEEN

The stone-faced warriors held their weapons on John Stranger, and Wundan relieved him of the Colt .45 and stuck it under his own belt. He then wheeled and spoke to one of his warriors in Apache, telling him to ride to the camp and bring Mandano. He was to speak to no one else and was to tell Mandano only that Wundan needed him. Once the two of them were out of the camp, the warrior was to explain the whole situation to him.

The warrior leaped aboard his pony and put it to a gallop, raising a cloud of dust as he went. When Wundan turned back to Stranger, the tall man was speaking to Casco.

"I appreciate what you're doing to save my life. I hope your brother will be able to persuade your chief not to kill me."

Casco was dabbing at his bloody mouth with his fingers. Surprise showed in his eyes.

"You understood our conversation?"

"Yes."

"How is it that you know the Apache tongue?"

"Long story. I've been in Arizona many times." He laid a hand on the boy's shoulder. "Why don't you sit down? You look awfully weak."

Casco nodded. "Yes, I am," and eased down onto the sandy earth.

Stranger turned and found Wundan standing behind him, about to speak. Before Wundan could get the first word out, Stranger said, "Casco's wounds need attention. My horse is over there behind that boulder. I have water to wash him and salve to put on the wounds. If you'll allow me to go get him—"

"No! You would try to escape. If I let that happen, Janos would be very angry. I will send one of my warriors." He motioned to a warrior who stood near. "Orondo, go to the boulder and bring—what is your name, white man?"

"John Stranger."

Wundan squinted at him. "Go to the boulder and bring John Stranger's horse."

"Tell him not to try to ride him," Stranger said. "Just lead him."

"He is trained to allow only *you* to ride him, John Stranger?"

"Didn't have to train him. I'm the only man he's ever allowed to ride him."

"Lead the horse over here," Wundan said to Orondo.

Orondo headed toward the boulder, and Wundan fixed Stranger with steady dark eyes.

"It is interesting that you know our language. You say you have been in Arizona many times."

"Yes."

"No white man learns our language unless he spends much time with our people. You have dark skin. You are much taller than any Apache man...but is there some Apache blood in your veins?"

"You speak English quite well, Wundan. Did you learn it from white missionaries like so many of your people?"

"Yes, but you did not answer my question."

"Did those missionaries tell you of Jesus Christ, the Son of God?"

"Yes, but I am not interested in white man's God. My god is

the sun. You did not answer my question."

"My God created the sun, Wundan. He is the Maker of all the universe. He also sent His Son—"

"I said I am not interested! You still have not answered my question."

"If I did have Apache blood in my veins, would it change Chief Janos's attitude toward me?"

"No. It is the white man's blood in you that he hates. Janos would say if you have Apache blood, it is contaminated by the white man's blood."

A shrill whinny cut the air. Stranger turned to see Orondo leading the big black toward them. Ebony's ears were pricked up, and his eyes were fixed on his master.

"It's all right, boy!" Stranger said.

As Orondo drew up, Ebony whinnied again. Stranger stepped to him and patted his long neck.

"It's okay, big guy."

Stranger stepped to a saddlebag and pulled out a leather pouch laced across the top with a rawhide cord. He lifted a canteen from the saddlehorn, stepped to Casco, and knelt beside him.

"All right, young man, let's get you cleaned up. Then we'll put some medicine on those cuts."

The warriors watched Stranger carefully while he worked.

Wundan admitted to himself that this white man was different than any he had known. Of course, Wundan would never feel friendly toward him. He is a white man. Janos would say he is still bad. He talks of his Jesus Christ like the missionaries did. This is wicked. The Sky Father who lights the heavens by day, *he* is the true god. Wundan was glad the missionaries weren't in Apache territory any longer.

Stranger was just finishing the application of salve to Casco's cuts when Mandano arrived with the warrior who had gone after him. He slid from his horse's back and rushed to Casco, who was now sitting up. He gave John Stranger a glance, then knelt and looked with concern at his brother.

Casco's right eye was swollen almost shut, and the left one was drooped. His face was shiny with salve, and his lower lip was puffy.

Mandano looked at the three corpses lying nearby and said, "I am glad they are dead! I am sorry, little brother, for the wickedness of such white men. I wish all scalp hunters were dead!"

"Big brother, it was this man who kept the scalp hunters from killing me. He shot them down. His name is John Stranger."

The wrath faded from Mandano's face and the shadow of a smile tugged at his lips.

"I am in the greatest debt to you, John Stranger. Casco is my only brother, and he means more to me than I could ever tell you."

"I'm glad I came along at the right time, Mandano," Stranger said.

"But most white men would not have stopped them. Even if they did not like what the scalp hunters were doing, most white men would not have risked their lives to interfere. They would not have felt that the life of an Indian was worth it."

Stranger gave him a slight smile. "Well, I do."

"So you have shown us. I cannot thank you enough."

"John Stranger is friend to the Apache," Casco said. "When he held his gun on the scalp hunters, the one with red hair called him a scum—scum—"

"Scum-bucket," Stranger said.

"Yes. Scum-bucket Indian lover. He told John Stranger that as a white man, he should hate us. He called us dirty savages. John Stranger told him he should not call us savages. He…"

"Yes, Casco?"

"Tell my brother what you told the scalp hunter with red hair about calling us savages. Please?"

Stranger set his eyes on Mandano. "The man called Apaches dirty savages, Mandano, and it angered me. I told him nobody called Apaches savages before white men came in here, killed their people, and stole their land. I told him the Apaches were only fighting to protect what was theirs, the same as the scalp hunters would do if they were in the Apaches' place."

"I am glad you spoke the truth of it before you killed them, John Stranger," Mandano said.

Stranger saw something different in this young subchief. He did not have the hard look the other warriors carried. There was almost a tenderness in his eyes.

"Mandano," said Casco, "I asked Wundan to send for you because I wish to have John Stranger set free for saving my life and being a friend to our people."

Mandano's brow furrowed. "But I do not have the authority to set him free. It is only Janos who can do this."

"I know, but Chief Janos hates all white men. Even though he saved my life and spoke as friend of Apaches, Janos will kill him."

"And you want me to try to persuade Janos to spare his life and set him free."

"Yes. Chief Janos will listen to you. You must talk him into letting John Stranger go."

Mandano closed his eyes for a moment, then opened them. "You have my word, little brother. I will talk to Janos, and I will do my best to persuade him to let John Stranger live."

He turned to Stranger. "I promise you, John Stranger. I will do everything in my power to see that you are released unharmed. But you must understand that Janos holds a deep hatred for all whites. Even my influence may not be enough."

Stranger nodded. "I understand, Mandano. I appreciate that you will try."

Chief Janos listened as Mandano, with Casco at his side, told his little brother's story. John Stranger stood between Wundan and Orondo, facing Janos. Several hundred Tonto men, women, and children formed a circle around them and looked on. Serinda, the

mother of Mandano and Casco, stood on the edge of the inner
circle, listening intently.

Stranger let his eyes roam over the Apache stronghold. There
was no sign of Dan Wheeler. He could see the beginnings of several
canyons that led back into the depths of the Superstitions. Dan
could be in any one of them.

He brought his attention back to Janos and watched the
chief's eyes as Mandano told how the tall white man had stepped in
to save Casco's life. Janos showed no emotion. Nor did his expres-
sion change when Mandano quoted Stranger's words to the redheaded scalp hunter about Apaches being savages.

"This man also tended to my brother's wounds, Chief Janos,"
Mandano said. "Because he killed the scalp hunters to save Casco's
life and showed himself a friend to the Apache, I ask you to let him
live. I ask you to set him free."

Janos stiffened and his dark eyes flashed at Mandano's request.

"You let these things make you soft, Mandano! This man is
still our enemy...not our friend. Was he not trespassing on Apache
land when he came upon the scalp hunters? He is no better than
they. He is still a white man, and all white men are enemies of
Apache!"

Casco's entire body shook. "Please, Chief Janos, John Stranger
is our friend! He is Casco's friend. He saved my life! Please, you
must have mercy on him!"

"You do not address me, Casco! You are but a youth!"

The boy's countenance fell. He turned and looked at Stranger,
then stepped behind his brother.

"Chief Janos," Mandano said, "my brother would be dead
now were it not for John Stranger. You must see that all white men
are not evil and greedy. Nor are all white men our enemies. This
man deserves to live. He—"

"He deserves to die! He is white, and white is evil and greedy!"

Breathing heavily in his anger, Janos swung his gaze on
Stranger and spoke to Mandano from the side of his mouth.

"Build a fire in the fire-pit."

John Stranger knew about Apache torture. Fist-sized rocks were laid close together in the bottom of a pit and covered with broken tree limbs. The wood was set on fire and allowed to burn until the rocks were exceedingly hot and the limbs reduced to glowing embers. The victim was then stripped to the waist and staked chest-down over the pit…and left to die a slow, agonizing death.

John had already spotted the fire-pit earlier, and he could see it from where he stood. The sight of it sent a wave of dread washing over him.

Mandano pressed Janos again to think over what John Stranger had done.

The chief's face went black with rage. "Mandano, there will be no more talk about this! So he saved Casco's life. This does not excuse his trespassing on Apache land. Get the fire going!"

Janos commanded six warriors to hold their guns on John Stranger, and four warriors went to work to prepare the fire-pit. Mandano, true to his word, again interceded with Janos.

"Chief Janos, you know I am faithful and loyal to you. I am a true Tonto Apache warrior. But I must disagree with what you are doing! I know John Stranger was trespassing when he came upon the scalp hunters, but you have not asked him why he was on our land. Possibly he was just passing through and had no intention of doing us wrong. His words to the scalpers prove he is our friend. Is the great Janos so unfeeling that he can kill a friend just because he was riding across our land?"

"I said enough! I will hear no more of this, Mandano. Your words are as the squabbling of children to me!"

The fire was lit. Hundreds of Apache eyes looked on with keen interest. Smoke billowed from the pit as the flames consumed the dry mesquite and the rocks began to heat up.

Stranger eyed the flaming pit and the six muzzles trained on him. He realized that in God's wisdom, this might be his time to die. His mind flashed to Breanna Baylor. He wished he could see her once more before his life on earth was ended. And he prayed, asking the Lord to spare him and to help him rescue Dan Wheeler.

Stranger was held at gunpoint while the fire crackled and smoke billowed skyward. After a half hour, Janos walked toward the pit to inspect it.

"It is hot enough. Mandano, I want the white man staked over the pit now! Pick four men to do it."

Mandano stiffened. "Chief Janos, I cannot give the order to murder the man who saved my brother's life and has proven he is a friend to the Apache. Whatever the consequences, I refuse to do it."

Janos stared Mandano in the eye for a long time. Mandano did not flinch. Janos suddenly wheeled, and in a rage, called the names of four warriors, commanding them to seize John Stranger, tear off his shirt, and stake him over the pit.

"Chief Janos!" a woman cried.

The four warriors kept moving toward Stranger, but all others looked toward the woman who was coming from the mouth of one of the nearby canyons.

"It is Zareem, Chief Janos," the woman said. "He is dying! He asks to see you before he dies."

Janos turned and called to the four warriors. "Wait! I must honor Zareem's request. Do not put white-eyes over the pit until I return. I want to watch every moment of his suffering."

With that, Janos hurried away with the woman.

John Stranger's whole body had broken into a sweat. He could feel little rivulets trickling down his back as he wiped moisture from his brow.

Mandano stepped up to him. "I am sorry, John Stranger. I tried."

"I couldn't ask any more of you, Mandano. Tell me...this Zareem. Is he a warrior?"

"Yes."

"What is wrong with him?"

Mandano told him about Zareem's gunshot wound and his long struggle to get well.

"At times it seemed he would recover, but he took a turn for the worse a couple of days ago."

"Is he running a high fever?"

"Yes. For two days, he lies in a pool of sweat. The wound is festered and giving him much pain."

"Mandano, I have much experience with gunshot wounds. Maybe there is still a chance for Zareem to live. Please tell Janos that I will try to save Zareem's life if he will give me the opportunity."

"I will do it," Mandano said, and ran toward the opening in the rocks where Janos and the woman had disappeared.

Moments later, John Stranger knelt beside the wounded warrior in a cave. Janos, Mandano, and Zareem's mother, Yamina, stood over him, looking on. Zareem was conscious, but barely so.

After examining the wound, Stranger looked up at Janos and said, "The wound is seriously infected, but Zareem is not as near death as he supposed. I can save him if I have the proper medicine quickly."

"But we have no medicine," Janos said.

Stranger stood up, towering over the Apaches. "Janos, I noticed the butterfly weed among the desert plants that grow just outside these mountains."

"I do not know this weed."

"Nor do I," Mandano said.

Stranger looked surprised. "Ah, perhaps you know it as the orange milkweed."

"Yes, we know that plant," Janos said.

"If I can get its milky juice into Zareem's system quickly, I can save his life. It can kill the infection. You must have several warriors gather a large supply of the weed with no delay."

Janos's face stiffened. "How do I know you speak the truth, John Stranger? Maybe this weed will not help Zareem at all. Maybe—"

"Why would I risk my life to save Casco, then lie to you so I could let Zareem die?"

"There is wisdom in what John Stranger says, Chief Janos," Mandano said. "We must hurry and bring the orange milkweed."

Janos's features flushed. "All right. Bring the weed."

Mandano was gone in a flash. Janos and Yamina stood over Stranger as he did what he could to clean the wound and make the young warrior as comfortable as possible. Mandano returned after a time with a ball of butterfly weed, saying there would be much more shortly.

Stranger squeezed the milky juice into a tin cup and helped Zareem drink it. Other warriors came with more of the weed, and he had Janos, Mandano, and Yamina squeeze juice into other cups while he administered the thick fluid to the wounded warrior. Stranger wished Zareem was more alert so he could drink the juice faster, but he worked steadily getting it down him a little at a time.

Hours passed. By sundown, Stranger set the cup aside and said, "That's enough for a while. Mandano, I'll need more weed by midnight. After his fever breaks and I know the infection is under control, I can start tapering off the dosage."

"We will bring plenty more," Mandano said, and hurried out of the cave. He returned moments later and assured Stranger there would be no shortage of the needed plant.

"I think Zareem looks better already, John Stranger," Janos said.

"Maybe. He's not out of the woods yet, though."

Janos frowned. "Out of the woods?"

"I mean he's still in grave danger. He definitely was close to death, and probably would have died sometime tonight if we hadn't gotten the juice into him. If he makes it through the night, I believe he'll live."

Janos nodded woodenly.

"You have proven once again that you are a friend to the Apache," Mandano said. "How did you know about the orange milkweed? Our people have seen it on the desert for generations, but never knew its power to heal."

"Apparently the Apaches and the Navajos do not talk."

"No. We do not."

"Well, I learned about the butterfly weed from a Navajo medicine man when I was in New Mexico a few years ago. Watched him use it on a wound infected something like Zareem's. It worked beautifully."

Yamina was kneeling beside her son. "You are going to let John Stranger live now?" she said to Janos.

"I...uh...I will let him live for now, since he is needed to care for Zareem."

Thank You, Lord, Stranger said in his heart.

"He will need rest," Yamina said. "I will stay by Zareem's side through the night. I can give him the juice at midnight so John Stranger can sleep. If Zareem grows worse, I will send for John Stranger. Where will you keep him?"

"Mandano, take John Stranger to the cave where Dan Wheeler is held captive. The two white men can share the cave."

Mandano glanced at Stranger. "We are holding the governor's son captive, John Stranger. Chief Janos has demanded weapons and ammunition in exchange for Dan Wheeler. We need them to fight the Zunis."

"I see," Stranger said.

"Chief Janos, I am only a woman," Yamina said. "I am not supposed to speak my mind to a man, especially my chief. But I am asking that you let John Stranger go free."

"If Zareem dies, the fire will be rekindled. If Zareem lives, then I know the Sky Father is telling me not to put John Stranger to death, at least for now."

"For now?" Mandano said.

"John Stranger will be allowed to live until I see if Governor Donald Wheeler delivers the weapons and ammunition by the time I told him. If he does, I will let both Dan Wheeler and John Stranger go free. If not, both will be executed on the fire-pit."

"Chief Janos, I request a moment with you alone," Mandano said.

Janos gave him a stony look. "It is important?"

"Very."

The chief nodded toward the mouth of the cave and headed outside. Mandano followed. The two guards Janos had placed outside looked on as the two men moved past them and disappeared behind a massive boulder.

Janos drilled Mandano with hard eyes and said, "What is it?"

"I remind the great Janos that he promised me Dan Wheeler would not be killed even if your demands were not met."

"I assure you I will keep my promise. I want to keep John Stranger worried. That is why I said what I did. I like to see white men under strain."

"I wish my chief had even a small bit of compassion!"

"And I wish my number one warrior had none!"

TWENTY

Twilight was settling over the Superstition Mountains when Mandano appeared at the mouth of the cave carrying Stranger's black saddle on his shoulder. Stranger was seated on the dirt floor next to Zareem, who was sleeping. Yamina was seated on her son's other side. Two candles burned inside the cave, filling it with pale yellow light.

"I am to take you to the cave where we are holding Dan Wheeler," Mandano said. "I thought you might want your saddle for what you carry in the saddlebags."

Stranger gave him an odd look.

"Wundan searched the saddle bags and found your spare revolver," Mandano said.

"Did he take anything else?"

"Only the cartridges."

"Where's my horse?"

"Janos told me to put him in the rope corral with our horses. He has plenty of water and food. You can leave Zareem now?"

"Yes. He is resting well, and his fever seems to have dropped a bit. Yamina will call me if she needs me during the night."

"We will go then."

Stranger rose to his feet and followed Mandano outside. He

was surprised to find Casco waiting with a kerosene lantern in his hand. His face was still swollen, but he managed a slight smile in spite of it.

"Hello, friend," he said.

"Hello, Casco," Stranger said.

Mandano told the guards he and Casco would return soon, then told the boy to lead off. The three followed the lantern's light through a wide space between two giant boulders.

"You want me to carry the saddle, Mandano?" Stranger said.

"No. It is my pleasure to carry it for you."

They made their way into a nearby canyon, and Stranger heard water gurgling. Soon a small stream came into view, and then he saw lantern light coming from the mouth of a cave about the same size as the cave where Zareem was being kept. Two Apache guards stood near the entrance.

Mandano spoke briefly with the guards, but Casco entered the cave without slowing down. Stranger heard a male voice speak in a friendly manner to Casco, followed by a question about the cuts and bruises on his face.

"I went to Apache Junction today," Casco said. "Scalp hunters caught me and beat me up. They were going to scalp me and kill me, but another white man came along and killed them."

"I'm glad for that white man," Dan Wheeler said, rising from his sitting position on the cave's floor.

"His name is John Stranger," Casco said just as John moved inside. "This is him. Chief Janos is holding him prisoner."

The name came to Dan's ears at the same instant he saw the familiar face. A smile started to curve his lips, and then he caught the warning in Stranger's eyes and let the smile die.

"I'm glad you saved Casco's life, sir. He and his brother have been very kind to me. That's more than I can say for the others...especially their chief." He extended his hand. "I guess they've told you who I am."

"Yes," Stranger said, gripping Dan's hand. "And they told me why you're being held."

"Why are *you* being held?" Dan asked.

"Because Chief Janos wants it that way," Mandano said. "He can tell you more about it while Casco and I bring your supper."

The Apache brothers left the cave, but the two guards moved into the opening and leaned against the walls. Stranger told Dan why Janos was holding him prisoner, though not his reason for being on Apache land.

Soon the brothers returned, and the guards moved back out into the darkness. The smell of the food turned Stranger's stomach. He looked at it but was unable to identify what it was.

"You won't be insulted if I just eat some beef jerky and hard-tack from my saddlebags, will you?" he said, looking at Mandano.

Mandano assured him it was all right, and Stranger moved to the saddle and unbuckled one of the bags.

"Mr. Stranger, would you have enough beef jerky and hard-tack for me?" Dan said.

Stranger grinned at him. "You don't cotton to Indian food either?"

"No, sir."

Mandano smiled. "I do not blame you. Sometimes I myself do not like it."

"How about some water?" Stranger asked. "You didn't bring my canteens along."

"I will have Casco bring them to you."

While Stranger pulled out enough jerky and hardtack for himself and Dan, Mandano said, "I must caution you, John Stranger. Janos keeps sentries outside the cave at all times. If you should try to escape, they have orders to kill you."

"I figured as much, but thank you for the warning. And Mandano…"

"Yes?"

"Thank you for trying to persuade Janos to let me go."

"I am against murder, John Stranger. To fight and kill in battle is one thing. To put a person to death who is not fighting you is another."

"You are not like most Apaches."

"That he is not," Casco said. "My brother does not hate white men just because they are white men. He is a fierce fighter in battle, but he does not kill white-eyes when they are helpless to defend themselves. Like the Sky Father, my brother holds human life to be sacred. This is why the Sky Father wept before he put humans on the earth. He knew that greedy white men would kill each other for earthly possessions…even for his tears, the yellow rocks he put in the mountains."

"I know about the tears of the sun, Casco," Stranger said.

Mandano looked at John and Dan and said, "I understand that white man's God, like Apache Sky Father, frowns on murder."

Stranger's eyes lit up. "What do you know about white man's God, as you call Him, Mandano?"

"Maybe not much, John Stranger. Our father, Nodannay—who was killed in battle with Zunis five years ago—had been taught the English language by white missionaries in his youth. In turn, he taught Casco and me. He also told us the white missionaries had tried to turn him from the Apache religion. But our father believed white man's God and His Son did not care for Indians. Casco and I hold the belief of our father."

"With all due respect to your father, Mandano," John said, "our God very much cares for Indians. He gave His Son as a blood sacrifice for *all* men, that they might be forgiven for their sins." He returned to his saddle and pulled his Bible out of one of the saddle-bags. "Here, let me show you what God says in His Book."

Mandano and Casco exchanged glances. They knew about the white man's "Good Book" and had been told by their father to avoid it. Mandano was about to say they did not want to hear any-thing from the Book, but because of his respect for John Stranger, he remained silent.

Stranger flipped pages until he reached the third chapter of

John. He turned the Bible so Mandano could read it and said, "See these words I've underlined?"

"Yes."

"Would you read them to us?"

Mandano took the Bible from Stranger, glanced again at Casco, and cleared his throat.

"For God so loved the world, that he gave his only begotten Son, that whosoever believeth in him should not perish, but have everlasting life."

"Who did God so love, Mandano?" Stranger asked.

"The world," came the unsteady answer. The subchief was visibly nervous.

"That is the world of mankind," Stranger said. "Are Apaches part of mankind?"

"Yes."

"Then you will see that God so loved the Apaches—God so loved Casco and Mandano—that He gave His only Son for them."

Mandano closed the Bible and handed it back to Stranger.

"We...we must be going."

"Wait a minute," Stranger said, flipping pages again. "There's something else I'd like for you to read before you go. You both understand what sin is."

They both nodded.

Stranger stopped at Romans chapter five and again handed the Bible to Mandano. "Just the underlined words."

Mandano cleared his throat again.

"But God commendeth his love toward us, in that, while we were yet sinners, Christ died for us."

"Who did God show His love toward, Mandano?"

"Us, it says. Sinners."

"You and Casco are sinners?"

"It is really time for us to go, John Stranger," Mandano said.

"I realize you must go. But please understand that the *us* includes all sinners...Dan and me, even Mandano and Casco and all Indians. Please believe God when He says He loves Mandano and Casco."

Mandano nodded and started to turn away.

"Oh, one other thing," Stranger said. "You said earlier that your Sky Father frowns on murder. Let me show you what the God who created your Sky Father says about murder."

Stranger read from Genesis 9 and then the Sixth Commandment to show them that God is grieved when human beings murder each other.

"I am glad to see that, John Stranger," Mandano said. "Now, Casco and I must be going. We will see you in the morning."

Stranger and Dan Wheeler watched the brothers walk away from the cave and melt into the darkness. They could see the guards in the shadows next to a large boulder about forty feet from the mouth of the cave.

"It sure is good to see you again, Mr. Stranger," Dan said. "It's been a long time."

"Yes, it has. You've grown some since I last saw you."

"I was only what…sixteen?"

"I think so."

"So what brought you to this area? You must not have been far from these mountains to have come upon the scalp hunters and Casco."

Stranger took a step closer to him and glanced toward the mouth of the cave to make sure the guards weren't close.

"I was coming here to try to find and rescue you."

"Really?"

"Your dad found out that I was in Apache Junction and wired me there. The wire said he needed me real bad, so I hightailed it to Phoenix. I met your lovely wife and was told the whole story."

Dan closed his eyes and leaned his head back.

"How's Rebecca Ann taking it?" he asked with a quaver in his voice.

"Pretty hard. The girl loves you very much, Dan."

"And I love her the same." He took a deep breath and let it out in a gust. "I take it Dad isn't going to give in to Janos's demands. This is why he sent you, right?"

"He doesn't want to put that kind of fire power in Janos's hands. He knows that once the fight with the Zunis is over, Janos will use the weapons on his white enemies, including farmers, ranchers, and travelers, as well as the U.S. army. And as you know, Janos has no conscience about ordering the killing of women, children, and helpless old men. If they have white skin, they're a target."

"What do you think Dad'll do when you don't show up with me when the deadline's drawing near? I mean, if he holds back on those guns, you and I are so much buzzard meat. *Cooked*, of course."

Stranger smiled. "I'm not sure what he'll do. Since there's no way to get a message to him, he's going to have to do some guessing. It'll get pretty tight about Saturday evening."

"Yeah. He'll have to have those guns close by in order to get them here before Sunday noon. It'll be touch and go because he'll be wondering if you and I might show up at any minute."

"I've been in some tight spots in my time, Dan, but as someone has well said, 'Man's extremities are God's opportunities.' I was about to grab for an Apache gun out there, but just before I did, a woman came out of the rocks telling Janos that one of his warriors was dying and wanted to see him."

"The one they call Zareem?"

"Yes. Well, Janos decided to go to Zareem and told his warriors not to stake me over the pit until he returned. As it turned out, I was able to work on Zareem and make him better. I think he's going to live. God's got His hand on this whole situation, Dan. He allowed me to get caught by the Apaches for a reason…maybe several reasons. This seemingly impossible extremity is God's opportunity to show His mighty hand. He'll get us out of here safely in His own way and in His own time. We must trust him to do so."

"Mr. Stranger, I don't have your kind of faith." Dan's body

trembled as he spoke. "I'll be honest with you…I'm afraid we're doomed, you and me." Tears filmed his eyes. "That sweet Rebecca Ann is going to be a widow before she even has a chance to be a wife. All the plans and dreams we shared will never come true."

Dan broke down and wept. He fought it, ashamed to act that way in front of John Stranger, but unable to bring himself under control.

John put an arm around Dan's shoulder.

"It's going to be all right, Dan. The Lord is going to deliver us. He's got something in mind that I don't know about yet, but it's going to be all right. You just wait and see."

Dan Wheeler looked at John Stranger through fearful, tear-filled eyes, then turned and walked to the far side of the cave. He sat down and leaned against the wall. Tears ran in rivulets down his cheeks.

A new arrangement had been made in Phoenix. Rather than inconvenience the Wilsons by keeping them at the governor's house, Donald Wheeler asked Colonel Bradley Munford to assign a cavalry unit to the Wilson house. The houses were only four blocks apart. Colonel Munford rode back and forth between the two to check with his men, staying about an hour at each place.

At the time John Stranger was taken into the Apache stronghold to stand before Chief Janos, Rebecca Ann was in her upstairs room, pacing the floor and weeping. She had not eaten since Dan had been taken away.

At one point she stopped pacing and stood at a window that overlooked the front yard and circle drive. She saw Colonel Munford mount his horse while talking with the captain he had put in charge at the Wilson house. When the colonel rode away, heading back to the governor's place, she let go of the curtains and gave way to utter despair that she would ever see her husband again. Her loud wails covered the sound of footsteps in the hall, and she jumped with a start when the knock came at her door.

"Rebecca, may we come in?" It was her father's voice.

"Yes, of course."

Gunther and Martha Wilson moved through the door, and Martha took Rebecca Ann into her arms.

"You poor darling. I wish I could take this for you. You're really afraid if John Stranger doesn't get Dan out of there that he'll die, aren't you?"

"Yes, Mother. And why shouldn't I be?"

"Honey," Gunther said, "when it comes right down to it, the governor won't let the Apaches kill his son."

"You don't think so?"

"No, and besides, he has the utmost confidence in John Stranger. Let's not forget that. He really believes Stranger can get Dan out of Janos's hands and back in your arms. We can't give up hope."

The sound of a carriage rattling into the yard came through the window. Gunther went to the window and pulled back the curtain.

"It's Donald and Colonel Munford."

He hurried down the stairs and met the governor and the colonel at the front door.

"Hello, Gunther. How's my daughter-in-law holding up?" Donald asked as they moved inside.

"Not too well, I'm afraid," Gunther said.

Martha and Rebecca Ann appeared at the top of the stairs. They had paused long enough for Rebecca to dry her tears and compose herself.

"Good afternoon, ladies," Donald said as they began their descent. "I wanted to come by, especially for Rebecca Ann's sake, and let you know what we've been doing."

"There's no word from John Stranger, I assume," Martha said.

"No, ma'am. But I want you to hear what the army is doing."

"Let's sit down in the parlor, Governor," Gunther said.

When everyone was seated, Donald asked Colonel Munford to explain the new plan. Munford told Rebecca Ann and her parents that he had contacted the commandants of five other Arizona forts. Along with troops from Fort McDowell, they were going to converge on the Zunis and drive them back to their pueblo in New Mexico. He assured them that the army had enough men in the six forts to accomplish the task in short order, and they would begin immediately. It should take only two or three days.

Once the Zunis were out of Arizona, Chief Janos would no longer need the guns he had demanded. Munford would then take a small unit with him from Fort McDowell under a white flag and have a talk with Janos. Munford was sure when Janos understood there was no more threat to the Tontos from the Zunis, he would release Dan.

"That is, if Janos even has Dan by then," Donald said. "I'm confident John will have him out quickly."

"Colonel Munford," Rebecca Ann said, "how can you be so sure the army can drive the Zunis back to New Mexico so quickly?"

"I have every confidence in our troops, my dear. Our commandants are working together to move swiftly and methodically. The plan is being carefully drawn."

Rebecca Ann rose to her feet, wringing her hands. Tears surfaced and clung to her lashes. She moved to her father-in-law, who stood to his feet. A strangled moan came from her throat and the tears spilled down her cheeks.

"Dad Wheeler, those plans can go wrong. Please…have Colonel Munford take the guns to Janos right now! I want Dan back today! Please!"

"Mrs. Wheeler," Colonel Munford said, "you must realize that we are going at this situation in a sensible way, and—"

"What do you mean, *sensible?*" Rebecca Ann screamed. Her breath was coming fast, irregular and rasping. "The sensible thing is to take those guns to that bloody Janos and bring Dan home!" She broke into uncontrollable sobs.

Gunther rushed to his daughter and wrapped his arms around her, pulling her close to him.

"Mr. Wilson," Colonel Munford said, "you've got to help your daughter understand that we're doing our best to save Dan's life as well as the lives of hundreds of other potential victims if the Apaches get those guns."

"I'll try, Colonel. Right now, I think her mother and I need to be alone with her."

Gunther thanked the governor and the colonel for what they were doing and for coming to let them know about it. Both men assured him they would keep him informed. Donald Wheeler spoke again of his confidence that John Stranger would solve the whole thing for them shortly.

On Tuesday morning, Wundan appeared at the cave where John Stranger was shaving. He fixed Stranger with hard eyes and said, "Janos sent me to bring you to the cave where Zareem is kept."

"Give me just a minute, Wundan," John said. He noted that both his revolvers were tucked under Wundan's belt.

When Stranger stepped outside the cave, he saw that Wundan had brought three other warriors to accompany him, and two more guards had been added at the entrance. It was going to take the hand of God to make a way of escape.

Yamina smiled at Stranger when he entered the cave. He greeted her warmly and knelt down beside Zareem. The wounded warrior's eyes were open and not as glazed as they had been the day before.

"Remember me?" John said, smiling at Zareem.

Zareem nodded and licked his lips.

"Good! You're fever's down a little. Let's see how the wound looks."

The anxious mother watched as Stranger removed the bandage and examined the wound.

"Looks better," he said. "Not a lot, but a little better. We'll give him some more milkweed juice today and watch him close."

Stranger poured a full cup of the juice down Zareem a little at a time, then changed the dressing on the wound. He told Yamina he would be back soon to check on his patient.

Yamina nodded and smiled.

When Stranger stepped out of the cave, he found a crowd of Apaches, with Janos standing beside Wundan. He wondered where Mandano might be. Janos, his face like granite, stepped toward him.

"How is he?"

"He's a little better, Chief. Yamina and I will watch him closely. We'll need some more of the orange milkweed brought in this morning."

Janos turned immediately to a group of men and told them to go gather more of the milkweed.

"Chief Janos," Stranger said, "I would like to go see about my horse."

Janos granted permission and sent four warriors with him to the rope corral. Ebony nickered at his master's approach, and Stranger patted him and spoke to him in soft tones. There was plenty of grain for the horses, and they had the stream that wound its way out of the canyons for water.

As he was about to leave the corral, Stranger's attention was drawn to a group of young warriors being taught hand-to-hand knife fighting by Mandano. Casco, along with some other boys, was watching the training session. Mandano happened to look Stranger's way, and nodded at him. Stranger nodded back.

On Wednesday and Thursday, Janos's search parties returned at sundown to report that they had not seen any Zunis. This puzzled the chief. On Friday, he sent them to check on the Zuni camps, knowing where some were located. The warriors returned at sunset to report that the camp sites had been vacated. They could find no Zunis anywhere. Saturday came, and Janos sent his search parties to find out where the Zunis had gone, if possible.

The chief watched the warriors ride out in their groups, then went to the cave to see how Zareem was doing. John Stranger was there as the chief moved past the guards to the mouth of the cave. He stepped inside and saw Stranger standing over Zareem, with Yamina by his side. There was a pleasant look on Yamina's face.

"How is he?" Janos asked.

"He's doing fine. The infection is almost gone, and he has no more fever. Your warrior is going to live."

Zareem was awake and clear-minded. From where he lay, he looked up and said, "My life is spared because of John Stranger, Chief Janos."

"I am glad you are going to live, Zareem. Soon you will be riding patrol again."

"Yes. The Sky Father has smiled upon me by bringing John Stranger to our camp."

"You must now return to your cave," Janos said to Stranger.

The sun was setting as Dan Wheeler and John Stranger sat in their cave and discussed the possibilities of escape. Suddenly Mandano entered the cave with Casco by his side.

"John Stranger...Dan Wheeler...Chief Janos wants me to bring you to him."

An escort of six warriors besides Mandano and Casco took the prisoners to the entrance of the Apache stronghold. Janos was standing on top of his favorite towering rock. He motioned to Stranger and Wheeler and said, "Climb up here."

When they both were standing beside him, Janos pointed to the northeast and said, "Fort McDowell is that direction. Do you see any sign of the army coming with guns and ammunition?"

Both men said they did not.

"I would think that if the governor was going to meet my demands, he would not wait until so close to the deadline. Perhaps,

Dan Wheeler, your father is willing to sacrifice you rather than give me the weapons."

Dan licked his lips nervously but could think of nothing to say.

"If the army is not here with the guns and ammunition by high sun tomorrow, the fire-pit awaits both of you."

CHAPTER

TWENTY-ONE

Janos descended the rock behind his prisoners and told Mandano to take them back to their cave. When they arrived at the cave, Mandano dismissed the escorts and entered the cave with them. John went to his saddlebags and began to pull out some more beef jerky and hardtack.

"Suppertime, Dan," he said over his shoulder. "You want some, Mandano?"

The subchief declined. "I am sorry the army has not come with the guns yet, my friends."

"Poor Rebecca Ann," Dan said. "How horrible for her to become a widow so early in life. John, where is God's deliverance? I don't want to die!" Dan thumbed tears from his eyes. "Mandano, what'll they do with our burnt bodies? Will they bury us or throw us out for the vultures to pick our bones clean?"

But Mandano was more intent on John Stranger's calm demeanor.

"John Stranger, you are not afraid of death?" Mandano asked.

"No, Mandano, I'm not. Let me show you why."

John reached in the saddlebag and brought out his Bible. The subchief listened intently, as did Dan Wheeler, while Stranger read Scripture after Scripture about salvation and the peace that can only come from knowing Jesus Christ. Soon the Word began to cut into Mandano's heart, and he became very uncomfortable.

"I must be going now," he said, moving toward the mouth of the cave. "For your sakes, I hope white man's God will give you deliverance from the fire-pit."

After Mandano left, John and Dan ate their cold supper. Dan was strangely quiet. John tried to encourage him, but his words fell on deaf ears. Dan Wheeler was terrified of dying, and it was all he could do to maintain his composure.

Soon Stranger doused the lantern, and they lay down for the night. A small bit of light from the stars came through the cave's opening. Stranger was almost asleep when Dan said, "John, you awake?"

"Mm-hmm."

"John, I'm not ready to die. I…I'm afraid. Would you go over what the Bible says about salvation once more?"

John sat up. "I thought you were a Christian."

"I don't know what I am," Dan said with a quaver in his voice. "Up until you started talking to Mandano about being saved, I've always considered myself a Christian."

"You must've heard the salvation message in your church. Hasn't your pastor preached on repentance and faith toward the Lord Jesus Christ?"

"Yes, he preaches the cross and the blood…and Jesus as the only way of salvation. But I guess I've really not applied any of it to myself because I've always looked at myself as in the fold."

"Always? You mean as far back as you can remember?"

"Yes. As far as I know, I've always been a Christian."

"Dan, nobody's *always* been a Christian. There must come that time of repentance and faith when the sinner turns to Jesus from his unbelief."

A match flared and Stranger lit the lantern, filling the cave with yellow light. All four guards crowded up to the mouth of the cave, holding their carbines ready.

"What are you doing?" one of them demanded.

"Just having a little talk," Stranger said. "We need light to read something."

The Apaches backed away, returning to their post.

Dan was sitting up, and Stranger dropped to one knee beside him and pulled the lantern close. He placed the Bible in Dan's hand and said, "I want you to read some verses to me. Turn to Acts 20:21."

The governor's son fumbled with the Bible, looking for the book of Acts.

"Let me help you," Stranger said. When he had found the page, he pointed to the verse and said, "Read me what Paul preached both to the Jews and to the Greeks."

"He said he was testifying 'repentance toward God and faith toward our Lord Jesus Christ.'"

"Repentance is changing your mind about sin, Dan. That includes your unbelief. You turn from it and put your faith in Jesus Christ, believing that He died for your sins, went to the grave, and rose from the dead on the third day, just as the Bible says. Repentance is a change of mind that results in a change of direction."

"I guess I never really understood that before."

Stranger flipped back to Isaiah 53, then handed the Bible to Dan and said, "Read me verse six."

"'All we like sheep have gone astray; we have turned every one to his own way; and the LORD hath laid on him the iniquity of us all.'"

"Who did God lay our iniquity on, Dan?"

"It says 'him'—is that referring to Jesus?"

"Yes, it is. Now notice the first half of the verse. It says that all of us have gone astray, and every one of us has turned to 'his own way.' Since this sinful human race has gone astray, our own way would be away from God, just like our father Adam did, right?"

"So we automatically go *away* from the Lord because we're all sinners."

"That's right. But Jesus calls for us to come to Him. In John 6:37 He says, 'him that cometh to me I will in no wise cast out.' We're headed the wrong way, Dan. How are we going to get to Jesus?"

"We have to do a one-hundred-eighty-degree turn."

"That's it. Look over in Isaiah chapter fifty-five."

Dan turned to it quickly.

"All right, look at verse seven. Keep in mind that the 'wicked' and the 'unrighteous' in God's eyes are those who have never been saved. Read it to me."

"'Let the wicked forsake his way, and the unrighteous man his thoughts: and let him return unto the LORD; and he will have mercy upon him; and to our God, for he will abundantly pardon.'"

"When does the pardon come?" John asked.

"When the lost sinner changes his mind, forsakes the direction he's going, and turns to the Lord."

"So what's for you to do now, Dan?"

A broad smile spread over Dan Wheeler's face. "Turn in repentance of my sin and unbelief and call on Him for salvation."

"All right. Let's bow before the Lord, and you do that very thing."

After Dan Wheeler had called on the Lord to save him, he wept and said, "John, I'm wondering about Rebecca Ann. We've talked a lot about it, and she says she's always been a Christian, like I've always said."

"Well, tell you what, Dan. I have perfect peace that the Lord is going to let us get out of here alive so you can lead Rebecca Ann to Jesus."

"I hope you're right. One thing's for sure…though I can't really explain it, my fear about our predicament is gone. I've got peace for the first time. Now I know why you weren't panicky like I was."

John grinned. "You're learning fast. You see, you were one of the reasons the Lord let me get caught by the Apaches. It took this situation—your hearing me talk to Mandano about salvation—to bring you to Jesus. Now if only Mandano would trust in Him too. What do you say let's pray for him right now."

Stranger led in prayer, asking the Lord to work in Mandano's heart and draw him to Himself.

The lantern was put out, and both men settled down for sleep. Dan was asleep first. Stranger lay in the darkness and thanked the Lord for Dan's salvation. Once more, he prayed for Mandano to be saved, then fell asleep praying that the Lord would help him be alert to His plan for their escape if the guns were not delivered by high noon tomorrow.

While John Stranger was falling asleep in the cave in the Superstition Mountains, Colonel Bradley Munford was at the gate of the stockade wall at Fort McDowell. Lanterns on the posts illuminated the area where weary troops were riding in on tired horses.

Lieutenant Cy McCarty was first through the gate. He swung his horse out of the way of the riders coming in behind him and dismounted near Colonel Munford.

McCarty wiped dust from his face and said, "All the men from the other forts are headed home, sir. Did my runner make it back this afternoon?"

"Yes, he did. I appreciate your letting me know what was happening. I was starting to get concerned."

"Sorry it took so long, sir, but we kept finding more Zuni camps. Like you, I thought the job could be done in a couple days...three at the most." He sighed. "Well, at least we got it done. So what's the status here?"

Munford nodded to a rider who greeted him as he passed by.

"We've got the guns and ammunition ready to pull out at the governor's command. When I had heard nothing from him by nine o'clock tonight, I wired him, asking if he had heard anything from John Stranger. He hadn't. Said since there was no word, he had to assume the Apaches have captured Stranger and are now holding both him and Dan hostage…or by this time, Janos might have killed Stranger."

"So what's he want us to do?"

"Said to plan on taking my small unit under the white flag and tell Janos his Zuni enemies are all back in New Mexico, so he doesn't need the guns and ammunition he wanted."

"Why a small unit, sir? Wouldn't it be better to go with some strength?"

"No. If I took every man in this fort, we'd still be outnumbered three to one by the Tonto warriors. Say Janos doesn't believe we drove the Zunis back over the border…he might figure we came ready to fight if he called us liars and refused to turn Dan over to us…Stranger, too, if he's still alive. If I have only a few men, Janos is more likely to believe me, knowing we're in no position to fight him."

"Makes sense. So why do you have the guns and ammunition ready?"

"Just in case the governor decides to play it safe and orders me to take the guns."

"Wouldn't that have been the best thing to do in the first place?"

"Not in the governor's eyes. He's had an awful time wrestling with turning that many guns over to Janos. He doesn't want the inevitable results on his conscience or on his record."

"I see what you mean. Tough decision."

"Well, anyway, if I don't hear from Governor Wheeler by eight o'clock in the morning, I'll take my five men and head for the Apache camp. At a steady trot, we'll be there by ten. That'll still be a couple of hours this side of the deadline."

"Is Captain Norton going with you, sir?"

"No. He'll be in charge here at the fort."

"Well, sir, I'm dead on my feet. I've got to get to bed."

McCarty started to walk away, then paused and turned back.

"I'd sure feel better about Dan and that Stranger fellow if you were taking the guns and ammunition to Janos."

"For that part of it, I would too, Lieutenant. But Governor Wheeler is calling the shots. See you some time tomorrow."

At the governor's house in Phoenix, Donald Wheeler sat at the kitchen table, his blond hair tousled. A lantern lighted the room from a nearby cupboard. Abigail stood over him, a hand on his shoulder, and said, "Why don't you at least come up to bed, honey? I know neither one of us is going to sleep tonight, but at least you can get some rest lying down."

Donald was staring at the wall on the opposite side of the room, and didn't seem to hear what she said.

"I just can't believe we haven't heard from John, Abby. I was so sure he'd go in there and have Dan home within a couple of days at the most."

"I know in Flagstaff we got to thinking of the man as if he were some kind of immortal, honey, but he's only human. Something went wrong. I just hope he didn't get killed."

"If we find out he got killed trying to rescue our boy, I'll never get over it."

"Come on, honey. Go to bed and get some rest, even if you don't sleep."

The Wheelers tossed and turned all night. At sunrise, the governor sat up and turned toward Abigail as she lay beside him. He saw her wiping tears with the corner of the sheet.

Before he could say anything, she sniffed and said, "You did say you told Mr. Madden to sleep next to the telegraph key in his office?"

"I gave him specific orders not to leave that key…that a message could come through from Apache Junction at any time."

Abigail laid the covers back and rose to a sitting position.

"Donald, we're not going to hear anything from John. Something's gone wrong." She looked at the clock on the bedstand. "It's almost six-thirty. If you wired Colonel Munford right now, there would still be time to get those guns to Janos."

Donald Wheeler did not reply. He rose from the bed, walked to the closest window, and looked at the army tents next to the house. Abigail saw his shoulders bunch, and then droop. She hurried to him, took hold of his arm, and looked into his face. He was fighting tears.

"Darling," she said, "please send those guns. You and I both know that Janos is a proud man. I don't think telling him the Zunis are gone will be enough to persuade him to give Dan back to us. He laid down his terms, and I believe he'll stick by them. No guns and ammunition...no Dan."

The governor took hold of the hand that was on his arm and squeezed it hard.

"I'm going to do it. I can't let our son die. I just can't!"

Abigail burst into tears. "Oh, thank you! Thank you!"

Governor Wheeler dressed quickly and dashed down the stairs and out the door. He called for Corporal Henry Pitts and sent him to the telegraph office with a message for Colonel Munford to take the guns and ammunition to Chief Janos.

Corporal Pitts borrowed an officer's horse and galloped to Phoenix's business district. When he arrived at the telegraph office, he found a note on the door informing him that Madden was at the doctor's office and would return as soon as possible.

The corporal galloped to the doctor's office and found that Zeke Madden had fallen down the stairs to his apartment and had broken his left leg. Madden had tried to crawl to the general store next door and awaken the proprietor, but he had passed out. It wasn't until over an hour later that a couple of townsmen out for an early walk found him. When they reached the doctor's office, Madden asked them to write a note and put it on his office door.

The doctor told Corporal Pitts that it would take at least an hour to splint the leg. There was no one else in town who knew how to operate the telegraph key. The message would have to wait until Madden could get back to his office. Madden assured him he would have it to Fort McDowell by eight-thirty.

Pitts gave Madden the message to be sent to Colonel Munford and returned to the governor's house. Upon arriving, Amanda told him that the governor and Mrs. Wheeler had gone to the Gunther Wilson home to tell the Wilsons that the guns were on their way to Janos.

Pitts hurried to the Wilson home and found Rebecca Ann and her parents in a state of elation. The news that the wire would be delayed upset Rebecca Ann, but the governor assured her that there would still be ample time to deliver the guns to Janos before noon.

At Fort McDowell, Captain Wayne Norton received the wire from Governor Donald Wheeler at 8:45. As planned if no message had come by 8:00, Colonel Munford had led his unit of five men out of the fort under a white flag and headed for the Tonto stronghold.

Norton knew that it would take at least three hours pulling the Gatling guns and a wagon bearing rifles and ammunition to reach Janos's camp at the northern tip of the Superstitions. They would have to hustle to make it by high noon.

The captain assembled his men and led them out of the fort with the Gatlings and the wagon. He sent a rider ahead to try to catch the colonel before he reached the Tonto stronghold and let him know of the governor's wire and that the guns were on their way.

The morning passed swiftly for Chief Janos. He had his warriors perched on high rocks, watching for any sign of the army.

John Stranger checked Zareem's wound, making sure it was still healing all right. He was pleased that it was doing fine. Zareem was growing stronger, and he expressed his appreciation to Stranger for saving his life.

Dan Wheeler was in his cave, nervous about the outcome of the day. He had hoped the army would arrive early with the guns, but there was no indication from the guards that they had. Though Dan now had peace about where he would go if the Apaches killed him, the thought of the slow, torturous death over the burning fire-pit was disconcerting.

The sun climbed higher and higher. Chief Janos paced at the base of his favorite rock, growing angrier by the minute. He thought about the Zunis, wondering if the empty camps were only a ruse to make him think they had left the territory. Were they planning an all-out assault on his stronghold? He must have those rifles and Gatlings!

John Stranger returned to the cave to find Dan Wheeler doing his own pacing. He told Dan the Lord had His hand on the situation. They must trust Him.

Out on the desert, the rider sent by Captain Norton reached Colonel Munford just before he and his men topped a rise where they could be seen by the Apache lookouts.

When Munford heard the news, he lifted his hat, sleeved sweat from his brow, and said, "From what you tell me, I'm afraid the Gatlings and the wagon might not make it in time."

"Captain Norton realizes that, sir. I'm sure he'll push those horses as hard as possible."

"Well, you ride back and tell him to do just that. Go!"

As the rider galloped away, Munford turned to his men.

"We'll wait here out of sight until just before noon. If the wagon and the Gatlings are not in sight, we'll ride in and tell Janos they are on their way…and hope he believes us."

The sun soon approached its zenith. Still there was no sign of the army unit bringing the guns.

Colonel Munford sighed and said, "We can't wait any longer, men. Let's put these animals to a gallop. We've got to tell Janos his guns and ammunition are not far behind us…and pray for Dan Wheeler's sake that he'll take our word for it."

At the Tonto camp, Chief Janos eyed the position of the sun, then turned to subchief Kimut.

"Bring Dan Wheeler to me! His father has defied me! We will not take time to fire up the pit. We will shoot him like white man's firing squad. And bring John Stranger. I want him to watch Dan Wheeler die. John Stranger will die over the pit before the sun goes down!"

TWENTY-TWO

J ohn Stranger was held at gunpoint by his own Colt .45 Peacemaker as Wundan stood behind him. Stranger's other revolver was still tucked under Wundan's belt.

The entire camp was present as Dan Wheeler was backed up against Janos's favorite rock and his hands tied behind his back. The warriors who served as lookouts watched from their high perches. Terror swelled the muscles of Dan's throat. He looked at Stranger with questioning eyes and gasped for breath.

Stranger was praying. Lord, this is cutting it awfully close. Help me to know what to do! He made a partial turn to get a look at Wundan. The subchief was within a step of him, with the Peacemaker cocked and aimed directly at his back.

"Turn around and watch the execution, John Stranger," Wundan said. "Yours will come at the fire-pit before the sun goes down."

Janos commanded three of his warriors to stand ten paces from Dan Wheeler. At Janos's command, they would shoulder their carbines, aim at the white man's heart, and fire.

Mandano, who had been visiting Zareem at his cave, suddenly burst on the scene. He looked at Dan Wheeler, then at the three executioners working the levers of their carbines, and ran up to Janos.

"What are you doing?" he said.

"I am putting Governor Donald Wheeler's son to death, as I promised him I would if the guns were not delivered by high sun today." He raised a hand toward the sky. "It is high sun."

"Chief Janos, you promised me this would not happen! You made me believe that you would not kill Dan Wheeler even if his father did not send the guns. Is the great Janos going back on his word?"

There was a gasping among the Tontos. Mandano would dare to speak to the venerable chief in such a manner? Mandano's heart beat fast, and he heard the sound of it in his ears, a drum counting the measure of his building fury.

"Chief Janos is a shame to the Tontos and all Apaches! He makes a promise, then breaks it! I asked you to spare John Stranger's life, too. You said you would. Are you going to break your word a second time?"

Janos lashed out with his fist and knocked Mandano down. He stood over Mandano and commanded four warriors who stood close by to seize him. Two grabbed each arm and jerked him to his feet.

"You will pay for speaking to your chief in such a manner, Mandano!" Janos said.

Suddenly there was a wild wail. "No-o! You cannot do this to my brother!" It was Casco, and he left his mother's side, dashing forward to stand beside Mandano.

"Get the boy out of here!" Janos snapped.

Casco yanked a large knife from a sheath on his waist and spread his legs in a fighting stance. He swung the razor-sharp blade at the warrior who came at him first. The warrior dodged it and grabbed for Casco's wrist, but missed. The boy swung the knife again. This time it slashed the warrior's rib cage, drawing blood. The warrior screamed and punched Casco in the jaw, sending him rolling and the knife flying from his hand. He landed behind Mandano and the warriors who held him. The warrior went to his knees, clutching the long cut on his side.

There was a murmuring among the crowd, upset to see violence among their own people. Serinda wanted to rush to her young son, but she knew she must not interfere.

Casco sprang to his feet, yanked a knife from the sheath of a nearby warrior, and charged the men who held Mandano. As he ran, he drew back the knife, aiming it for the back of one of the four, yelling, "Let go of my brother!"

A shot rang out, and Casco went down. His mother screamed and ran to him, kneeling by his side. A warrior with a rifle on the inside of the crowded circle had shot the boy.

Mandano fought his captors, trying to break loose to go to Casco. He ejected an angry wail when he heard his mother scream that the boy was dead.

He glared at Janos and yelled, "Do you see what your broken promise has caused?"

Janos turned to Kimut and commanded him to give Mandano a beating while the four warriors held him. There was pleasure in Kimut's eyes as he approached Mandano and stood for a moment in front of him. Then the blows began.

When Janos saw that Mandano's face was a bloody mass and that he was sagging against the hands of the warriors who held him, he called for Kimut to stop. Then he told the four warriors to hold Mandano upright.

"Mandano, do you hear me?" he said.

Mandano looked at Janos with glassy eyes and gave a short nod.

"You are to leave this stronghold and never come back. For defending a white man and insulting your chief, you are now an outcast. You are no longer a Tonto Apache! Word will spread, and you will soon be an outcast with *all* Apaches!"

Serinda rose to her feet beside the lifeless body of Casco and quietly melted into the crowd. Janos watched her until she passed from view, then raised his fists over his head and shouted, "Death to all whites! They are our enemies! Death to the whites!"

Most of the crowd joined in the chant.

AL LACY

When the chanting died down, Janos pointed at Mandano and said, "Go, now, Mandano! And take your mother with you!"

Serinda suddenly broke from the crowd behind the three executioners and ran toward the one on the right, her eyes wild. Someone cried a warning, but the executioner did not react in time. Serinda yanked the carbine from his hands and aimed it at Janos.

Wundan swung John Stranger's Colt. 45 on her and fired. The slug hit her a split second before she squeezed the trigger. Her shot missed Janos and struck a warrior who stood a few feet to Janos's right. The warrior went down dead, as did Serinda.

The instant the Peacemaker fired, John Stranger moved with the swiftness of a cougar and snatched it from Wundan's hand. He punched Wundan on the jaw and made a lunge for Janos. Before Janos knew what had happened, Stranger had him in a choke hold with the Peacemaker cocked and pressed against his head.

The crowd stood frozen in place. Wundan lay flat on the ground.

"Nobody move!" Stranger said. He knew that Janos was practically a god to the Tontos. They would do nothing to endanger his life.

"Let go of him!" he said to the four men who held Mandano. They did so instantly.

"Drop your rifles!" he said to the executioners. The two who still held theirs let them fall to the ground.

"Untie Dan Wheeler!" While the cords were being removed from Dan's wrists, Stranger said, "Mandano, that revolver under Wundan's belt is my spare. Get it."

Mandano's face was bloody and swollen, one eye so puffy it was practically closed. Yet he acted quickly and pulled the Colt .45 from under the stunned subchief's belt.

"I know my brother is dead," he said, looking at Stranger. "I want to check on my mother."

"She is dead, Mandano," said an older man who was kneeling

beside Serinda. "The bullet hit her heart."

Mandano set his eyes on Janos, who was firmly in the crook of John Stranger's arm.

"You didn't kill my mother and my brother with your own hands, Janos, but they are dead because you have broken your word. I am sure the Sky Father will weep more tears this day, but not over the greed of white men. He will weep over an Apache chief who caused the deaths of three of his own people because he broke his word to a subchief who trusted him."

"Janos is still our chief, Mandano!" a warrior shouted. "You have no right to speak to him as you do. You are an outcast! You are no longer Apache! You are a filthy white man!"

"The four of us will be leaving now," Stranger said, running his gaze over the faces of the crowd. "If you make any hostile moves toward Mandano, Dan Wheeler, or me, Janos will die. If we get out of these mountains and reach a place of safety, I will let Janos return to you unharmed. If he dies, it will be because you did not heed my words."

"Shoot him!" Janos bellowed. "Shoot him!"

The warriors looked on wide-eyed and fearful.

"Chief Janos," Kimut said, "we cannot shoot him without his bullet killing you. It is better for us to give up Dan Wheeler and John Stranger than to lose you. I will be glad to see that outcast gone, though I would like to see him dead!"

Several voices came from the crowd, agreeing with Kimut.

John Stranger looked toward the rope corral and gave a shrill whistle. In one seemingly effortless leap, Ebony cleared the single rope and trotted to his master.

"Dan, take the reins and lead him," Stranger said. "We'll go to the cave and get my saddle."

Dan led Ebony as they started toward the split in the boulders that led to the cave and beyond to the maze of canyons. Mandano wiped blood from under his nose and from a split in his lip. Stranger walked backwards, keeping his eyes on the angry Apaches.

Janos stiffened and made Stranger drag him with his heels making grooves in the sand.

Soon they were out of sight from the Apaches and near the cave where John and Dan had been held prisoners. Dan retrieved Stranger's saddle and cinched it on Ebony.

"John Stranger," Mandano said, "it will be safer for us to escape through the canyons than to travel all the way on the open desert. I know it appears that the Zunis have left the territory, but we have no guarantee of it. If the Zunis *are* still around and should see Janos and me traveling with two white men, they will attack."

"I see your point," John said. "Of course we'll still have open desert to travel once we're out of the mountains."

"Yes, but much less of it if we stay in the mountains and come out just east of Apache Junction. I know these canyons well. I can get us out in good time."

"All right, but we've got to get some horses for you and Dan."

The crowd was still collected as Stranger and the others emerged from the rocks into the open area. Still holding the gun to Janos's head, Stranger called out, "We're going to take two horses! Do not interfere!"

"Shoot him!" Janos said. "Shoot him!"

But no one moved.

Moments later, Stranger, Janos, Wheeler, and Mandano left the fierce-eyed Apaches and moved into a narrow canyon, leading the horses. When they were a good distance from the camp, they mounted up. Though it made Ebony nervous, Janos rode him with John Stranger seated behind the saddle, his gun pressed to the chief's head. Astride his painted pony, Mandano led the others deep into the winding canyons.

"I expect them to follow," Stranger said. "They'll no doubt try to come up with some way of rescuing their chief."

"They will," Mandano said.

Dan Wheeler's thoughts went to Rebecca Ann, and he tried to visualize their reunion. They weren't out of danger yet, but he was convinced that what Stranger had told him was true. The Lord was going to deliver them in His own way.

John Stranger spoke to the Lord in his heart, thanking Him that they had made it safe thus far and asking Him to take them all the way to Phoenix unharmed.

After about an hour, they came upon one of the many streams that flowed through the Superstitions. They stopped long enough to let the horses drink and allow Mandano to wash his face in the cool water. Just before mounting again, Mandano stood still and looked back eastward.

"Hear something?" Stranger asked.

"No. Just looking that way because I know some of the warriors will be on our trail."

"You think they'll try to attack us?" Dan asked.

"Only when John Stranger removes his gun from Janos's head. They'll follow unseen and wait for their opportunity."

"I'm not going to give them one," Stranger said. "Before I take this gun from his head, I'll let you do a little scouting to be sure no Tontos are within striking distance."

"You are a fool, John Stranger," Janos said. "You will not get out of these mountains alive."

"We'll see about that. All right, let's move out."

Three hours passed. The sun's smooth arc changed the shadows in the rock-walled canyons. Little desert animals skittered across their path from time to time. Twice they saw diamondback rattlesnakes among the rocks.

Janos rode in silence but smiled to himself from time to time as he saw Mandano look back over his shoulder and glance to the high rims of the canyons in search of any movement.

They came around a bend in the canyon, and Dan Wheeler said, "John! Look up there!"

They were approaching the mouth of a cave that led to a gold mine in the bowels of a mountain. Two miners lay on the ground. One was face-down, and the other was crumpled in a heap, a gunny sack near his hand. Several gold nuggets were scattered on the ground. The one that was face down still had his revolver in his hand. The other one's gun lay in the dust a few inches from his body.

Dan slid off the painted pony and hurried to them. Mandano dismounted and followed.

"They're both dead, John," Dan said. He moved to the mouth of the cave. "Several more sacks of gold nuggets in here. And a couple boxes of dynamite."

Stranger looked at Mandano. "How about climbing up on that tall rock over there? Check the area. If you don't see any Tontos, we'll take a few minutes rest."

It took Mandano only seconds to scurry to the top of the rock. He scanned the area, shading his eyes from the sun.

"There is no one, John," he called down.

"Okay, let's take a few minutes. Get down, Janos."

Stranger slid off Ebony's back, keeping the Peacemaker trained on Janos. It felt good to the chief to have the muzzle away from his head. He dismounted and stood looking at the canyon rim in the direction of the Tonto camp.

"Guess we ought to bury those miners under some rocks," Stranger said. "We don't have time to dig graves."

Mandano bent over and picked up a handful of the gold nuggets that had spilled from the sack. He held them so they flashed in the sunlight.

"Tears of the sun. Shed because of greedy white men."

Janos saw John Stranger and Dan Wheeler looking at the nuggets in Mandano's hand. Janos sprang away from Stranger and ran for Ebony. Mandano gasped and was shocked to see Stranger holster his gun.

"Aren't you going to shoot him?" he asked.

"Won't need to. He's not going anywhere."

"He'll steal your horse, John!" Dan said.

"Watch."

Ebony saw the chief running at him full speed and nickered. Janos vaulted into the saddle, snapped the reins, and shouted, "Hyah!"

Ebony ejected a wild whinny and bucked. Janos flew into the air and came down hard on the saddle. The horse did a quick circle with his hind legs, moving dangerously near a jumble of sharp-pointed rocks and throwing Janos off balance. Then he bucked again. Janos flew into the rocks, striking his head on a sharp point.

The three men dashed to Janos, who lay in a lifeless heap, his skull caved in on one side. Movement on a high promontory to the east caught Mandano's eye.

"John Stranger…Tontos."

A half-dozen Tonto warriors were looking down at them, the wind toying with their long black hair.

"They saw what happened," Mandano said. "There are no doubt many others with them. They will come in full force now with massacre on their minds."

"How long do you think it'll take them to get down into the canyon from up there?" Stranger asked.

"I would say about twenty minutes. We had best move fast."

Stranger ran a quick panorama of the area. "We've not been able to move very fast because of these winding canyons, Mandano. If we could block this canyon up behind us, is there another one they can use to get to us?"

"No. If somehow this canyon was blocked between us and them, we could be out of the mountains and safely into Apache Junction before the warriors could ever get to us."

"Okay," Stranger said. "You two ride on and take my horse with you. I'll catch up to you shortly."

"What are you going to do?" Dan asked.

"I'm going to take some of the dynamite over there and climb up to that pile of boulders about three-quarters of the way up the side of that cliff. On that rocky shelf." He pointed to the spot. "See them up there?"

Both men nodded.

"Time's wasting, fellas. Take Ebony and go."

Even as he spoke, Stranger ran to the mouth of the cave. He picked up several sticks of dynamite, along with some matches that lay in a small box nearby, and ran toward the cliff.

Dan and Mandano mounted their horses. Mandano took Ebony's reins in hand, and they headed on down the canyon.

John Stranger reached the bottom of the towering rock wall and began working his way upward. He glanced toward the promontory where they had seen the Tonto warriors. They were gone.

Ten minutes later, Stranger reached the point he had chosen. From its lofty height, he looked down into the canyon eastward. He could see the Tontos, about two dozen of them, working their way his direction.

He worked fast, placing the dynamite sticks strategically amid the boulders. The fuses were long, for which he was thankful. He fired a match and hurriedly lit all the fuses. They hissed like coiling snakes, and he climbed a little higher, leaped to the level rim of the canyon, and ran westward as fast as he could.

He had run about a hundred yards when the first stick exploded. The others exploded in succession, like giant firecrackers. The earth shook under Stranger's feet. He stopped and looked back. Massive billows of smoke rose skyward, and the sound of boulders tumbling into the canyon filled the air. Behind the billows of smoke came huge dust clouds.

"Thank you, Lord," Stranger said. "You really did work it all out, didn't You."

He wheeled and hurried toward the west. He would find a way down into the canyon again and meet up with his friends. Behind him, the bodies of Janos and the two miners were buried in the rock slide, along with the sacks of gold.

CHAPTER
TWENTY-THREE

———◆———

D an Wheeler and Mandano were waiting a half-mile down the canyon for John Stranger. Before he came around a bend looking for them, he heard Ebony nicker. Both men smiled as Stranger came into view, and Ebony nickered again.

"Sounded like the whole canyon was falling down, John," Dan said.

"They won't be coming through there after us, I guarantee you," Stranger said and grinned. "They could climb up and over on the rim, but their horses can't. On foot, they'll never get near us."

The trio mounted and headed west.

"I have to confess, John, my faith was pretty weak," Dan said. "But the Lord did it, didn't He?"

"He sure did! I can't wait to see Rebecca Ann, not just because I miss her, but because I want her to know Jesus, too."

"How about you, Mandano?" Stranger said. "Have you considered what I showed you in the Bible about your need of salvation?"

Mandano had indeed considered it. The Scriptures John Stranger had read to him kept coming to his mind, and he struggled with his thoughts.

What if what John Stranger has shown me is true? What if Jesus Christ really did die for my sins and there is a place called hell where I will go if I die without Jesus Christ in my heart? I must not believe this! I am Apache! I serve the Sky Father who shines on me at this moment. It was the Sky Father, not Jesus Christ, who delivered us from death back there.

Mandano shook himself and said, "I have considered it, John Stranger, but I am Apache. Sky Father is my god. He will take care of me when I die."

Stranger once again quoted for Mandano the Scriptures he had used before, and several more besides. Mandano listened for a time, then said, "This has been a very difficult day for me. Not only did I lose my mother and my brother, but my own people shed my blood, and they have rejected me. I am an outcast, John Stranger. I have no home. I have no people. I do not know what I will do or where I will go."

"The Lord Jesus cares about you, Mandano. If you will allow it, He will provide a new home and a new people for you."

"When we found those miners who had killed each other, we saw the tears of the sun...the tears of my god. My Sky Father is much more compassionate than your God or His Son, John Stranger. Neither your God nor His Son ever weep over men like the Apache Sky Father does. Where are their tears?"

John Stranger had prayed much for wisdom, desiring to lead his Apache friend to the Lord. Suddenly he had it!

"Let's stop right here," he said, hauling up.

"What for?" Dan asked.

"I want to show Mandano something. Let's get off the horses."

There were some flat rocks in the shade of a massive boulder nearby. Stranger left the saddle and pulled his Bible out of the saddlebag while the other two were dismounting.

"Come, Mandano," he said, moving toward the rocks. "Sit with me over here." Dan followed and sat down on Stranger's other side.

"Mandano, I've told you how God sent His Son, Jesus Christ, to provide forgiveness for sins and a place in His heaven for all who will repent and put their faith in Him for salvation."

Mandano nodded.

"You asked me where His tears are, Mandano. Let me read it to you."

Stranger read how the people of Israel had despised and rejected the Lord Jesus Christ, who had come to give them salvation. He showed Mandano the scenes where the Jews took up stones time and again to stone Him to death. Then he took him to Luke 19 and showed him how Jesus wept over Jerusalem as he rode the donkey colt down the side of the Mount of Olives, knowing He was returning to the city to be crucified.

"Do you see those tears on His face, Mandano?" Stranger asked.

The Apache swallowed hard. "Yes."

"Those are the tears of God's Son as He wept over sinners who rejected Him."

Stranger then turned to the crucifixion scenes in the gospels and read them to Mandano, reminding him that all of this was planned before the foundation of the world as God's only means of salvation and forgiveness for sinners.

Mandano was moved when he pictured the crown of thorns, the lashes on Jesus' back, the cruel hands that beat him about the face.

"You can identify with some of this, can't you?" John said.

Mandano nodded. Something strange was happening deep within him.

Mandano was moved even more when Stranger explained that what Jesus suffered was for *Mandano*. He was crucified for *Mandano*. He arose from the grave so He could save *Mandano*.

Stranger saw the evidence of the Spirit's conviction in Mandano's dark eyes. The struggle he was experiencing in his heart showed on his face.

"Mandano, you have spoken of the tears of the sun in the Apache religion."

"Yes."

"You have seen here in the Bible that Jesus Christ wept over sinners."

"Yes."

"Can you see the tears coursing down His cheeks, Mandano?"

"Yes."

"Those are the tears of the Son...God's Son. Do you see that?"

"Yes."

"I've already shown you Scripture after Scripture that Jesus died for all sinners so that all could be saved if they would. This includes you, right?"

Mandano swallowed hard, nodding. Stranger saw a tear in his eye. Dan Wheeler's heart was pounding.

"So you see, Mandano," Stranger went on, "you speak of the tears of the sun shed for men who kill one another in greed. Here are the tears of the *Son,* shed for men who are lost and without hope unless they repent and put their faith in Him to save them. If you're willing to turn to Jesus in repentance right now and call on Him to save you, He will do it. The Bible says so. The tears of the Son were for *you,* Mandano."

Mandano was now silently weeping. The tears of God's Son and the bloody death Jesus had died for him were enough to break down all resistance. He wiped tears from his cheeks with the back of his hand and said, "I will call on Jesus to save me."

Dan Wheeler wept as John Stranger led Mandano to Jesus.

With joy in their hearts, the trio mounted up a short time later. They pushed the horses as fast as possible and soon were out of the Superstitions. The sun was now in the bottom half of the afternoon sky. They drew rein, let the horses blow, and agreed that a hard ride at a full gallop would have them in Phoenix in little more than an hour. They were about to put the horses into a run when Mandano pointed northward and said, "Look!"

Six riders in blue were galloping toward them, waving their

hats. As they drew nearer, Stranger said, "That's Colonel Munford in the lead."

When the cavalrymen came to a halt in a dust cloud, Munford said, "Dan...Mr. Stranger! I figured we'd catch you about here. I'm so glad to see you both alive and well!"

"How did you know we'd be here, Colonel?" Dan asked.

Colonel Munford explained that when he and his men drew near the Tonto stronghold, they heard an uproar in the camp. Under the white flag, Munford spoke to one of the Tonto sentries, asking if he could see Chief Janos. The sentry informed him that two white men who had been prisoners in the camp had taken Chief Janos hostage and headed eastward through the mountains. Munford galloped away with his men and turned the Gatlings and the wagon back to the fort. Then they headed for the west side of the Superstitions, hoping to meet up with Stranger and Wheeler as they emerged onto the desert.

"This isn't Janos," Munford said, looking at Mandano.

Stranger introduced Mandano to the colonel and told how he had been brutalized and declared an outcast by the Tontos because he dared to stand against Janos in an attempt to save both white men's lives. He then told of finding the dead miners and how Janos was killed trying to escape on Stranger's horse.

"So you're about to head for Phoenix?" the colonel asked.

Stranger nodded. "Dan's eager to see his wife and his parents."

"We'll escort you there. But I think we should let them know as soon as we can that Dan's alive and well. If it's all right, I'll send one of these men into Apache Junction to wire the governor so they can all stop worrying. While he's doing that, we'll see how fast we can get to Phoenix."

"Send him...and let's ride," Dan said.

"Colonel, something's been on my mind the last couple of hours," Stranger said. "It's concerning Mandano. I haven't even said anything to him about it."

Mandano gave Stranger a puzzled look.

"He's without a home and a people," Stranger said. "He's an Indian without a job in a white man's world. I know you have ex-Apache warriors who serve as army scouts. They receive room, board, and pay, right?"

"Yes, they do."

"Like I say, I haven't talked to him about it, but if he's willing, could you find him a spot in the army as a scout?"

"I'm in need of another scout at Fort McDowell. How about it, Mandano? You want the job?"

A broad smile worked its way across Mandano's face.

"Yes, sir!" he answered, his eyes sparkling. "I will take it!"

"Good! Then the job is yours starting right now. We'll get you a uniform when we return to the fort."

Mandano turned and smiled at John Stranger.

Colonel Munford quickly dispatched a corporal to ride to Apache Junction and send the message to Dan Wheeler's wife and family that he was alive and well and on his way home.

The sun was setting, casting a golden hue on the desert as the three men and their army escort approached the eastern edge of Phoenix at a full gallop. Suddenly John Stranger pointed forward.

"Hey, Dan! Look there!"

Dan's mouth fell open as he beheld Rebecca Ann, her parents, and his parents standing with the soldiers who had been guarding them at their homes. The group was collected just outside of town alongside the road.

"Yahoo!" Dan shouted, and lashed the Indian pony with the reins.

Colonel Munford laughed and signaled for his men to slow up. John Stranger and Mandano followed suit.

"That there is one happy young man, Colonel!" Sergeant Clyde Holman said.

Rebecca Ann Wheeler wiped tears as she watched her husband riding toward her on the painted Indian pony. Both sets of parents were weeping, too. When Dan was within fifty yards, she broke into a run, throwing her arms open wide. Dan reined the horse in and quickly slid from its back.

"Oh, darling!" she said as they came together. "Thank God you're alive!"

They held each other for a long moment, then kissed tenderly, mingling their joyful tears. Dan took his wife by the hand and led her to where the others waited. There was a tearful reunion with his parents and the Wilsons. Even some of the soldiers were crying.

When Colonel Munford's unit drew up, along with John Stranger and Mandano, Dan leaned over and said in Rebecca Ann's ear, "I have something special to talk to you about, sweetheart. A wonderful thing happened to me while I was in the Apache camp. I'll tell you about it tonight."

She gave him a look of eager expectation and laid her head back against his shoulder.

Then with Rebecca Ann at his side, Dan stood before the group and introduced Mandano, explaining how he was beaten and made an outcast by his people because he dared to stand against Chief Janos to save Dan's life. Those gathered cheered Mandano as a hero.

Dan then told how John Stranger's courage and ingenuity brought them safely out of the Superstition Mountains. There was a cheer for John Stranger.

Colonel Munford told his men that Mandano was now an army scout, and Governor Donald Wheeler thanked Mandano for what he had done to save his son's life. Abigail clung to her son, along with Rebecca Ann, and the Wilsons told Dan how glad they were that he was back safely and asked questions about his treatment at the Apache camp.

When the conversations began to trail off, Governor Wheeler looked around for John Stranger. He was nowhere to be seen.

Wheeler went to his family and the Wilsons and asked, "Do you know where John went?"

"Why, no," Abigail said, looking around. "He was here just a moment ago."

"He's got to be here somewhere," Dan said.

Sergeant Holman walked up and said, "Mr. Stranger rode away a few minutes ago, folks. He left something with me to give to Dan and to Mandano."

The sergeant placed a silver medallion in the hand of each man.

"What is it, Dan?" Rebecca Ann asked.

"It's a silver medallion." Dan held it up for all to see.

"Exactly the same as mine," Mandano said. "It has a star in the middle and words engraved around the edge: *THE STRANGER THAT SHALL COME FROM A FAR LAND— Deuteronomy 29:22.* This must be from the Bible."

"It is," Dan said.

Sergeant Holman pointed eastward and said, "If you'll look quick, you can still see him."

In the purple hue of the desert sun's last light, they saw John Stranger riding his big black horse across the rolling hills. Then the twilight swallowed horse and rider from view.

EPILOGUE

Arizona's Superstition Mountains are the most mysterious and storied range in North America. Over a period of nearly two hundred years, many spine-tingling stories have come from those mountains' shadowed canyons. From the early days of the nineteenth century, men have ventured into the twisting, steep-sided canyons of the Superstitions and never returned.

The most enduring story is that of Don Miguel Peralta's Sombrero Mine, later claimed by Jacob Waltz, the "Dutchman." From the early 1870s through the 1880s, Waltz worked the mine without ever revealing its location. Some treasure-seekers tried to follow Waltz to his mine and either became lost or were murdered. As recounted in the story you just read, Waltz's partner, Jacob Weiser, met with an untimely demise. Though many believed Weiser died at the hands of the Dutchman, it was never proven.

Jacob Waltz died in 1891, and to this day no one has found his "Lost Dutchman" mine. The Superstitions seem determined to preserve their secret. A curiously large number of people have died in those mountains. Some have been climbers and hikers who fell to their deaths, but many others were on the trail of the Lost Dutchman mine when they were murdered or simply disappeared.

In the 1930s, a Dr. Adolph Ruth arrived at Apache Junction,

claiming to have a map of the mine. He ventured into the Superstitions one hot summer day and never returned. Several months later, his skeleton was found. The buzzards had picked the bones clean, and there was a bullet hole in the skull.

In spite of the risk, gold-seekers still climb and paw through the Superstitions. Among them is Arizona's recently retired attorney general, Bob Corbin, who has been systematically searching for the Lost Dutchman mine since 1957. He has not found it, but he has managed to elude becoming a statistic. I have no doubt, however, that even the fortunate ex-attorney general of Arizona would say if you enter the Superstitions, you do so at your own risk.

OTHER COMPELLING STORIES BY
AL LACY

Books in the Battles of Destiny series:

☞ *A Promise Unbroken*

Two couples battle jealousy and racial hatred amidst a war that would cripple America. From a prosperous Virginia plantation to a grim jail cell outside Lynchburg, follow the dramatic story of a love that could not be destroyed.

☞ *A Heart Divided*

Ryan McGraw—leader of the Confederate Sharpshooters—is nursed back to health by beautiful army nurse Dixie Quade. Their romance would survive the perils of war, but can it withstand the reappearance of a past love?

☞ *Beloved Enemy*

Young Jenny Jordan covers for her father's Confederate spy missions. But as she grows closer to Union soldier Buck Brownell, Jenny finds herself torn between devotion to the South and her feelings for the man she is forbidden to love.

☞ *Shadowed Memories*

Critically wounded on the field of battle and haunted by amnesia, one man struggles to regain his strength and the memories that have slipped away from him.

☞ *Joy from Ashes*

Major Layne Dalton made it through the horrors of the battle of Fredericksburg, but can he rise above his hatred toward the Heglund brothers who brutalized his wife and killed his unborn son?

Books in the Journeys of the Stranger series:

☞ *Legacy*

Can John Stranger, a mysterious hero who brings truth, honor, and justice to the Old West, bring Clay Austin back to the right side of the law...and restore the code of honor shared by the woman he loves?

☞ *Silent Abduction*

The mysterious man in black fights to defend a small town targeted by cattle rustlers and to rescue a young woman and child held captive by a local Indian tribe.

☞ *Blizzard*

When three murderers slated for hanging escape from the Colorado Territorial Prison, young U.S. Marshal Ridge Holloway and the mysterious John Stranger join together to track down the infamous convicts.

Books in the Angel of Mercy series:

☞ *A Promise for Breanna*

The man who broke Breanna's heart is back. But this time, he's after her life.

☞ *Faithful Heart*

Breanna and her sister Dottie find themselves in a desperate struggle to save a man they love, but can no longer trust.

Available at your local Christian bookstore